Lucky
IN
LOVE

Lucky IN LOVE

CAROLYN BROWN

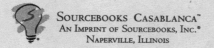

SOURCEBOOKS CASABLANCA™
AN IMPRINT OF SOURCEBOOKS, INC.®
NAPERVILLE, ILLINOIS

Published by Sourcebooks Casablanca, an imprint of Sourcebooks, Inc.
P.O. Box 4410, Naperville, Illinois 60567-4410
(630) 961-3900
FAX: (630) 961-2168
www.sourcebooks.com

Printed and bound in the United States of America
QW 10 9 8 7 6 5 4 3 2 1

To Morgan, Inc.,
Trisha, Isabella,
Kurtis, Destiny,
Lilybet, and Hope

Chapter 1

BEAU STOMPED THE BRAKES AND JUMPED OFF THE three-wheeler, anger boiling up from somewhere down deep in his scuffed-up cowboy boots. "What in the hell do you think you're doing?" he shouted at the back of the skinny, short stranger on the other side of the fence. The fool held the reins of a jet-black horse and was looking out across the pasture at several white-faced heifers and his prize Angus bull that nobody *ever* borrowed for free, not even his best friends or his favorite neighbors.

"You idiot! That's my stud bull you've cut this fence and let through!" he continued to rant as he passed through the tangled barbed wire. Jim Torres had hired very few dummies in his life, and when he did, they didn't last long. This man would be riding his big black horse into the sunset before nightfall once Jim found out about this. If Jim Torres didn't fire him on the spot, then Beau fully well intended to string him up in the nearest oak tree. Considering how little the fellow was, he could do it single-handedly. The man must have cow chips for brains to deliberately cut a fence and let an Angus bull in with purebred white-faced cattle. Either that or Beau had just walked in on the first step of a rustling job, in which case the man could look forward to spending a long time behind bars.

Milli heard a commotion behind her and turned to see if Alice Martin or maybe even Buster had come to help. Her grandfather, Jim Torres, was going to have the kind of hissy fit seen only in the front gates of hell if that big Angus critter actually bred one of these cows. Thank goodness the big black bruiser was just eating grass and didn't seem to be interested in the cows milling around him.

She'd only arrived yesterday, to help her grandfather while he was recovering from hip-replacement surgery. A cut fence and a big, mean Angus bull in the pasture weren't exactly what she had in mind for her first day's work.

Milli gasped when she saw the man, yelling at her instead of the bull. She put her hands on her hips and glared at him.

"What are *you* doing here? And why in the hell did *you* cut the fence and let that stupid Angus bull in with pure-bred white-faced heifers? Don't you have any sense at all? Wait 'til Alice finds out that she's got a cowhand that don't know purebreds from culls. You might just as well crawl up on your play pretty back there and go pack your bags, 'cause Alice Martin is going to fire you by nightfall."

She pointed toward the three-wheeler and shook her finger under his nose, amazed that she could utter a single word to the blond-haired man. Just how in the hell did he get from Louisiana to Oklahoma, and why had Alice Martin hired a drunk like him? One thing was sure, he could pick up his paycheck, because he'd just pulled the damnedest stunt in history.

Beau stopped dead in his tracks, not three feet from the stranger who turned out to be a feisty woman instead of a short man. Her brown eyes flashed with as much anger as danced in his steel blue ones. She'd jerked her hat off in the middle of her tirade and hair as black as the bull grazing in the pasture had fallen down to the middle of her back. Her lips were full and sexy and her eyebrows arched in pure rage. A tingle on the nape of his neck said he'd met this hellcat somewhere before, but he damn sure didn't know where.

He might be a sucker for dark hair and big, brown eyes, but no one was cutting his fence and using his prize bull without paying stud fees. To be threatening him on top of her stupidity was adding insult to injury, and Beau wasn't in any mood to explain to this upstart female that the Bar M was his ranch now, not Alice Martin's.

He pointed his finger at her. "Don't you lie to me. You've cut this fence and thought you'd take advantage of my prize bull. That bull is worth a whole pasture of those ignorant cows and I don't let him breed nobody's cattle for free. Not even Jim's—even though he's my neighbor and friend. Either that or you're lying your way through an attempted rustling."

She slapped his finger away. "Get back on your land. And don't point at me or yell at me again. I didn't cut the fence, but I'm damn sure going to repair it so your horny bull won't be on Lazy Z ground again. And I am not a cattle rustler."

She shoved her hand in the pocket of her tight blue jeans and hoped it didn't burn a hole right through the denim. Just touching him brought back memories she'd buried and long since tried to forget. It all went to show just how damn fickle her body could be. One touch and she was a melting pot of passionate hormones again.

"You ain't repairing a thing. I'll fix the fence as soon as I get my bull back in my own pasture." He turned abruptly and stomped back to his three-wheeler, crawled into the seat like it was a saddle, and started toward the fence. Where had he seen her before? When she touched his finger, desire shot through his body like he'd only known one time before. But that wasn't possible. That had just been a drunken man's dream that set him firmly on the sober wagon for all eternity.

She pulled a .22 rifle from the sheath fastened to the side of her saddle and before he had gone ten feet, she fired twice, dusting up the gravel in front of him. That got his attention.

He growled deep in his throat. "You stupid bitch. You could have killed me! Put that gun down right now."

There was no way that spitfire of a woman had been in his dreams. Maybe in his worst nightmare, but damn sure not in any sweet dream like he remembered when he thought about a night in paradise with a lady named Amelia.

"If I'd wanted to kill you, you'd be dead. And if you want to be dead, you just tell me what part you want shot first and where you want to drop and I'll make it as painless as possible. And don't you *ever* call me a bitch again. You get a warnin' the first time, but the second time I just let my anger have its way."

She drew a bead right between the sexiest blue eyes in the whole world. What on earth had brought him to Oklahoma? She'd left him in southern Louisiana after that fatal night when she had let her hormones ride roughshod over her better judgment.

Beau glared at her. Stupid woman had no business shooting at him. Either she'd just escaped from a mental institution or else Jim had started hiring gunfighters. But why? He and Jim had always been best friends. They played poker together with other area ranchers once a month at the bunkhouse. At least Jim had joined them until last week, when he'd had his hip replaced. Beau figured it was just a matter of a few weeks until Jim would be at the head of the table dealing cards and sipping Jack with them again. He would be willing to bet his Saturday night silver spurs that Jim didn't have any idea who was out here on his land with a gun laid on her shoulder and pointed right at him. She probably really was a cattle rustler and bluffing her way through getting caught. She had cut the fence and waited for a truck to arrive to steal his bull and however many of Jim's cows she could haul away at one time.

He put up his hands. "Whoa, wait a minute. Put that gun down and let's talk sensible." He started toward her slowly, fully intending to grab the weapon, take her to Jim's house just over the rise, and see if he had indeed put someone as impulsive as an erupting volcano on the Lazy Z payroll.

She lowered the gun slightly and dusted the gravel again, so close that the tarnished silver spurs wrapped around his boots jingled like a doorbell. "Don't you take another step, cowboy. Just crawl up on that tricycle you rode in on and get on out of here. I'll take care of this pesky bull. He's on Lazy Z property. And I'll fix this damned fence, too. I didn't cut it, but I'll see to it that it's fixed right proper, so get your sorry old scraggly ass out of here before I get really mad."

The next bullet wasn't going to make the dust fly or his spurs jingle. She looked crazy enough to make buzzard bait out of him. It wasn't easy to back down from a woman, but Beau wasn't totally stupid. He turned around very slowly so as not to excite the lunatic, crawled up on the seat of his three-wheeler, and started the engine just as slowly, all the while resisting the urge to wipe the nervous sweat off his brow. One squeeze of her finger and there wouldn't be any more poker games. There wouldn't be any more sitting on the porch swing on a hot summer night with his arm draped loosely around Amanda's shoulders. There would just be a zingy pop and Beau would be no more, and it would probably be late evening before Buster or one of the other hired hands came looking for him. It wouldn't take that long for the buzzards to find breakfast, though. He wouldn't even have time to pull the cell phone from his pocket and make a call for help. He patted his shirt pocket and moaned—he'd left it at home.

He drove the vehicle through the pasture and over a small rise before he braked, drew a pair of binoculars from the saddlebags, and eased back up the hill on his belly to see what was going on. Would the crazy woman rustle Jim's cows and his bull, or would she really put that rangy, mean-spirited bull back in the right pasture and fix the fence? He cocked his elbows up to make a brace and peeped through the glass to watch her cut the bull away from the cows with the finesse of a well-trained cattleman. She edged him back into Bar M pastureland and then went back to the fence. She took a small kit from the worn saddlebags on her horse, which bore a strange brand Beau had never seen before. It looked like a T lying at a thirty-degree angle. Not straight up. Not really lying down. She whipped a new piece of barbed wire from one orange steel post to the other, wrapped it tightly and snipped it. She repeated the process two more times before she plucked the wires like he did his guitar strings to check them for tightness. He almost expected to hear a melodious twang float across the pasture to his ears.

"Well, I'll be damned," he muttered, inching backwards down the hill.

Buster yelled from the back porch when he parked the vehicle in the bunkhouse yard. "Hey, Tyler Spencer called and said he found a cut fence this morning 'tween us and the Lazy Z. Bunch of younguns he knew was out lettin' their dogs chase coyotes last night and he figures they probably cut the fence to get their three-wheelers through to keep up with the dogs. That's where you keep your stud bull, so thought maybe you'd better send someone over there to fix it before he gets in with the Torres cattle. Jim would have a stroke if an Angus bull ever bred one of his white-faced cattle and even though the bull might have a good time, you'd lose the price of a stud fee." Buster chuckled, his smile creating even more wrinkles in a face that already looked like a road map of Texas. "Kids these days ain't got no respect. Bet they spooked the hell out of that bull lettin' coyotes chase past him with a bunch of dogs a-howlin'."

"Fence is fixed. Who's the woman Jim's hired?"

"Jim ain't hired no woman. Far as I know he ain't never hired women to work the ranch. Just Hilda to cook, and she and Slim are family, they been there so long. Oh, bet you're talkin' about Milli. Was she out there? She's his granddaughter. Pretty, ain't she? She used to come around here some in the summer when she was a little girl. Knew she'd grow up to be a looker. Biggest brown eyes in the whole state of Texas. Comes from out around Amarillo. Little town north of Hereford where her folks have a ranch. The Lazy T. She come out to help Jim 'til he's back on his feet." Buster's green eyes sparkled. "She's full of spit and vinegar, that girl is. She could tell a man to go to hell on a silver poker and make him look forward to the trip."

Beau pulled out a pack of gum and offered Buster a piece. "You can say that again. Jim's granddaughter, huh? How come nobody ever said anything to me about him having a granddaughter who could shoot the eyeballs out of a rattlesnake at a hundred yards? She whipped that rifle out of her saddlebags so fast I figured Jim was hiring gunslingers these days. She peppered the rocks in front of my toes and told me to get back on my tricycle and go back where I came from, then she mended that fence back together in record time."

Buster shook his head, his eyebrows knit together in a gray, bushy line. "If I can't chew something stronger than that stuff, I'll do without. Just what'd you do to make Milli pull a gun on you, boy?"

Beau shrugged his shoulder in exasperation. "Well, hell, Buster, I thought she cut the fence. I didn't know if she was a rustler or just a crazy bitch."

"Don't you never call Miss Milli that in front of me again, boy, and expect to keep all your pretty white teeth. You might be my boss but you ain't goin' to talk about Miss Milli like that. She's a pure lady and comes from fine folks."

Beau held up both hands like he was being robbed. "Sorry. Looks like I've done backed into a rattlesnake nest when I thought it was a gopher hole. And I guess I've really got off on the wrong foot with Jim's grand-daughter, too."

"Yep, reckon you did, son. You might need to dust off that new pickup truck of yours and ride over there and apologize for any ill feelings you caused," Buster said.

Beau couldn't believe his ears. "*Me*, apologize! She didn't tell me she was his granddaughter! She didn't tell me nothing, just started firing that cannon at me and issuing orders. I didn't do nothing to apologize for— except for calling her a bitch, and she set me straight about that pretty damn quick. Said the first time was on the house, but the second time she'd let her anger take control and I didn't ask what that meant."

A deep chuckle started down in the bottom of Buster's beer belly and erupted into a full-fledged roar. He pulled a red bandanna from the hip pocket of his bibbed overalls and wiped his eyes. "I'd give my eye teeth to have got to see that. Some little old girl putting a big feller like you around the corner. Boy, you just ain't got a damned bit of sense when it comes to handling women folks. You 'bout as lucky as Mr. Midas himself when it comes to running this ranch and making money, but when it comes to women, you damned sure ain't lucky, Beau."

"What's so funny?" Rosa, the cook at the Bar M for the past thirty years and Buster's wife two more than that, appeared on the back porch of the main house. She wore a starched white bibbed apron tied around her short, stout body and her jet-black hair was tied back with a bandanna. Buster didn't lose a minute's time beating a path over to the porch to tell her about Beau meeting Milli and how she whipped out a gun on him. Beau shook his head and went on to his office at the far end of the bunkhouse. He might be the talk of the ranch for several days, but he'd been the butt of jokes before and he had a tremendous sense of humor. Today it was his turn to make them laugh; next week it would be someone else's turn. And they were sure right about one thing. As they were always saying, he wasn't lucky in love. But that was changing, and he had a diamond ring in a little velvet box sitting on his dresser to prove it. Next week, when he was engaged properly to Amanda, they could all eat their words.

Milli Torres spotted the binoculars by the glint of the sun's rays reflecting off them. Things must have changed over at the Bar M. He acted like he owned—or at least operated—the ranch. But where was Alice Martin? Poppy hadn't mentioned anything happening to her, but if she was able to run the Bar M, she sure wouldn't hire a foreman. Especially an egotistical male chauvinist who jumped to conclusions and let his dump-truck mouth get ahead of his bicycle butt. And besides, just how did Beau Luckadeau get from Louisiana to Oklahoma, anyway? The last time she'd seen him he was drunker than Cooter's owl. Thank goodness for that. At least he had been so drunk he didn't remember meeting her that disastrous night, which seemed like eons ago. The episode couldn't have affected him like it did her. If it had, he would have noticed the smoke rising from his hand when she slapped his pointing finger away from her face. His insides would be something akin to warm, quivering jelly and he wouldn't be watching her from the back side of that little rise. He'd have gotten a soft look in his eyes and gathered her in his arms so tightly she could hear his heart beating too fast through his chambray work shirt. No, sir, Beau did not remember and that was a good thing.

She finished the job, checked the wire for tightness so he would see she was able to do exactly what she set out to do, mounted her horse, Wild Fire, and rode back to the house, leaving only a cloud of dust, a herd of white-faced heifers, and a million unanswered questions in her wake.

She rode hell-bent for leather into the barnyard at the ranch. "Slim? Would you please unsaddle Wild Fire and rub her down? I've ridden her hard and…"

Slim, the tall, lanky ranch foreman with graying hair and gaunt cheeks grabbed the reins. "You're right about one thing, Miss Milli; you rode this horse too hard. A kid from over on the Spencer place called and said some young fellers were out last night letting their dogs run the coyotes. Said he thinks maybe they cut the fence between us and the Bar M. It's over there where Beau keeps that prize bull of his, and you know Jim would rise up out of that bed and kick that bull to hell and back if it got next to one of his cows. Not to mention what Beau would do if he thought someone was trying to get a free standing out of his bull. Brags all the time about how much money he makes in a year off stud fees with that bull. Says the critter is the same as ownin' a good-pumpin' oil well. Thought maybe you'd want to check it out, or at least send one of the boys."

She made a beeline toward the house. "I already fixed it."

"Granny?" she called out at the door. "Where are you?"

A small, lightly brown-skinned lady with gorgeous brown eyes, short graying black hair, and a spry step that belied her sixty years, peeked around the door into the utility room. "Right here, child. What do you need?"

"What is Beau Luckadeau doing on the Bar M?" Milli asked bluntly as she plopped down on the tiled floor and removed her boots.

"Beau? Why, he's the owner. Alice Martin got Alzheimer's disease a while back and when she realized what it could do to her, she willed everything she owned to Beau, since he's her favorite nephew, and then when things started getting bad, she checked herself into a nursing home over in Ardmore. Smart woman. I see her every so often, but she doesn't know me anymore. How did you know Beau?" Mary Torres asked.

"Didn't 'til now," Milli lied. "Sorry sumbitch thought he was going to order me off the land until I dusted up the gravel in front of his boots with my rifle. Treated me like I was some kind of hired hand who didn't know straight up from backwards on a sunny day."

"You shot at Beau?" Mary exclaimed. Why was Milli lying to her? Three signs always gave a liar away: breathlessness, high color, and shifting eyes. Nothing got past Mary Torres. "Why in the world would you shoot at Beau? He's the easiest-going one of all those Luckadeau boys. That's why Alice liked him best. He's got green thumbs when it comes to growing things and a sixth sense when it comes to cattle. Lord, he wouldn't hurt a fly. Now why would you shoot at him?"

"Because he made me mad. He yelled at me."

"He's one of your Poppy's best friends. He used to visit Alice in the summertime. Surely you met him at a barn dance or something when you come back here to visit?"

She tugged off her socks. "Nope, I did not. I didn't even know he was kin to Alice until right now."

"Maybe you better get in your truck and drive over there and make things right," Mary suggested.

"Me? I didn't do nothing. It was *his* stupid bull in our pasture, and he started the fight, yelling at me like some kind of idiot. Come through that cut fence like somebody died and made him God. Called me a bitch, even," Milli said.

"Have it your way."

Something wasn't right. Mary felt as if she was looking at the pieces to a jigsaw puzzle and had no idea where to start fitting them together. There had been questions Milli would never answer, not when all three of her brothers pitched a fit that could be heard all the way from Amarillo to southern Oklahoma. Not even when her mother threatened to throw her out on her ear if she didn't tell them who the baby's father was. Mary didn't know the details, but the first piece of the puzzle glowed brightly.

Milli knew Beau, and that was the corner piece to the whole puzzle.

"Where's Katy?" Milli asked. She padded across the room in her bare feet, untucking a blue chambray shirt to let it fall on the outside of faded blue jeans that fit her so tightly she looked as though she'd been melted and poured into them. Mary remembered a time many years before when she filled out a pair of jeans like that: when all the male eyes in a room followed her as she walked across a room. Milli might look like her mother, but she was sure built like Mary had been at twenty-three: full bosom, tiny waist, rounded hips. Evidently Beau really had let his temper get ahead of his hormones if he yelled at her, instead of admiring all the curves under her jeans and shirt.

"Katy is entertaining your Poppy. I put her in the playpen and she's been throwing her toys out over the top. He picks them up with his cane and tosses them back inside. It's a good game for both of them," Mary answered.

Milli headed for the den, where a hospital bed and lift chair had been installed for her grandfather when he came home from the hospital, and where he ruled the ranch with an iron fist even yet. At least Mary let him think he was king of the Lazy Z. Mary had as much of the ranch sense in the Torres family as her husband. They worked as a team and she was wise enough to let Jim wear the crown.

A pretty little toddler with a head full of gorgeous blonde curls looked up and squealed, "Mommy! Ride, peas?"

The baby raised her chubby little arms. Milli picked her up, squeezing her tightly to her chest. She talked fast to hide the quiver in her voice and the tears welling in her eyes. "We'll go for a ride later, Katy Scarlett. Have you been taking good care of Poppy while Momma's been out checking the cows?"

Katy wiggled down into her mother's embrace and giggled.

"Course she's been taking care of me," Jim said from

his recliner. "Best nurse a Poppy could have. If she wants to ride, then take an hour and go ride with her. We have to encourage her to keep her a cowgirl."

A smile lit his weathered brown face and his soft brown eyes glittered as he watched his only grand-daughter. He enjoyed having them both at the ranch so much that he'd begun thinking in terms of healing slower so they wouldn't go home at the end of the summer. Perhaps he could offer to build them a home of their own. Give Milli a hundred acres or so and bring her herd of cows out from west Texas. The ranch needed the laughter of a child again, and Katy fit the bill just right.

"Poppy, that's all I hear: 'Ride, peas.' She'd keep me on a horse twenty-four seven if I'd let her. She loves to ride."

"I think it's cute the way she says it. 'Body didn't know better they'd think she was wanting to ride peas rather than a horse. Wasn't that her first words? Stands to reason she'd say them often. It brings her something she likes and it's easy for her to say."

Mary stood in the door and that funny feeling rose again. Milli's long black hair covered Katy like a natural blanket when she hugged her tightly. Katy's blonde curls bounced as she wiggled in her mother's arms and it was the second that she looked at Mary that it became so evident. It was those steel blue eyes that everyone noticed when they first looked at Katy. They looked so out of place with her lightly toasted skin from genera-tions of Mexican blood on both sides of the family. Why hadn't she seen the resemblance before?

Milli hugged Katy even closer. "*Ride* was actually her first word. I wanted her to have manners so I said,

'Say ride, please.' Turned into 'Ride, peas.'"

"Ride, peas, now!" Katy drew her eyes down.

"And you shall, after lunch," Mary said.

She eyed mother and daughter. Two years ago Milli had broken up with her fiancé when she'd caught him in a motel with another woman. Then she'd gone back to college at Waco that fall, only to return home at Christmas with a baby on the way. When her brothers had wanted to square off with her ex-fiancé, she had told them the baby wasn't his, and when Katy was born there was no doubt she was telling the truth. Her fiancé was from an old Mexican family and didn't have a drop of Caucasian blood in him. His hair was black as a raven's and his brown eyes were like two lumps of coal set in his well-chiseled, fine-boned face. He had been handsome and rich from the day he was born, with a bank account only slightly smaller than his ego.

At the end of April, when she gave birth to Katy, Milli declared the baby was hers and didn't have a father. Even when her mother threatened her, she stood by her decision not to tell, but now that Mary looked at the baby, she wondered if she really didn't know what gene pool Katy Scarlett dipped into to inherit those blue eyes and blonde curls. As she stared at the child with a puzzle piece now firmly in place, she saw other features that supported her theory. Curly blonde hair. Tall for fourteen months. Sweet natured. The exact replica of her father, with only a little of her mother's skin color, determination, and temper showing through. Oh, all of it could have come from Milli's other grandmother, but somehow, Mary Torres didn't think so.

"What are you staring at so intently, Mary?" Jim asked. "It looks like heaven just opened up and you got a glimpse of an angel."

Mary smiled sweetly. "That's exactly what happened, sweetheart. Milli, bring Katy out in the yard and we'll put her in the swing for a while before dinner. She needs to get some fresh air, and your chores are done for the morning. We'll put old crip here in his wheelchair and push him out to watch her giggle. That'll probably heal the hip quicker than any medicine the doctor can prescribe anyway."

Jim and Mary sat side by side in the backyard, him in a wheelchair, her in a rocking chair, as Milli pushed the baby in a swing that hung from the first limb of a tall hackberry tree. "What happened back there?" Jim whispered.

Mary shot a look toward the swing. "Shhh, she'll hear you. When I get it all figured out, I'll tell you," Mary leaned over and whispered in Jim's ear.

"Is it about Katy?"

"Yes, and you're going to love the story when it all gets worked out. She's lovely, isn't she?"

"Yes, she is. Sure you don't want to tell me a little bit of it? You know I've always trusted your sixth sense," he teased.

She took his hand in hers, kissing his fingertips. "Not now. Later."

Milli sent up a silent prayer as she listened to Katy's squeals. *Lord, help me to pretend I don't know him if he's ever in my presence again. I need about ten thousand angels right now just to help me keep my sanity, Lord, so if you've got any to spare, send them to southern Oklahoma. Just touching his hand about made me melt in a puddle at his feet—again. I'd be grateful for a miracle, because that's what I'm afraid it's going to take if I have to stay here all summer.*

Chapter 2

BEAU DRAGGED A FOLDING LAWN CHAIR ACROSS THE YARD and melted into it. "Mornin', Jim. Looks like we're going to have another hot one, don't it? How's that hip? Been meanin' to get over here all week, but things has been hectic over at the Bar M. How you been, Miss Mary? Keeping everybody in line with this old codger out of your way?"

"Oh, he still takes care of most things. He and Slim can boss from anyplace on the ranch."

"And I'm better now that my granddaughter and her baby are here to help me out. Slim could probably do the work. Goodness knows he bosses the boys around as much as I do. But Milli needed a break from the Lazy T and she's almighty good help," Jim said.

Beau nodded. "I see."

So that T listing off to one side was the brand from her father's ranch. Beau remembered Jim mentioning his son ranching somewhere out in the panhandle of Texas. He'd married a woman from that area and they'd located out there. Beau wrinkled his brow in a frown, trying to remember all that Jim had mentioned about the ranch while they played poker, but nothing else rose to the surface of his memory pool.

"Met your granddaughter this morning out in the pasture. Some fool kids cut the fence and my bull got over on your land. Don't think he did any damage. Just ate a few bites of your grass," he said casually.

Jim grinned. "Guess I can spare that, son. Milli didn't mention meeting you."

One minute Milli was pushing Katy in the swing and listening to her squeal. At least she could enjoy the exuberance of her daughter, the sweetness of her grandparents' love, and the mid-morning summer breezes. By afternoon it would be so hot the horny toads and grasshoppers would be carrying parasols and canteens. Granny and Poppa were holding hands and had their heads together as they whispered like newlyweds. Someday she was going to have a marriage just like that. Someday when she found a man she could trust. One who didn't say the words, "I love you," the same way he asked, "Do you like white wine?" That's about how much the three words meant to Matthew. He said the right things at the right time—and didn't men love women before they proposed to them?

Apparently not all of them.

She shook off the bad memories and lifted her eyes toward the cloudless blue sky to thank the Almighty she'd found out just what kind of man Matthew had been before she married him. A flicker from the sunlight dancing on Beau's blond hair caught her attention before she could even phrase a quick word of thanks. When she looked over her shoulder at her grandparents, expecting to see Granny either blushing or Poppa whispering sweet words again—there was Beau sitting in a lawn chair beside them.

The heavens had opened up and dropped him down in her sight again, for the second time in one day. Heavens, nothing. If anything had dropped him, it would be the pure old devil himself. Maybe he was the devil incarnate. With clear blue eyes and tight-fitting jeans that made her blush when her eyes went from his sexy mouth, down his hard chest rippling with muscles beneath a skin-tight T-shirt, to his belt buckle and below.

His gaze traveled from her bare feet up to her face, blushing crimson—but there was no recognition in his eyes. Not a single blink and then a slow smile to say, "Hey, I remember you. I remember that night when…"

Good grief. She'd come to Oklahoma to get away from everything. This wasn't going to be a summer of peace; it was going to be a summer of pure turmoil straight from the bowels of hell's furnace.

"Milli," Jim called. "Come over here and say hello to our neighbor."

She had the sudden impulse to grab Katy, load Wild Fire back in her red and white horse trailer, and make a beeline back to west Texas. Or forget the horse trailer and just get in her little airplane out on the north forty and let one of the hired hands bring Wild Fire home next week. She was sitting on top of a keg of dynamite with a short fuse and the explosion was going to rock the world. On second thought, even an airplane couldn't get her out of Oklahoma and back into Texas fast enough. She wished she could twitch her nose like that witch on television when she was a little girl, and presto, Beau would be a toad frog or an Angus bull. He could be the best-looking cowboy in the whole world twenty-four hours after she was gone, but just let him be a bull long enough for her to get Katy out of southern Oklahoma. Suddenly, a ranch in

Australia looked good. Or even in South Africa. She'd raise chickens in a Louisiana swamp if she could just get away from Beau.

Louisiana, she moaned silently. She didn't ever want to set foot in that state again. They could give the whole state to the Cajuns and make it a separate country for all she cared.

Not a single one of these options had a foot in reality, and if she didn't want to upset Poppa, she'd have to go over there. However if that man went and recognized her, she was going to grab Katy and run. She gave Katy one more push to keep her swinging and crossed the yard to where Beau was sprawled out in a lawn chair like he belonged to the Lazy Z Ranch.

"This is Anthony Beau Luckadeau," Jim said. "He inherited the Bar M from Alice. Does a fine job of running it. We just call him Beau—he's not too fond of Anthony."

"Mr. Luckadeau?" She tried to smile but it came out more like a grimace. Lord, Almighty, but he was good-looking. Those clear blue eyes and all that blond hair, not to mention the way he filled out his blue jeans or the way his chest and arm muscles strained the seams of his faded blue T-shirt. The last time she saw him he was dressed up for a wedding, but even in his work clothes, he'd make any woman's panty hose crawl down to her ankles.

Stop it. This is a crucial time and if he looks up and says anything about Texarkana two years ago, I'm in deep trouble.

He stood up, towering above her five foot four inches, and stuck out his hand. "Just call me Beau. I really don't like Anthony. Guess we got off on the wrong foot this morning. I should have introduced myself instead of assuming you knew me."

A jolt of electricity glued her to the ground when she put her small hand in his big one, and a new burst of anger boiled in her heart. She had been determined never to let anyone make her feel like this again. Men weren't to be trusted. They were all fickle and few cared what happened when the good time was finished.

She nodded coolly, ignoring the hot, fiery emotions. "Beau, it is, then. I should have introduced myself, too. It was just a crazy mix-up. Now, if you'll excuse me, I have to take Katy inside."

"That your little girl?" Beau hated to let go of her hand. Those brown eyes were familiar. He'd met lots of women in his thirty years and he was a complete sucker for brown eyes, especially since an experience at a wedding a couple of years before. But that woman was just a figment of his overactive and drunken imagination. She didn't really exist, or so his relatives said. If she did, she might have looked a little like Milli. That's probably why he felt so drawn to her. She was physically like his Amelia: the lady who had stolen half his heart one hot, steamy night in Louisiana. Amelia had had a soft southern voice like pure clover honey with just a faint hint of good whiskey to cut the sweet taste. She'd lain in his arms and taken his soul to paradise and then disappeared: an angel no one remembered and he couldn't find the next morning.

She nodded and turned away from him. "Yes, that is my daughter, Katy."

"Your husband here, too?"

"No," she said over her shoulder as she took Katy out of the swing and started toward the house with Mary following close behind.

Beau didn't want her to leave. "Is he coming later?"

She pretended she didn't hear him.

"She hasn't got a husband," Jim said. "Set back down here, son, and keep an old man company for a little while. Womenfolk think they've got to help Hilda put dinner on the table. Why don't you stay and eat with us? Hilda always makes plenty."

Beau shook his head seriously. "Can't, but thanks for the invitation. Rosa would have my hide tacked to the smokehouse door if I didn't show up for dinner today. She's made apple dumplings and they're my favorite dessert. Milli's divorced, then?"

"Nope, never married. Folks were upset at first, but Katy kinda wins everyone's heart so they got over it pretty quick. Milli's a top-notch hand. She can work hard as any man and cook good as any woman. Her brothers can't hold a candle to her when it comes to cattle. She got a sixth sense about it from her granny. Mary's always been smarter than me about ranching, but she's a good enough woman to let me think everything is my idea. Milli was engaged to a fellow who did her dirty and then she went away to college and got pregnant. Wouldn't ever tell who the father was. Just said the baby was hers and she was a single mother."

"I see," Beau said, a whoosh of air escaping from his lungs. Relief filled him. He didn't want Milli to be married, and yet couldn't understand why. Amanda, his current girlfriend, the woman he intended to propose to the very next night, was everything he needed in a wife. Tall, blonde, feminine. A kindergarten teacher at the Wilson school. He'd dated her for six months and it was time for him to settle down and raise a son to take over the Bar M someday. So why did he care whether or not Milli Torres was married?

"Well, I better be gettin' on back. If I'm late Rosa will complain for a week. Looks like you'll be back at the head of the poker table before long," he said.

"Sure hope so. Don't be a stranger, son. Come back soon. Guess we'll see you at the Spencer barn dance tomorrow night? Mary says I can go if I'll sit in the wheelchair. Won't be easy for an old two-stepper like me. Reckon I could beg you into askin' my wife to dance one time? Doc says it'll be a few weeks before I can do much dancin'," Jim said.

"Be honored, sir. See you there. And listen to the doc. You can dance later."

"That's hard for an old feller like me to do." Jim waved as Beau disappeared around the front of the house.

"Now, what was that all about?" Jim muttered as he drew his eyebrows down into a solid black line over his brown eyes. "Something is brewing around here. I can smell it, and by damn, Mary knows something, too. And I think it might have to do with Beau. Milli acted like she'd rather touch a rattlesnake than shake Beau's hand, and she ain't never even met him. Well, Mary better get ready to tell me what's going on or I'll get out of this wheelchair and throw a stompin' ravin' fit."

"Nice man, that Beau," Mary said. "Hilda, don't you think Beau is a nice man?"

The gray-haired cook nodded as she stirred a pot of pinto beans boiling on the back of the stove. "Yes, I do. Always been polite and a downright nice gentleman. Don't know what he sees in that Amanda girl, though. She's uppity if you ask me. Course, it ain't a bit of my business. Rosa says when she comes to the ranch she's got her nose so high in the air that if it rained, she'd drown. But if that's who he's got picked out, guess we'll have to live with it. Like I said, it ain't a bit of my business if Amanda turns the whole ranch into some kind of social club, and you mark my words, that's exactly what she'll do. Anyway, that's Beau's business. It sure ain't mine."

"Who's Amanda?" Milli asked, then was instantly angry for caring. Whatever Beau did or didn't do wasn't any of her concern. She'd only met him one time before and that was a strange situation that he wouldn't ever remember, and every day she wished she didn't either.

"Why, that's his girlfriend. Talk has it that he's about to propose to her," Mary said. "She's a schoolteacher up in Wilson. She's a tall blonde and pretty as a picture, but so snooty and snobby, no one around here thinks much of her. Beau brought her to the last barn dance over at the Spencers' place and she acted like she was afraid she'd step in something nasty all evening. Barely would even two-step with Beau."

Milli fought a batch of tears damming up behind her eyes. She didn't shed a tear the day the doctor told her she was pregnant. She didn't cry when she told her parents and her mother ranted and raved for an hour about how she'd disgraced both the Jiminez and Torres names. She didn't even cry when she was in labor for sixteen hours and delivered an eight-pound daughter. So where in the hell did a bucket of tears come from now?

Hilda talked as she cooked. "Rosa says that Beau is as lucky as they come. Says he can make a cow have a healthy calf and the alfalfa grow tall as a barn, but he's just plain stupid when it comes to women. She says he's lucky in everything—but he ain't lucky in love. So I guess if he really asks this Amanda to marry him, he'll have a pretty showpiece for his ranch, but she won't be worth much more than tits on a boar hog. She might be a good teacher, but she's worthless when it comes to ranchin'."

Mary saw her granddaughter's big brown eyes swimming in tears. Maybe it was just the stress-filled morning. It couldn't have been easy to find that big, black bruiser of a bull in her grandfather's pasture. It would have been hard to face Beau out in the yard after she'd yanked out her gun and shot at him—to realize he was indeed a good friend of the family. But Mary really believed that her granddaughter, Camillia Kathryn Torres, was facing something bigger than her pride today.

"I think Katy needs her diaper changed," Milli choked out a few words and disappeared up the stairs of the farmhouse with her daughter.

She set Katy on the bedroom floor to play and plopped down on her bed to stare at the swirls in the textured ceiling. If she'd known Beau Luckadeau was anywhere near southern Oklahoma, she certainly would not have accepted the offer to work for her grandparents all summer. Now that she was here, how in the world would she ever be able to go back home without an excuse? The only thing she could do was endure the summer, hopefully with her emotions and senses intact.

Katy picked up a pyramid of brightly colored rings stacked on a rocking base. Milli continued to stare at the ceiling, remembering the summer two years before.

She'd fallen in love with Matthew the first day she laid eyes on him at the Lazy T cattle sale. His grandfather and father had come from the Rio Grande Valley to look at a Torres bull for his grandfather's ranch. She could envision that day even yet. She had walked into the barn and his eyebrows had raised a full inch.

"Well, is someone here going to introduce me to this lovely lady?" Matthew had asked softly. "Or did an angel just fall out of heaven and no one knows her?"

"My daughter, Camillia," her father had thrown over his shoulder and went back to talking with the elderly gentlemen about the bull.

He'd bowed deeply and kissed her fingertips. "And I am Matthew. I'm sure they can decide whether this bull is of the quality they need for our ranch. Come, walk with me and show me your ranch. This country is very different than our valley."

She was smitten from the moment he bent over her hand and heard his soft Texas drawl with just the faintest trace of Spanish accent. They bought the bull and before they left, she had a date with Matthew for the next week. He flew into Amarillo from south Texas and took her to a steak house. Her mother said they made the cutest couple in the world, and Matthew treated her like a China doll.

Two months later he'd proposed, drawing a three-carat diamond solitaire from his pocket. "My darling, I love you with my whole heart," he whispered seductively and kissed her passionately. "I want things to be right between us, but I don't want to wait forever to hold you in my arms and make love to you."

She almost told him at that very moment that he didn't have to wait any longer than it would take them to drive to the nearest motel, but his family and hers wanted one of those old-fashioned real weddings where the bride wears white and deserves it. "I know. Let's have a short engagement and get married soon. A huge wedding with satin and roses and the whole works. Our mothers will love it and we'll be so busy the time will go fast."

He'd wrapped his arms around her. "With a reception afterwards at the Lazy T. We can leave at dark, just as the sun is setting, and go to Amarillo, where we will fly to an island paradise and stay for days in a cabin. Just the two of us making wonderful love."

It was perfect. Not one thing could ever go wrong.

Until one of Milli's friends called one evening.

She had been coming home from a dinner date in Canyon when she saw Matthew slipping into a motel on the outskirts of town. A tall blonde was hanging on him as they opened the door to a room. At first Milli didn't believe a word her friend told her, but the friend was adamant. So, more to appease her than anything else, she drove fifteen miles to the motel. She parked beside his Mercedes and must have sat there an hour, staring at the motel door. Her wedding dress hung in the guest bedroom from a hook in the ceiling—the train falling from a bow in the back and reaching all the way across the room.

She wiped the sweat from her forehead just like she had when she had slipped into the dress in the bridal shop. She had giggled with her sisters-in-law that day about how hot satin could be.

"It'll be hot in the church. Can't get it cool enough for a bride. Must be the thoughts of what is going to happen later that night," one of them had teased with a twinkle in her eye.

Anger replaced numbness in front of the motel as Milli looked at her engagement ring, an emerald-cut diamond solitaire. Without love, it was nothing but a glass cutter. It sparkled by the light of the moon, but glitter didn't bring trust. She moaned. Her mother was going to crucify her. Just yesterday her engagement picture had been in the newspaper. Now everyone in the panhandle of Texas would know that she was engaged and then, suddenly, not engaged. Maybe she should forgive this indiscretion. After all, they weren't married yet. She hadn't gone to bed with him when he mentioned not waiting forever to get married because he wanted her so badly.

What was the matter with her? Great God in Heaven, was a diamond and a newspaper article worth going through life without trust? No sir! It was not.

She would not marry a man and pledge to love him until death parted them, if she couldn't trust him. She wanted the kind of marriage her grandparents had—both her Torres grandparents in Oklahoma and her Jiminez grandparents in Rio County, Texas. The kind her parents had. She didn't want to wonder every time Matthew called to tell her he was working late, or every time he left for a few days on business, if he was in a cheap motel with some other woman.

She knocked on the motel room and listened to the

giggles and heavy breathing, then knocked again, this time louder.

"Who is it?" Matthew's voice was breathless.

She called loud and clear, "Room service."

"Just a minute," he said.

She heard shuffling and imagined him finding his expensive pants among a pile of tumbled clothing on the floor.

His eyes were big when he opened the door and zipped his pants all at the same time. His chest was bare and dark circles showed on his neck where the blonde had marked him during sex.

"What in the hell are you doing here?" he demanded roughly.

She handed him the ring. "I came to bring you back your property."

"Damn it, Milli," he said. "This don't mean nothing. We can't do anything until we're married. You can't expect me to do without for six months."

She looked him right in the eye and didn't blink. "It means something to me, Matthew. It means a lot to me. Don't call me. I never want to see you again."

"It's a deal!" He slammed the door.

It was the last time she had seen the man. His father called her father with an apology, but Matthew never called. The dress went back to the bridal shop and most of the gossip mongers quit talking a few weeks later.

Two weeks after the engagement was broken, she received an invitation to attend a high school friend's wedding in Texarkana, five hundred miles away on the other side of the state. She and Lisa had been friends from junior high until graduation two years before. Lisa had gotten a scholarship to East Texas State University and Milli was enrolled at West Texas State University. Milli RSVP'ed the very day she got the invitation. It was exactly what she needed to get over the Matthew-doldrums. She would fly into Texarkana for the wedding and stay in a motel for a couple of nights.

Lisa Thomas married Darrin Luckadeau, an air force captain, on Saturday night, and Milli envied her the wedding, the love, and the marriage. After the reception another party was held at the Luckadeau ranch and Milli went with a whole group of Luckadeau cousins, their relatives and friends. Sometime during the course of the evening a tall, good-looking cousin glued himself to her side. He was drinking too much champagne and talking much too loudly, but he was the exact opposite of Matthew Sanchez.

"Mommy?" Katy said, breaking into her thoughts.

Milli opened up her arms and Katy toddled toward her. "Come here, baby."

Katy laid her face on Milli's chest and stuck her thumb in her mouth. In a few seconds she was sleeping soundly. Milli sat down in the big, comfortable rocking chair in the corner of the room and let her thoughts go back again to the night of Lisa and Darrin's wedding.

"Who is that man?" She'd asked a girl when the good-looking stranger left her side for a few minutes.

"That's Beau Luckadeau. Cousin of the groom. Handsome old thing, isn't he? All them Luckadeau men are good-lookin'. They come from down around Shreveport. Big family of them. His daddy is one of about six or eight boys and only one girl. And there's a whole scad of Luckadeau brothers in Beau's family. Lord, it'd be impossible to remember all their names. But they're all damn good-lookin', blond and blue-eyed. All except for Griffin, the one with the white streak in his black hair. He's the oddball. Beau usually doesn't drink much. Somebody said his latest girlfriend dumped him for another man. Guess he ain't so lucky when it comes to love," the girl said and headed toward the champagne fountain.

"Understand your name is Jiminez," he'd said when he sat back down in the chair beside her. "Lady over there told me your last name. But I don't know your first one."

"Camillia," she said softly. "And they call you Beau and your family is from Shreveport."

"My dad's family is. I'm from wherever the wind takes me. I might just be from Timbuktu next week." He slurred his words. "Why don't me and you get away from this place and go over to my cousin's trailer where I'm stayin', and talk where it's nice and quiet?"

She was playing with fire. She was using the man to get even with Matthew, who didn't give a damn if she got revenge or not. She didn't even know him. He could be a prisoner on parole. He could be married, despite what the girl had said. Right then she didn't care. She tipped back the champagne he'd handed her and smiled up at him.

"All right. It is pretty noisy here, isn't it? I can't even hear myself think."

He'd handed her the keys to his truck. "You better drive. I don't usually drink and I never drive when I do. Trailer is a mile down the highway. First turn to the right and second trailer on the left."

"Okay," she'd said.

Memories continued to tumble around her as she nuzzled her face into her sleeping daughter's soft hair. Sometimes at night when she awoke, her body ached for his touch, her mouth wanted to be kissed like that again, but it was all a fairy dust night. He hurt because he'd been dumped. She hurt because Matthew couldn't be trusted. In their pain they'd found each other for one night only.

He'd used a key to open the trailer door and when they were inside he wrapped his arms around her and kissed her passionately. She remembered feeling a jolt unlike anything she'd ever experienced before or since, until today when he shook her hand out in the backyard. Matthew's kisses hadn't affected her like that, and neither had any of the other boyfriends she'd had along the way.

She'd shaken her head when the kiss ended. "Whew, that champagne is some potent stuff."

He led her to the sofa and pulled her down to sit on his lap. "I think I saw some stars. Don't know if it's the liquor or the kiss."

A hundred kisses later, they found their way to the bedroom at the back of the trailer, where he threw his white western shirt and freshly starched and ironed jeans in a heap on the floor with her off-white, lace dress. An hour later he was snoring loudly beside her and she was staring at the ceiling wondering what she'd just done.

Sex. It was more than she'd ever expected. Even the pain of the first time didn't dull the glow all around her. She pulled the sheet up to cover her nakedness, as if he could see through shut eyes and a drunken haze. He looked more like a little boy than a grown man, with blond ringlets framing his angular face. Heavy eyelashes brushed the top of his cheeks, which needed to be shaved again. She ran a finger over the rough beard, an anomaly for a blond man. Most of them had little facial hair. She was about to tangle her fingers in the fine curly brown chest hair when she heard the front door rattle and someone, presumably another cousin, came in. That jerked her into reality so quickly she drew back her hand as if she'd been scalded.

Just before daylight the trailer was finally quiet. Using the dim light of the moon, she found the number of a cab service in the directory under the phone on the nightstand. Very gently she crawled out of the bed and slipped into her lace dress. She firmly resisted the temptation to kiss him on the forehead and eased out of the trailer to patiently wait on the porch for the taxi.

She drove from the church parking lot to the motel where she'd stayed the night before and changed into traveling clothes. She checked out at daybreak, gave the rental car back to the Hertz folks, and waited for two hours until she could board her plane, taking her back across the state to Amarillo.

The next month she went back to college for her junior year. She hadn't even finished the first nine weeks when the doctor confirmed her suspicions. She was pregnant. She couldn't believe it. Chances of pregnancy the first time out of the chute were slim to none—or so she'd thought.

Beau Luckadeau wouldn't even remember her name. He sure wouldn't remember that night she laid in his arms and saw a whole galaxy of stars explode as they made wild, passionate love. He certainly wouldn't want to be forced into a marriage with a woman who was so easy all he had to do was kiss her and she fell into bed with him. Not even if that woman was carrying his child. Whoever said you didn't get pregnant the first time had cow chips for brains and even though the idea of abortion flitted through her mind—to save the family from embarrassment—she didn't think about it very long. She had acted without a lick of common sense, and now she'd pay the fiddler for her actions.

She'd gone home at Christmas and told her family she was pregnant. In April, Katy Scarlett Torres had been born in Canyon, and before she was a week old, she'd had the whole Torres family wrapped firmly around her little finger.

Milli remembered that night in Louisiana often but she'd never uttered a word about Beau Luckadeau. She'd come close to having a full-fledged heart attack when she turned to find him cussing a blue streak about his precious bull. Thank goodness there hadn't been the faintest sign of recognition in his eyes. She'd just have to be very careful that he didn't see too much of Katy. Because if he ever looked at her close, he'd have to be blind as a bat not to know he was looking at his own child.

Chapter 3

"I THINK I'LL JUST STAY HERE WITH KATY," MILLI said when the talk got around the supper table about the Spencers' barn dance. "She's not quite used to the place."

"She'll be fine with Hilda. You need to get out and socialize with the folks. Bet you haven't been dancing in months. The Spencers have a barn dance four times a year. We have one four times a year and the Bar M has one four times a year. So we've got something going once a month to keep us all from going plumb crazy. Katy will be asleep most of the time we're gone anyway, and Hilda's been rocking her to sleep for her afternoon nap, so she won't be afraid." Mary didn't leave room for argument.

Besides, Mary wanted to see Beau and Milli in a social setting. She'd noticed the sparks when he shook her hand out in the backyard, and she also saw the sheer fear in Milli's eyes. It was as if a magnet drew Milli to him while her good sense wanted her to bolt and run like a jackrabbit. It was the first time in all her life that Mary Torres had ever seen her granddaughter fear anything, anyone, or anywhere. She could ride a bull, barrel race with the best of the best, and make her little airplane do stunts that took a person's breath away. So why would she be afraid of Beau?

Milli nodded, afraid to put up too much of a fuss, and listened halfheartedly all through supper about cows and

who would be at the dance. It would probably do her a
world of good to see Beau dancing and flirting with his
girlfriend, Amanda, who was as worthless as tits on a
boar hog according to Hilda. Even that thought couldn't
conjure up a smile.

Later, she opened the closet doors and stared at the
hangers without seeing anything. Finally she pulled out
a pair of tight-fitting jeans and a sleeveless, turquoise
and hot pink western-cut shirt and tossed them on the
bed. She chose turquoise and diamond stud earrings
and a small T-drop necklace encrusted with diamonds
hanging on a gold chain. She tied her long, dark hair
back with a turquoise bandanna, and lightly dusted her
nose with powder.

"Long as I can keep him from recognizing me,
I'm fine. But what the devil difference does it make,
anyway? He was so drunk he probably doesn't even
know he spent part of a night with anyone. He just woke
up the next day, grabbed his aching head, and thought
he'd had a dream. Probably even a nightmare, because I
sure didn't know what I was doing. Just whatever came
natural when a girl is mad as the devil and hotter 'n the
furnace door in hell."

Jim whistled through his teeth when she came down
the stairs. "Whooeeee! If you don't cause a couple of
fights out behind the barn tonight, I'll be surprised."

She lit up in a brilliant smile—but it didn't quite
reach her eyes. "Oh, Poppy, you just love me. Besides,
cowboys don't fight over women like that anymore."

"Yep, I love you, but I ain't blind. And don't fool
yourself darlin'. Cowboys still draw lines, spit on their
knuckles, and decide who's goin' to court a good-lookin'

woman. Mary, let's go visit the neighbors and show off my favorite granddaughter," he said.

"Poppy, I'm your *only* granddaughter other than Katy," Milli reminded him.

"Yep," he said. "And when she gets to be twenty-three years old you might have to move over and she'll be my favorite. But tonight you're the fair-haired child."

Milli laughed, her spirits lifting. "Fair-haired? That's something you sure can't ever call me. Maybe you can call Katy fair-haired, but I've got too much of your blood showing through to be your fair-haired baby. I'm a black-haired, brown-eyed Mexican."

A live band played country music from a platform in the south end of the Spencers' biggest barn. Fresh hay covered the floor and several couples were already out on the floor when Mary pushed Jim in his wheelchair through the doors and settled him in front of a table. She kissed him on the forehead and said she'd find him a tall glass of tea to sip on while he listened to the music.

"I don't want tea," he said. "Bring me a longneck beer."

She shook her head. "Not with your medication. In a couple of weeks you can have a beer, but not now. Remember: no alcohol or dancing."

"Don't remind me," he groaned. "I feel like an invalid. No dancing, no beer, no nothing."

"You'll survive, and just think how much fun it'll be when you can dance again," Milli said when Mary headed toward the refreshment tables. "I'm going to the ladies' room and don't you be flirting while I'm gone."

When she came out, she stopped in the shadows. She had spotted Beau right away, dancing with a tall, fair woman who must have been Amanda. The woman looked as out of place as a hooker in the front row of the church in a revival meeting. She wore a pink business suit with high-heeled shoes to match, and a triple strand of pearls around her neck. Her expression told everyone there that she'd as soon be in bed with a migraine as dancing the two-step with Beau.

"Oh, well," Milli muttered under her breath. "That's his stupid business."

A voice behind her made her jump. "Talkin' to yourself? It's all right. I like to stand back and watch things myself. Sometimes I've even been known to mutter a bit. Ain't seen you in a few years, Miss Milli."

She hugged the man. "Buster, you come near to scarin' me into heart failure. Thought I was the only one hiding in this corner. Tell me what's been going on with you and Miss Rosa and all the crew. And how's Alice?"

"Poorly. Alice don't know anybody. Ain't much use in goin' in that place to see her anymore. She'd rise up and shake the liver outta that boy out there if she knew he was courtin' that woman. Amanda ain't ranchin' material. She's liable to be the ruin of Beau," Buster frowned.

"Why?" Milli asked.

"Just something I feel in my bones and see with my eyes. But even if I was stone-cold blind and couldn't see a thing, I could still feel it. Just look at her, Milli. She's window dressing for town livin'. Boy's smart about everything but women, but when it comes to them he ain't got a lick of sense. You better get on out there on the dancin' floor. Pretty girl like you don't need to stand in the shadows all night. I'll dance the first one with you and then I'll step aside and watch the young fellers beat a path to your side. You sure are a pretty sight."

"I'll just stand here and watch," Milli said.

Buster grabbed her hand and pulled her out in the middle of the floor, then picked up her hand and put it on his shoulder. "Over my dead body. Now smile and make this old man feel real good, just thinkin' he's done beat all the good-looking feller's time with the prettiest woman in the barn."

Beau looked over Amanda's shoulder and saw Milli. Buster looked as if he had died and gone straight to heaven. A surge of jealously filled Beau from the silver-tipped toes of his light-gray eel cowboy boots all the way to the top of his feathered-back blond hair. His eyebrows knit into a solid line across the top of his big, round blue eyes, and his square jaw set in a firm line. Two forces battled inside him and all he could think was run… and run… and run. He needed to go out to the back forty or to Lake Murray, lie flat on his back, and sort out all these crazy emotions. He hadn't been so confused since the night Darrin got married. The night he met the lady of his dreams: Amelia Jiminez.

He remembered leaving her side for a minute at the party after the wedding.

"Who's that beautiful woman?" he'd asked an older relative.

"That's one of the Jiminez girls' daughters from west Texas. Those Jiminez girls were all pretty. The grandfather married a white woman, and they had three or four girls, or maybe it was five or six. A whole passel of them, anyway. Seems like she might belong to the oldest one."

Here he was about to ask Amanda to marry him and a spitfire from west Texas falls out of the sky to torment his mind and body. It was just because she reminded him of the lady at the wedding, and she was nothing more than a figment of a drunken imagination.

What was it Buster said? Milli was full of spit and vinegar. Well, he could sure enough believe that. Even when he'd dreamed about her last night, she'd been a pure witch. She'd had that rifle on her shoulder and was looking down the barrel, just daring him to take one step toward her. He had awakened in a cold sweat with desire surging through his veins. He'd wanted to take the gun away from her and kiss her fiercely to see if he'd get the same response as he did when he kissed Amelia that hot Louisiana night. He'd reminded himself one more time that Amelia didn't even exist except in his imagination. It was a long time before he went back to sleep.

Amanda wanted to finish the silly dance, put in enough of an appearance to keep Anthony from getting angry, and then plead a headache so she could go home. Lord, she hated these backwoods boonie affairs, and as soon as they were married, they'd never go to another one. That was a fact, and they could drag out the stone, chisel the words into it, and prop it up beside the ranch house porch post. Country music gave her a headache and the only thing she hated worse than barns was that old ranch foreman who was dancing with the dark-haired gypsy-looking woman.

After she and Anthony were married, the foreman would be the first thing to disappear from the ranch.

God, she hated the way he looked at her. Even the six months she planned to stay married to Anthony before she filed for divorce and took half his property was too damned long to put up with that old man.

A tight little smile turned up the corners of her mouth—but it didn't last long. Buster tapped Beau on the shoulder and said something. Then suddenly Amanda was dancing with the old man.

Beau put his hand on Milli's back and a strong jolt of chemistry rattled around in his tall, lanky body like a dynamite blast in the side of a rocky mountain. "Miss Torres? So how's Jim today?"

"Fine." Her heart pounded.

"You know, it seems to me like I've met you somewhere before. I used to come to the Bar M when I was just a kid—did I see you here back then?"

"No. I visited Granny and Poppa every summer, but I never met you here," she said honestly. He danced well and she fit into his arms as well vertically as she had horizontally. High color filled her cheeks at that thought.

The song ended and Beau tipped his hat to Milli. "Thank you for the dance. Be seein' you around."

"You're a fine dancer. It was my pleasure," she said.

Amanda wasted no time crossing the floor and grabbing Beau by the arm. "Anthony, take me home and don't you ever ask me to dance with that old fool again. You know how I feel about him. He stinks like tobacco and cheap shaving lotion and I hate him."

Milli wanted to slap the woman until she was cold for

talking about Buster like that and had to hold her hands tightly behind her back. The Bar M was in big trouble if Beau didn't wake up soon.

"Now, Amanda, darlin', don't say things like that about Buster. He's been on the Bar M so long he's family. Stay a little longer, honey. I've got a surprise for later. And please call me Beau," Beau pleaded.

She tossed her blonde hair back with a sweep of the hand. "Only an hour. I'm going to sit at that table and in an hour I'm going home. And I will never call you Beau. It sounds like a redneck hick name. You'll always be Anthony to me."

He put his arm around her and started to lead her to the floor. The singer crooned a song by Martina McBride, "Safe in the Arms of Love." Amanda set her pink, high-heeled shoes firmly in the fresh hay and refused to be led back to the middle of the barn.

"Dance with me again?"

"No, I'm sitting down until you are ready to take me home. This is not my idea of a social outing. You know I hate these things."

He shook his head. Surely, she would change when they were married. Given a little time she'd be shopping in the western stores for something new to wear to the barn dances once a month, and she'd get excited when a new baby calf was born. She'd learn to like Buster and love Rosa and maybe after this next year she'd even be ready to quit teaching and stay home to raise their son. The first one would be a boy, and probably all the rest after that. Luckadeaus just didn't throw girl babies. As much as his mother would like to have a granddaughter, it wasn't about to happen. Luckadeaus made boys, and that was a fact.

"Looks like that woman is feelin' as out of place as she looks," Jim whispered to Mary. "I sure wish that boy would boot her on out of his life and find someone who'd fit in with his way of livin' a little better. She's got dollar signs in her eyes instead of love."

Mary nodded but didn't say anything.

A young man stopped at their table and tipped his hat toward Mary and Milli. "Evenin' Mr. Jim. How's the hip? Like you to meet Cindy. She goes to school with me. Folks has got a little spread up over by Lone Grove. I saw where you had a fence cut the other morning. I should've stopped and fixed it, but I didn't have my fencing stuff with me. Did you get it taken care of?"

Jim nodded. "Pleased to meet you, Miss Cindy. Make this boy bring you over to the Lazy Z and we'll show you around."

"I'll do it. Hear you raise some white-faced cattle. My dad likes that brand, too. He's got a few Angus, but he's partial to the white face. We had a calf last week and I had to crawl out of bed at four o'clock and help pull the stinker. It was a fine heifer, though, and I'm glad we could save it," Cindy said.

"Well, we gotta get on around the room and make Cindy known. Both my sisters, Amy and Rachel, are comin' in next week for a visit, you know. I expect they'll run over to say hello. Ask Hilda to brew up some peach cobbler and I'll even come with them." Tyler Spencer patted Jim on the shoulder and the two young people went on to the next table.

Milli tried to watch the dancers. She tried to listen to the band. She tried to think about cattle, Wild Fire, West Texas—anything but Beau. But it didn't work. She watched Amanda pull away from him and start toward the ladies' restroom on the south side of the barn. Milli was still itching for a catfight, so she followed her. Amanda and a red-haired woman were both leaning toward the mirror above the lavatory, reapplying mascara, opening their eyes wide and seeing nothing but their already-caked eyelashes. Neither of them appeared to know that the door had opened and there was another woman in the restroom. Milli went into the first stall, put the lid down on the potty, and sat down.

"So how much longer you stayin'?" The redhead asked.

Amanda's voice was high and shrill. "One hour. Not a minute longer, Brenda, and I wouldn't agree to that but he said he had a surprise for me. I figure he's going to propose tonight, so I'll stay around for that. If he doesn't, then I'll be damned if I ever come to another one of these country bumpkin affairs. God, I hate the whiny country music and the smell of hay. Only thing I hate worse than country music and barns is kids."

"And you a schoolteacher?" Brenda chuckled.

"Yep, but I can put on a fake show for the administration and send the little urchins home at three thirty. And I don't plan on being a teacher all my life. It was just something to get me through college while I looked for a husband."

"What do you intend to do after the wedding? He's got a ranch, you know," Brenda asked.

"And he can keep his ranch. God knows, it makes enough money—I damn sure don't want him to give it up. But he can commute every day from Ardmore if he's going to sleep with me. I've got a sweet little brick house in mind. Not too big, just two-story with a triple garage with the maid's quarters over it. Only time I'm living on that ranch is while the paperwork goes through for us to buy something else. And that half-wit foreman of his is getting his walking papers the first week. I'll live here a month and then we're going to town. Six months after everything is signed and legal, Anthony is giving me half of his kingdom. Then I'll go looking for a *sophisticated* husband number two. By the time I get to number five, I might even marry for love."

"Well, good luck." Brenda giggled.

Milli had to hold her hands tightly in her lap to keep from knocking down the restroom door and charging out like a bull from a riding chute. Forget fight! God wouldn't even lay murder to her charge if she shot that sorry excuse for a woman and laid her carcass out for the coyotes to feast upon. Poor, poor, ignorant Beau.

When the two finally left and she could trust herself to stay within the law, she opened the stall door and stopped long enough to check her hair in the mirror, surprised to find a haunted-looking woman staring back at her.

"Oh stop it," she muttered. "You knew you'd never see him again from the beginning, and he's never, ever been yours, so just stop it. Katy and I will go back to west Texas at the end of the summer. You'll only have to see him three times this summer and he's going to be so wound up with his wedding plans he won't even know you are around. You knew what you were doing when you let him lead you back to the bedroom of that trailer. So get on back out there and dance with that tall, dark fellow who's been trying to catch your eye ever since you got here. In ten years, Beau will be just a pleasant memory."

And you're a damned liar.

She ignored the comment from her conscience and went back out to the table where her grandmother and grandfather sat, holding hands and acting like two young people in love.

"Can I claim your granddaughter for another dance?" Beau asked just as Milli sat down. "We didn't get a whole dance last time. And then I'd like to ask permission to dance with your wife, Jim?"

"Sorry, I was just about to call it a night, and go home," Milli said.

"Oh, posh," Mary chided. "We ain't nearly tired out, yet. Go on and dance. Loosen up and relax. Enjoy the evening."

Milli figured she'd be more relaxed in a den of hungry rattlesnakes. "Okay then, Mr. Luckadeau, let's dance."

"I know I've met you before. I think I might even have danced with you before. I can almost remember holding you in my arms, and I wouldn't forget someone as pretty as you," he said.

"I would remember dancing with someone as smooth as you, Beau. And we've never danced before tonight." She didn't lie. They hadn't danced. They'd spent the night wrapped up in each other's arms, but they definitely had not been dancing.

"You ever been to Louisiana?" he asked.

"Flew into the airport one time," she said.

"Well, I sure thought I knew you."

Everyone stopped dancing and formed a circle around them, watching as they kept perfect time. His hand on her back guided her so well that she knew exactly what his next move would be before he turned and she moved gracefully with him. When the song ended, everyone clapped and whistled for them.

"Wonder who the bitch is?" Amanda asked her red-haired friend, Brenda. "I'm thinking she better go on back across the border where she belongs or I might have to kick her that far. I haven't worked six months on this project to have some dark-haired bimbo step in on my territory and take what's mine."

Brenda tapped her on the hand. "Don't worry. Anthony's only got eyes for you. He's not interested in anyone else. It's just a dance. Can you just see him bringing something like that to the Bar M? The woman is Mexican! Their kind might be friends with Alice and Anthony, but to marry one... hey, get real, girl."

"That's the truth. After Anthony proposes tonight, I guess that little hussy will know that he's taken and she'll quit lookin' at him like she could eat him up."

"Jealous?" Brenda asked.

"Hell, no!" Amanda exclaimed. "Just protecting my new house and that new Jag I've got my eye on. He's not about to get out of my clutches. Six months after the "I do," I'll take my half of the ranch in cash."

The woman fanned herself dramatically with her hand. "Looks like you got things figured out really good."

"Yes, I do," Amanda smiled sweetly and waved at Beau.

He grinned back at her and went to the bandstand where he commandeered the microphone. "Ladies and gentlemen, this next song is for Miss Amanda, sitting over there looking beautiful. Honey, if you'll join me for one more dance while they sing our song?"

Amanda whispered behind a fake smile. "I guess it's

going to be a public announcement. Oh, well, the things we women have to do for future security."

She walked toward Beau, who waited in the middle of the floor. The band played "The Battle Hymn of Love," and she swayed to the music, but it wasn't the graceful sight he and Milli had made when they danced together.

The song ended and he dropped down on one knee, still keeping her hands in his. "Amanda, I want to ask you to be my wife," he said loudly enough for everyone in the barn to hear.

A pregnant stillness floated down from the rafters that reminded Jim of the day he heard the announcement on the radio that Pearl Harbor had been fired upon. No one clapped. No one rushed to their side. He choked on a bite of barbecue and swallowed several times before he could make it go down. He should've talked to the boy. Now it was too damned late.

Mary's big brown eyes almost popped right out of her head. His mother was off in Louisiana and neither of his parents had met Amanda, so they didn't know he was about to make a big, big mistake. She should have gone over to the Bar M and made him listen to her. She picked up her beer mug and downed the whole thing, froth and all, without coming up for air, to get the bitter taste out of her mouth.

Milli's chin quivered. She wanted to hit something. Anything would do. A brick wall. Amanda's nose, preferably. Beau's sexy mouth. She looked at the rough wood ceiling of the barn as she tried to get her bearings before she disgraced herself in front of her grandparents by letting tears stream down her face. Things were so quiet that a feather floating through the air to the straw-strewn floor could have been heard a block away.

Amanda played it to the fullest, smiling like a beauty queen in the middle of an eight-foot walkway on the way to get her crown. "Why, darling Anthony, you've caught me totally by surprise. But, of course, I will marry you, darling. I've been in love with you forever. I thought you'd never ask." She bent down and kissed him gently on the cheek.

She squealed when he pulled the box from his pocket and snapped it open. "It's lovely. Look, everyone, what this sweet man has given me." She pivoted all around the room, a huge diamond solitaire flickering in the sparkling lights of the candles set in the middle of the tables.

"You've made me very happy," Beau said with a big grin on his face as he stood to his feet and signaled the band. He put the ring on her finger and drew her close for a slow dance around the floor. Still no one clapped. Few people even breathed. It wasn't really a surprise—he'd been dating her for months. But it wasn't right and everyone was stunned speechless.

"Let's go home," Mary said staunchly. "I might have to get used to this, but I sure don't have to like it, and I'm going home before he expects me to congratulate them tonight. Maybe next week, when the whole thing has sunk in a little better, I can fake a congratulations, but tonight I can't."

Beau had the microphone again. "In two weeks we're having an engagement party at the Bar M. On Saturday night. Rosa and Buster will barbecue a side of beef and you're all invited."

Milli heard the invitation and swore she wouldn't be at that celebration if it absolutely harelipped the president himself. Beau might be about to make a fool out of himself, but she didn't have to participate in the thing. Maybe she'd be fortunate enough at least to be back on the Lazy T before the wedding. Knowing what she did, she could never sit in the congregation at the church and watch him marry a woman who was already planning to take him to the cleaners. He might be blind, but he sure didn't deserve that kind of treatment.

Mary fumed all the way back to the Lazy Z and found a new ear to bend in Hilda, who was reading a romance novel. "Well, he proposed right out there in front of everyone and God. She acted just like you'd expect. We made a hasty getaway before he started bringing her around for everyone to see the ring and tell them how happy they were. Lord, lightning would have come down out of the blue skies and struck me down if I would've uttered such words."

She sucked in a lungful of air and started again. "That fool. Can't he see she's just a gold digger? If he didn't own the Bar M she wouldn't give him the time of day. Why, Tyler Spencer's got more sense than that boy. At least the little girl he had on his arm tonight knew the difference between a bull's balls and the udder of a nursing heifer."

Jim waited until Mary folded her arms across her chest and put his two cents worth into the pot. "Bet that girl wouldn't touch a bait of calf fries if they were served up to her on a silver platter. I sure can't see her helping him run the Bar M. She belongs out here like a horse apple in a church social punch bowl."

Hilda clucked like a hen gathering in her chicks during a storm. "I'm just glad Alice Martin *knew* the boy didn't have much sense when it comes to women-folks. Buster said that she fixed it so the ranch can't never be sold and there's some kind of agreement the lawyers will make her sign before they get married. It says she won't never, ever be able to get a square foot of the Bar M. Be right interesting to see if she signs those papers."

Mary threw up her hands. "I'd forgotten about that. Alice did tell us when she went to the nursing home, but it slipped my mind. Well, now that puts a whole new spin on the merry-go-round. Bet you dollars to donuts that the engagement will be off the day she finds out."

Milli climbed the stairs without saying good night to any of them. Amanda might not have a leg to stand on when it came to making Beau sell the ranch, but she could stay married to him, make his life miserable, and bleed him dry as she demanded more and more material things. In the end, the ranch wouldn't be worth much, anyway.

She found Katy curled up in her crib, a thumb in her mouth and a floppy, old teddy bear drawn up close to her chubby little body. She leaned on the crib and wondered just what Beau would think of his daughter. Would he make a good father?

But those were questions that would never be answered, because Beau—or Anthony, as Amanda seemed determined to call him—and Amanda would be married in a few months, and the only children he would ever know about would be those they produced. The ones that Amanda already declared she would hate. Even if she didn't love him and even if she hated his way of life, she would probably realize the way to keep the money rolling in for fancy houses and expensive cars would be to appease him occasionally. A child would glue her to his side so tightly that he would never leave her, even when he figured out he'd made a bad mistake.

And what about when Katy is eighteen and she comes to you demanding her right to know who her biological father is? her conscience nagged.

"I'll either cross or burn that bridge when I get to it," she whispered.

Chapter 4

MILLI AWOKE THAT FINE TUESDAY MORNING BEFORE dawn and padded down the stairs in her faded Mickey Mouse nightshirt. She carried a glass of orange juice to the deck and sat down in a chaise lounge, enjoying the morning sounds of a ranch waking up from a night's rest. A hungry calf was crying for its mother somewhere in the distance, and the crickets were singing in fine form. A couple of tree frogs added their voices to the cricket's concerto and she thought she heard a faint whisper of a Spanish accent when a fat toad frog put in his baritone croaking.

Pulling her muscular legs up under her, she sat cross-legged, Indian fashion as she sipped the icy cold juice. She flipped her tangled hair over her shoulder and wiped the sleep from big, brown eyes. It might be half-decent cool right then, but the day was going to be another scorcher and the first of June was nothing to what July and August would be in southern Oklahoma. In August, the horny toads, rattlesnakes, and green grasshoppers would be hunting the shady side of a fence post. But the morning air was pleasant, and she marveled again at the peace in the hours just before the sun peeped over the trees on the eastern horizon.

Five years before, she'd graduated from high school and gone away to college. She couldn't wait to get to the city where she didn't have to look at cows; where she could wear fancy shoes instead of boots and nice dresses instead of jeans. A month of dorm life had proven what was really important in her life, and by the end of the semester, she had ached for the smell of a cow lot in the early morning hours. Three years later she went home for Christmas and stayed. She'd never regretted her decision.

A whimper floated down from her bedroom and she quickly drank the rest of her juice before heading back upstairs to change Katy's diaper and bring her down for breakfast. No, she wouldn't trade the joy of her daughter for anything this world had to offer, and raising her on the ranch, just like she'd been raised, was the best gift she could give her. Katy might not have a father, but she had two uncles who doted on her, a grandfather who thought the sun came up each morning just to shine upon her fair hair, and a great-grandfather who was deeply in love with her. She certainly did not lack for a male role model in her life, even if she didn't have a real daddy around twenty-four hours a day.

By the middle of the morning, Milli and Wild Fire were on their way to fix another section of fence those pesky kids had cut while they were out chasing coyotes with their dogs. She'd like to give those boys a piece of her mind… maybe even a piece of leather applied firmly and harshly across their backsides. They had to be city boys who had absolutely no idea what chaos could be created when fences were cut. They might even be related in some way to Amanda, as stupid as they were.

Milli moaned aloud. "Why did I have to even think her name? It's too pretty a morning to mess up with thoughts of that varmint."

She found the cut fence and was mending it when she noticed the big, black cow on the other side of the fence. She was evidently in labor, so Milli eased over to her side.

She crooned to the heifer, whose eyes rolled in fear. "Hey, pretty baby. It's all right, old girl. This must be your first time around," she kept talking as she petted the cow's head. "Hurts like warmed-over hell before breakfast. Kinda makes you wonder if all that short-lived good time was worth it, don't it? I'm going to check this out, now, lady, and see if everything is going like it should, then I'll back right out of here and let old Mother Nature and you do your jobs."

Milli rolled up her right shirtsleeve, baring her whole arm, and had it shoved shoulder deep up into the cow's uterus when Beau rode up on his three-wheeler.

"That's my cow. What in the hell are you doing?" he yelled as he dismounted from the vehicle and set his jaw in a firm line.

She pointed her left index finger at him. "Stop shouting. She's young and she's scared and this damn calf is too big. What'd you do, breed her to that big fancy bull? Bet you didn't even think about how big the calf would be, did you? She's wore out from labor and if you don't help me, you're going to lose her and this baby calf, both. There's rope on my saddle horn. Go get it." She barked the order like a military captain to a green recruit.

"What makes you think you're so damned smart?" He threw the rope back to her.

"I'm not arguing with you right now. Get back here and help me."

"This is my land. This is my cow and that's my calf." Anger stewed in a bubbling rage inside him. How could this woman be so sweet at a dance and so abrasive when she was out in a pasture and close to that horse of hers? And now she'd cut his fence just to come onto his land… to poke her nose into his business and tell him how to do his job.

"If you don't help me all that will be left is your damned land, because this calf and cow are going to be dead. I've got the rope around it and I'm going to monitor the contractions. The next time she's got energy to push, you're going to pull. And damn it, you better pull hard."

"I happen to know how to pull a calf. Who died and made you God of all the Angus in the world?"

She took off her shirt and wiped the slime from her arm. She wore a grungy, old grayed T-shirt under it and there was a long bloody smear across the right arm. "Nobody… yet!"

She patted the cow, "Now, Bossy, work with me, baby…"

He held the rope. "Her name is Betsy, not Bossy."

She cut her eyes around at him. Now where had he seen that look before? Mercy, but he knew he'd seen Milli before somewhere, and it was right on the edge of his mind. Any minute he was going to remember dancing with her at…

She yelled at him even though he was only two feet away. "Pull, damn it, pull hard! She's pushing with all she's got left. Didn't do much good, did you? You're going to have to pull harder than that or I'll hook the rope up to your tricycle and you can back it up."

"You sure are bitchy this morning. Don't you like to get out of bed and face the morning?"

"I probably do a day's work before you ever even open your baby blue... pull again, and this time put some muscle into it," she shouted.

He pulled and felt something give. One second he was jerking on a rope and the next he sat down hard on the baked earth and a baby calf was on the end of the rope. Milli was everywhere at once. Swabbing the calf's nose and mouth with her shirt and barking orders at the cow and Beau both.

She slapped the calf. "Breathe, damn it. Your momma didn't lay here and hurt like hell all these hours to have a dead calf."

Beau figured he'd breathe if she slapped him that hard. By damn, if it was him lying there, all wet and slimy and she said for him to breathe, he'd suck up enough air to fill his lungs in a New York minute.

Finally the calf sighed, took its first breath and bawled all at the same time, and Milli giggled. A light chuckle at first that erupted into a belly laugh of happiness. She wrapped her arms around Beau in a bear hug and knocked him backwards, laughing the whole time. "We did it, Beau. We did it! It's alive."

He hugged her back, reveling in the magic of birth. "We damn sure did. Look at her, Milli. She's a fine new heifer and next year, she'll be big as her momma."

He kept his arm around Milli even after they'd stood up.

"Where'd you learn all that? You're pretty damn handy to have around, even if you are bossy as hell."

"I'm a ranch girl, and I'm not bossy as hell. I just happen to know what to do and you were being obstinate. I've been pulling calves since I was a kid... or at least helping. Daddy said I could get a rope around a calf better than the boys," she said.

"I believe it. If you hadn't come along when you did, I might've lost that cow and calf, but couldn't you just have crawled under the fence or jumped over it? Did you have to cut it?" He moaned as he looked at the tangled barbed wire.

She glared at him. "I didn't cut your fence. Tyler called Poppy this morning and said those same kids who chase coyotes had cut it. If I ever catch them, I'm going to put the fear of Milli Torres into them so deep they'll circle the whole state to keep from cutting my fences again."

He let out a whoosh. "Whew! Well, let's get the sumbitch fixed before our cattle mix it up and me and Jim have a bunch of half-breeds."

"Okay, and I'm still not bossy as hell."

"Yes, you are. Only person in the whole world bossier than you is Aunt Alice. I'll get my wire and—"

"Don't forget the stretcher," she said.

"See… bossy as hell."

Her knees turned to jelly. "Oh, hush!"

Someday he was going to remember just where he'd seen that sassy piece of baggage, and the two of them would laugh because neither of them had remembered it before. They worked together just like they danced. She held the wire while he stretched it tight, and she clipped it. When they finished the job, he was on his property and she was on the other side, on her grandfather's land, with four strands of barbed wire between them.

And that's the way it will always be, she thought. *He'll marry that bitchy Amanda and she'll eventually cause him to lose everything his feet are standing on. And I'll always be close enough to see him... but separated from him by barbed wire.*

His tongue was suddenly glued to the roof of his mouth and the moment turned awkward. "Thanks, again."

She pointed and he turned to see the calf making her wobbly legs support her while she stood for the first time and found her mother's udder. The cow was on her feet and licking the calf.

"Everything's well that ends well," she said.

"Philosophical, as well as a good ranch hand."

"Thank you," she said.

He felt a sudden urge to keep her there, and recapture that memory of just where he had met her or someone who looked a whole lot like her. "You just come by all this natural, or did you go to school for it?"

"Both, I guess," she said. "Poppy and Granny were both ranching folks, and they raised my dad right here on this place. John Torres—don't know if you ever met him or not? He'll be sorry to hear about Alice if he doesn't already know. Granny might have already told him and I just didn't get the message."

"Nope, never did meet him. Heard Jim talk about him a lot at the poker games. You'd think he had a halo or something."

"Well, he married Angelina Jiminez from down in the valley and they bought a spread out in west Texas back before I was born. It's all I ever knew. I went to college and majored in business the first semester, then changed it to vet-tech with an agri-business minor the second semester. I've got an associate's degree in vet-tech, but I never finished up to get my bachelor's. But, honey, I could pull a calf without a piece of paper in my hands saying I knew which end it was coming out of."

"Well, I'm glad you were here today," he said.

Jiminez? Wasn't that the name the man had said in connection with Amelia? Maybe it was. Maybe it wasn't. Jiminez, like Torres and Gonzalez, was as common in Mexico as Smith, Jones, and Williams were in America. The day he put the ring on Amanda's finger was the day he'd made up his mind to completely forget the brown-eyed lady whose memories made his heart ache and set his body on fire with desire. "Guess you'll be at my engagement party Saturday night?" he asked.

It was her turn for acute awkwarditis. "Don't know. Katy hasn't felt real good this week, and Hilda may want the weekend off."

"Katy? That would be your daughter?"

"Yes, and she's teething. Hilda's good with her, but if she can't stay then I wouldn't want to leave her with a stranger," Milli walked away from him toward Wild Fire. "Congratulations, though. I hope you are very happy."

"Oh, I will be. Amanda will learn to fit right in when she spends a little more time out here. Thanks again, and tell Jim and Mary hello for me."

"Will do." She waved as she and Wild Fire disappeared over the rise.

So much for thinking she wouldn't have to see Beau except at a few social affairs. Evidently all the guardian angels in the whole sky had gone on vacation and left her to her own defenses, because not a single one seemed to be around when she was in desperate need. Drat their little naked, winged bodies anyway. She was about to get to the place where she didn't believe in angels, anyway. If they were really up there, she would never have met Matthew Sanchez, and if she'd never met him, she wouldn't have been so angry when she went to her friend's wedding. If she hadn't been mad, then she wouldn't have fallen into bed with Beau and wound up in this bed of thorns today.

Beau watched her until he couldn't even see Wild Fire's tail anymore. It would sure be wonderful when he and Amanda could bring a calf into the world like he and Milli just did. When Amanda would whip off her shirt to wipe off her arm and wouldn't even notice the blood-stains on her T-shirt.

When pigs fly and don't crap on your head, his conscience told him bluntly. *Amanda will never, ever ride a horse or a three-wheeler, and she will never get close enough to a cow to pet it, much less take a rope inside a cow s uterus to help bring a calf out.*

"She might," he stuck his chin defiantly in the air. "She loves me, and when she realizes how much it means to me to have her by my side all the time, she'll learn, and that's a fact. And when our son is born, she'll see how much he loves the land and by then she'll be as at home as Rosa and Buster," he said with determination, leaving no room for that niggling little voice to bother him anymore.

Slim was in the corral when Milli rode in. "Get that fence fixed?"

"Yep," she nodded.

He noticed the blood smudge on her sleeve. He grabbed her arm and checked it as she crawled down off Wild Fire's back. "You hurt yourself on the barbed wire, Milli? Let me see. You need stitches?"

"I'm fine. One of the Bar M cows was down and I helped Beau pull a calf while I was out there."

"Well, go get a shower." He ordered her around just like he'd done since she was a little girl. "I'll take care of this horse. She likes me better than she does you, anyway." He grinned, showing off two oversized front teeth with a big split between them.

Milli laughed with him. "When cows fly. She's just like me. She tolerates men but she doesn't like them."

"Hmmph. Calf make it?"

"Of course. I was there."

"Good thing Beau's woman wasn't there. She'd of scared it to death. One look at a newborn calf and she woulda set up a caterwaulin' to scorch the hair off Lucifer's horns. I still say that boy is out of his monkey-assed mind if he thinks he'll ever turn her into a ranch wife. Lord, even a deaf and dumb, blind fool knows you can't turn a sow's ear into a silk purse. Did you see her face at the barn dance? She hated bein' there worse than anything in the whole world."

"Thanks for taking care of my horse."

Halfway to the house Milli could still hear him, muttering about Amanda. Everyone in the county could see the mismatch mistake but Beau. Evidently he wasn't very lucky in love. At that point, it didn't matter what kind of luck the man had or lacked. He'd made his choice and he was cowboy and man enough to stand beside it. He'd marry that woman no matter how worthless she was because he'd given his word, and that was a fact as solid as the ones Moses brought down from the mountain.

"Lands, child, did you hurt yourself?" Hilda exclaimed when Milli pulled her dirty boots off at the back door. Hilda and Slim were as different as night and day. Where he was so slim a good north wind could blow him all the way to the Gulf, she was short and stocky with a big, round face. They'd been married forever and never had any children—other than claiming Milli and her two brothers, and they only had come for a while in the summer when they were younger.

"Nope, just had to pull a calf while I was out."

Hilda stirred a pot of chili on the back burner. "Did it live?"

"Sure it did. I was there. You think I'd let it die?"

"Well, go tell your Poppy he's got a fine, healthy calf, and don't track up my clean floor. Shake the dust off your jeans right where you stand. You want jalapeño corn bread with this chili for dinner?"

"You bet I do, and double the peppers. I like it hot enough to make my nose run. But it's not Poppy's calf. It was one of the Bar M cows."

"Then call Beau and tell that idiot he's at least lucky when it comes to ranchin'. Tell him Hilda said he's not lucky in love, though. Tell him if he got any unluckier than he is right now, he could just call the undertaker and arrange his own funeral, because he's just as good as dead if he really marries up with that blonde-haired witch. Tell him…"

"You tell him. But he already knows about the calf. He arrived on that play pretty he rides on and I made him help me. He said I was bossy. But I'm not. I just know what to do and…"

"Well, you're the kind of woman he needs. You're the kind of woman the Bar M needs. And here you are right next door and he's blind as a bat and crazy as a drunk skunk. That Amanda is a city girl and she's got dollar signs all over her body. Why, she ain't no better than one of them high-dollar whores in the big cities. Them kind that stand on the street corner. They sell what's in their underpants for a dollar and she sells what's in hers for what she thinks she's goin' to get him to buy her. And by the time he gets through buyin' and buyin' there won't be a Bar M. It will be dead and gone. Just a few bunkhouses and a lot of weeds. She might not be able to touch the ranch, but she can sure bleed him dry. Just a high-dollar whore."

"Hilda, what do you know about a high-dollar whore?"

Hilda shook a spoon at Milli. "Never you mind what I know or don't know. You just go get cleaned up. You ain't comin' to my dinner table lookin' like a…"

"High-dollar whore?"

She shooed her away with the flap of her apron. "Get on out of here and quit your smart mouthin'. I can still bend you over my apron. Any kid what begs for a whippin' can find one. Get on up them stairs."

Milli bypassed the den, where she could hear her grandfather talking to Katy. If she went in, she'd have to hold the baby and love her, and she wasn't clean enough to do that. She peeled out of her work jeans, socks, T-shirt, and underwear and stepped into a hot shower, letting the water run down her back and through her hair.

The shower in the motel the morning after she'd spent the night in Beau's arms had felt like this. Hot and clean. But it hadn't washed away the guilty feelings she'd had that morning, any more than it washed them away this morning. When she had looked up and seen Beau riding toward her, she'd wanted to take her arm out of the cow and hug him. And after the calf was born, and she did hug him impulsively, her body had wanted to drag him down behind the trees and make love with him again. Just once more to see if it was as good the second time as she remembered it being the first time; if the look in his eyes would be as soft as when he pulled her to him, her naked breasts touching his furry chest, the sensation making her beg for another bout of lovemaking.

For that she felt guilty. He had asked Amanda to marry him, and it didn't matter what she or the rest of the ranching world around him thought of her, she was still the one he'd chosen. The one he truly wanted to wake up beside for the rest of his life, and Milli had no right to the feelings that surged through her.

She should be honest and tell him that she was the woman he'd slept with after Darrin's and Lisa's wedding—at least he'd stop asking where he'd met her. It was just a matter of time, anyway, because someday things would click and he would remember. Even in his drunken state that night, he would have remembered the next morning that he didn't spend the night alone in the back bedroom of that trailer. And something, somewhere would trigger a little memory, which would set off a chain reaction, and Beau would remember she was only a one-night stand. A woman who'd been willing to fall into bed with him without very much seduction, and who couldn't even blame her actions on liquor, since she had only had one glass of champagne and was stone-cold sober when she peeled that lace dress over her head. She'd have to tell him that she hadn't given a damn about him for anything except erasing Matthew from her mind and she'd used him as much as he'd used her that night. He would look at her with a different look on his face—one of disgust and shame.

She wrapped herself in a fluffy pink towel. She pulled a pair of jean shorts and a bright red knit shirt from the closet. This afternoon she and Mary were going to Ardmore to shop. When she used to come to the ranch as a teenager, Granny had always taken her there at least one day and they'd eat ice cream after they'd shopped until their feet hurt. They'd take Katy and the stroller and push her through the stores. Then maybe they'd have a banana split at the ice cream store before they came home. It could be a tradition thing… every time she and Katy came to Oklahoma…

She shook her head violently to erase the image. "Oh, no! Tradition ends right here. If I ever get back to west Texas without having to bare my soul, I'm not coming back here. I'll fly in by myself, pick up Poppy and Granny, and they can visit us in Hereford, Texas. And that's a fact."

But maybe if she and Granny got away and shopped a while, she would at least forget all about Beau and this precarious situation she was in. Even that much would be a blessing today. Just to look at baby clothing for Katy and maybe a pair of dress shoes or sandals for herself.

She rolled her eyes toward the ceiling. "Not pink high heels. I'd break my neck if I tried to walk in those things

Amanda wears. But I can get away from ranching and thinking about him."

Forget Beau? Good luck. Even if you do, it won't be for long. You'll remember him every day for the rest of your life, girl, because you can never look at Katy without remembering who her father is... and that he is right next door to the Lazy Z forever.

Chapter 5

Hilda shooed them out the door. "You get on outta here. Lord knows, you ain't been outta Jim's sight in weeks, and you girls need an afternoon out. Go find something new to wear to that party Beau is having this weekend. I'm glad I don't have to go. I'd just feel like it was my God fearin' duty to set that boy down and give him a talkin' to. But it ain't a bit of my business if he wants to ruin his whole life. You two just get on outta my way. Go eat a banana split at the ice cream store. It'll do you both a world of good."

"Are you sure, Hilda?" Mary asked for the tenth time. It had sounded like a perfectly wonderful plan when Milli came in asking if they could go shopping over in Ardmore. But she hadn't left Jim alone since he'd been home and she was having second thoughts about doing so right then. What if he tried to get up and do something stupid, like drive the truck out to the back forty to check on the cows? Or worse yet, heaven forbid, if he insisted Slim saddle up a horse?

"Yes, I'm sure," Hilda fussed. "It's just Ardmore, for goodness sake. You can see everything in the mall in an hour, eat your ice cream, and be home by suppertime. Now, go and don't worry. Me and Slim will watch one of those old John Wayne movies with Jim. We won't let him do anything you wouldn't."

"I worry too much," Mary said as Milli strapped Katy into the car seat in the back of her club cab pickup. "But if anything happened to him and I wasn't there…"

"He'll be fine, Granny. Now it's off to look at pretty stuff even if we don't buy a single thing. I'm not about to spend money on something to wear this weekend. You and Poppa can go if you want to, but I'm not planning on it. I just plain don't like that woman, so why should I go? She's a gold digger in the worst sense. Did I tell you what I overheard her say in the bathroom? She hates ranching, hates cows, hates the smell of a lot, and doesn't even like kids." She inhaled with intentions of keeping up the tirade but her grandmother butted right in on cue.

"Of course you're going. We're all going. It would be rude, even if we don't like the hussy. We'll be there with smiles on our faces for Beau's sake. But right now we're not going to worry about that. I'm not about to spend money on something just for that occasion, either. But it will be nice to run around a few dress racks. Maybe I'll find something new for church, and I'm looking forward to going to the ice cream store where we can gain twenty pounds and then bitch because we can't wear a single thing we've got in our closets."

"You're good for me," Milli patted her grandmother's hand—but she was not going to that party.

Maybe if she fell down the steps and broke a leg and couldn't dance? But then her sharp old Granny would probably just put her in Poppy's wheelchair and take her anyway. And to think, she'd actually thought she was coming to Oklahoma for a summer of hard physical work but that there wouldn't be any emotional strings that far from the panhandle of Texas.

Milli was busy pushing Katy and telling her she had to stay in the stroller, that she could not get out and run through the mall, and didn't even realize she'd walked right past Beau until her grandmother spoke.

"Well, hello, Beau," Mary said cheerfully.

Milli felt a slow, hot flame rising from her neck to her cheeks. By the time she turned around she had a high color she couldn't disguise and only hoped he thought it was the result of just coming inside out of the blistering summer heat.

"Whatever are you doing here?" Mary asked.

"Oh, Amanda wanted to shop after we went to lunch. I don't get into running around clothes racks a hundred times, so I'm practicing waiting out here like a dutiful husband."

He squatted in front of the stroller and touched Katy's chubby hand. "Hi, you little doll. You remind me of my nephews down in Louisiana with all that blonde hair and them big blue eyes. But you got your mother's pretty skin for sure."

Milli held her breath until her chest hurt. Surely, he would feel something when he touched his own flesh and blood. He stayed squatted down beside the stroller so long that Milli feared he had recognized his own reflection in the baby. Finally, he stood and she was dizzy with relief.

"So what are you doing in Ardmore this afternoon? Did you bring Jim out for a bit of different scenery?"

"Getting out away from the ranch for a little while. Left Jim at home with Hilda and Slim to watch John Wayne. Just hope he don't get any foolhardy notions like he can sit a horse just because I'm not there. Every once in a while we have to get out and be something other than cattle women, so we're going to run around those dress racks. And then we're going to Braums to eat banana splits until we groan and moan."

Milli was glad Mary kept up a running conversation. If she'd had to choose between saying a word or standing before a firing squad, she would just have reached for the blindfold and put it on herself.

"Well, don't be spending Jim's money on something to wear to my party. You two would look just fine in a gunny sack tied up in the middle with a piece of bailing twine. Too bad we already ate or we'd join you for ice cream."

"Don't you be flatterin' me. A gunny sack, indeed! Now, you might be telling the truth about Milli, and if I was thirty years younger, I might give her a run for her money when all those cowboys are just slobbering to get to dance with her," Mary said.

It worked. He set his jaw and drew his eyebrows down in a frown.

"We'll be seeing you," Mary waved. She'd gotten exactly the response she'd hoped for. There was chemistry between them, by golly, and she intended to fan the flames every chance she got. After all, all was fair in love and war and that hussy hadn't gotten him in front of a preacher man yet.

Milli gave a short, silent prayer of thanksgiving that Beau and Amanda had already eaten. She couldn't bear to sit so close to him that she could smell that wonderful aftershave and watch him drape his arm around Amanda while they shared a banana split. Amanda might even feed him a few bites, at which time Milli would upchuck right there in the middle of everyone's dessert. The very thought of him taking ice cream off the very spoon Amanda had eaten from made her stomach churn in agony. She didn't even let herself think about the fact that he'd probably kissed the witch quite passionately in the last few hours.

"Hey, Milli, why don't you let me walk around the center of the mall here with the baby? I need to walk off part of this supper and she's not a bit interested in all those dress racks. She didn't cry when I was talking to her, so I think she'd be comfortable with me," Beau offered.

"Oh, I…" Milli stammered.

Mary pushed the stroller two feet forward and put the handle in his hands. "How nice of you. If she gets fussy, just bring her to the store and we'll take her off your hands. She loves to ride so I doubt you'll hear a peep out of her."

"Sure thing. Now off to your right is a shoe store, sweetheart. You'll probably grow up to buy eighty million pairs of shoes and not wear any of them. You'd rather wade in the water in your bare toes, wouldn't you, honey? Of course you would—or else go out to the pasture in your boots and jeans and ride a little pony. I bet Jim buys you a pony by the time you can walk…"

"Now why did you do that?" Milli hissed when he was out of hearing distance.

"Because Katy will love it and so will he."

Mary looked as innocent as a newborn kitten. Maybe, just maybe, if he spent enough time with the child, he'd finally look down and see that she was the spitting image of him. And if he didn't, then someone might come along and say something like, "My, don't that baby look just like you," and then he'd wake up and smell the roses, or baby powder, or whatever new fathers smelled when their eyes were opened.

Milli wondered if she could get back to the panhandle of Texas by midnight.

They went into the store, past the perfume counter and to the lady's department. She flipped a couple of hangers around the round rack as she fought down the urge to turn around and confess everything to her grandmother. If Mary knew what was actually happening right under her nose, she might not be so eager to turn Beau loose with Katy, and she might even help her get away from the Lazy Z without too much fanfare.

"Well, hello, Amanda," Mary said in a sticky sweet voice. "Have you met my granddaughter? She was with us at the barn social the other night but I don't think you were formally introduced. This is Milli Torres, and this is Beau's fiancée, Amanda."

"I'm pleased to meet you," Milli said, but she couldn't even force a smile to her face.

Amanda wore a baby blue business suit with a very short skirt and a jacket with a wide white lapel. A gold pin shaped like an alligator with sapphire eyes crawled up the lapel on the left side and her engagement ring glittered in the fluorescent lighting.

"Oh, so you're the neighbor?" Amanda started at Milli's toes and sized her up, literally curling her nose by the time she got to her hair, which Milli had pulled back with one of those new plastic clips.

Milli bared her claws and got ready for the catfight. Granted, she wasn't very classy in her jean shorts and

T-shirt. But she wasn't sweating underneath panty hose and a business suit and the clip kept her long black hair out of her eyes. Even with a shot of self-applied confidence, she still felt like an ugly June bug that Amanda was about to step on with her fancy high-heeled shoe.

"When is the wedding? I suppose you're already up to your elbows in preparations and wedding books," Milli asked in a sticky sweet tone.

Amanda looked down on Milli, trying to intimidate her, but it wasn't working. Instead of shrinking and cowering like a little whipped puppy, Milli gazed right back up at Amanda.

"Oh, I'm not sure. Of course Anthony wants to get married tomorrow. He's so much in love with me it's just plain sickening. But I really must have a big wedding. You know all of Ardmore expects it. A social affair with a long, long honeymoon afterwards. Maybe the Bahamas or Paris, France. I haven't decided. Definitely something by early fall, though. I'm not going back to school this year."

Milli raised a dark eyebrow. "Oh, really."

"I suppose you will be busy at the ranch," Mary managed to say without too much acid. "There's a lot for the wife of a rancher to do. I know. I've been one for a long, long time. It's good that you'll be arriving in the slow season where ranching is concerned. At least you'll get your feet wet before the real busy part begins next spring."

"Oh, honey, I'd never live there. Not that far from civilization. I must have a social life or I'd just wither up and die. No ma'am, ranching is not for me. Anthony and I will live in town. I've got the cutest little two-story mansion picked out. We'll make a bid on it next week, and then…"

Milli couldn't believe her ears. The woman had said those things to her friend in the privacy of the restroom, but this was a very public place.

"Oh, I figured Beau would want to live on the ranch," Mary said.

"He probably does. God, I wish everyone would stop calling him Beau and refer to him as Anthony. Beau is so hickish," Amanda said curtly. "But what he wants and what he gets are most definitely two different things. He loves me. I hate cows and hay and the smell of barns, so he will do what I say. Besides he'll look so nice in a formal tux at social affairs. I've even looked at dress pants and suits in the men's section tonight. Of course, there's nothing there that's quite right. We'll have some real clothes custom made. Won't he just be delicious in Italian silk? I'm thinking chocolate brown. What do you think?"

"Frankly, I like blue jeans and a nice white western shirt. And you'll just have to get used to us calling him Beau. It's what we know him as," Milli said.

Amanda sniffed and raised her chin another inch. "Well, it takes all kinds. Not everyone can be born with good taste. I've got to run. He's probably just panting, thinking about me while he sits out there and waits so patiently. But it's wonderful training, don't you think? We're going to a movie tonight. Such a crazy way to spend an evening. When we're married there will be golfing and all kinds of social events we'll have to take in, but for now we'll just do things his way. Dinner and movies a couple of times a week. Such a simple little way. I just can't wait to remake him into a GQ man. All my friends will be so jealous when they see him decked out in the newest styles. Ta-ta."

Milli conjured up a picture of Beau in an Italian silk suit and a chuckle began down deep in her bosom, erupting as a full-fledged giggle which she had to stifle with the back of her hand. She got the hiccups and fanned her red face with the back of her hand.

"Guess we'd better go get our baby." Mary said.

"Good grief," Milli gasped. "She'll be fit to be tied if she finds him pushing a stroller around the mall. Beau with a baby, and she hates kids."

Amanda's heels clicked on the tile. "What the hell is that and where did it come from?"

He squatted down in front of the stroller and touched Katy's hair. "It's Milli Torres' little girl. Isn't she the cutest thing you ever saw, Amanda? Maybe by this time next year, we'll have one like her. Probably a son, though. Us Luckadeaus usually throw boy babies, but I wouldn't complain if we had one like this."

"I hope to hell not. God Almighty, I don't want a baby to ruin my figure and make me fat. You better be wishing for something else."

"Oh, you'll change your mind. Here comes your Mommy, sweetheart."

"I'm not changing my mind," Amanda said bluntly.

"Of course you'll want children. We'll get a nanny to take care of the baby when you go with me around the ranch, and you'll get your girlish figure back in no time. Riding is good for that, I'll bet. But for now we'll think about the wedding and the honeymoon." He kissed her on her neck.

She brushed the warmth of his kiss away. "Give that kid back and let's go."

Milli and Mary overheard the last sentence as they walked up behind them. Milli reached for the stroller handle and her hand brushed Beau's. The sparks were almost visible as they both jumped back. Mary saw them; Amanda didn't.

"Mommy, look!" Katy popped her thumb out of her mouth and pointed toward another child in a stroller.

Amanda snarled. "Slobbers. Yuck. There's a good enough reason right there for me never to want kids."

"Thank you for pushing her around," Milli said. "Amanda says you're off to the movies. We'll take her now so you won't be late."

"My pleasure. Anytime this girl needs a chauffeur you just call on me. I love kids."

Amanda jerked his arm possessively. "Come on."

"Be seeing you ladies." He tipped his hat and followed along beside her like a pet hound on a leash.

Mary frowned and grunted. Milli just watched, mesmerized. He must be drugged to let Amanda treat him like that. He surely didn't act like that when he was alone with Milli. That first day he'd acted like a madman, and when he found her helping the cow deliver the calf they'd had another shouting match. Just the brief touch of his hand made her knees go weak, and she could tell he was affected by it too. And all that Amazon witch had to do was tug on his arm and he followed two steps behind her like a servant. Something just wasn't right somewhere, and there wasn't a damn thing she could do about any of it.

Mary finally found her voice. "Well, I do declare. This has been an afternoon, now hasn't it? I can't believe Beau knows what that bitch has got planned, and I don't know who needs to tell him."

Milli put her hands up in defense. "Well, don't look at me. It's not any of my business if he wants to make a complete jackass out of himself."

Chapter 6

MILLI RODE THROUGH THE PASTURES TO COUNT COWS, see if there were any new calves, and check the fence lines. The sun was a piece of an orange ball on the eastern horizon and morning dew made the grass blades glisten like they'd been kissed by diamonds.

Diamonds. Now why did she have to think about diamonds and that ring Beau put on Amanda's hand last weekend? It was every bit as big as the one she'd handed to Matthew through the motel door. She wondered what her life might have been this fine summer morning if her best friend hadn't seen him going into the motel. But, that was water under a bridge that had been blown to smithereens long, long ago.

Two new bull calves were in the north pasture. She pulled a small notebook from the pocket in her shirt and wrote down the tag numbers of the cows who'd given birth since the first of the week. In the east pasture, she found a calf, just minutes old, with the umbilical cord still dangling as it tried to stand up on its wobbly legs to get its first taste of mother's milk. Again, she pulled out the notebook and wrote down which cow had given birth, remembering the morning just two days ago when she and Beau watched a calf do the same thing.

Poppy was going to be happy when she reported back to him today. And Granny, bless her heart, just might find something to talk about other than Beau and

Amanda. Granny and Hilda had talked it so firmly to death, Milli thought about having a funeral for the issue complete with a preacher and floral wreaths. Just bury the whole thing and get on with life. Jim just huffed and snorted around, declaring that when that gold digger got finished with Beau he'd be worth as much as a newborn kitten in the snow. And this morning as she was leaving the corral, Slim said again that the boy was just plumb out of his mind to be thinking about bringing a city slicker like that to the ranch.

She was sick to death of listening to it, and if they didn't stop, she and Katy were going back to west Texas, no matter what she had to tell Granny and Poppy. Just when she thought she'd gotten over it, there he was, bigger than life, sober as a judge on Sunday, and fussing about some Angus bull he thought was capable of sprouting wings and sitting right up there in heaven next to the angel Gabriel. Talk about a small world!

She crawled down off Wild Fire to check the fence she'd repaired and found it still as tight as it was the day she'd popped the barbed wire for Beau's benefit. How dare he hide up there like some kind of detective out of a book. She looked to see if there was the glint off binoculars that morning, but instead saw a three-wheeler lying on its side about halfway down the hill.

"Good enough for him. Depend on those big boy tricycles when a horse can do…" Then she saw a buzzard circle just above the tree tops and light not far from the three-wheeler. It waddled a few feet closer and she saw a tattered red shirtsleeve flap enough to send it back into the sky.

She put her foot in the stirrup and swung up into the saddle. Wild Fire cleared the fence with grace and kept trotting until she felt the reins tighten and Milli fly off her back.

"Beau, what happened?" She hurried to his side.

The three-wheeler had his left arm and leg pinned and he'd hit his head on a rock when he overturned. Dried blood covered his face, and only one eye opened a mere slit when he realized she was bending over him, then he closed it slowly and figured he'd really died and his soul was on its way to heaven. Instead of his whole life flashing in front of him, a mere portion of it played out again. He was back in Texarkana at his cousin's wedding. He knew he couldn't hold his liquor—but then who cared, anyway? Jennifer had just dumped him for his cousin.

"Hey, Beau, you better lighten up. You're going to have a demon headache in the morning," Darrin had told him.

"Good. Then I won't be able to think."

"Well, I won't be here to listen to you moan and bitch about it," Darrin said.

Then the most beautiful lady in the whole world dropped right out of the sky and sat down beside him. She wore an off-white lacy dress with a slit up the side and long, dangly, silver earrings shaped like teardrops. They'd left the party and gone to the trailer, where they wound up in the back bedroom. When he woke up she was gone.

He remembered stumbling out of the bedroom the next morning to find two of his cousins, Slade and Griffin, drinking coffee around the kitchen table. "Where's my dark-eyed lady? Is she in the bathroom?"

Griffin poured him a cup of hot coffee and handed it to him. "What lady? You must've drunk half the champagne at the wedding. There ain't nobody here but us boys and hasn't been all night. You drove yourself home and passed out in the bedroom. We could hear you snoring all night, and ain't nobody come out of there but you this morning. Didn't no one come home with you, Beau. You must have been dreaming."

"But she was here. She was wearing a lace dress and her eyes were big and brown and…"

"And I'm going to start drinking champagne if that's what you dream about when you do," Slade said.

"I swear it. She was here. Right there in my arms, and I fell in love. Just like that." He snapped his fingers.

"You fell in love with a dream. Have a cup of coffee and forget it. And remember what too much champagne does," Griffin said.

"I'll never drink again," Beau said seriously.

"I hope not. It's not worth it the next morning, is it?"

When he went back to the bedroom he found one of the teardrop earrings lying on the floor beside his boots and he knew down deep in his heart that it wasn't a dream. He remembered that someone said her name was Amelia Jiminez and she was from down in the valley. He talked to several people who had been at the wedding and one lady thought she remembered one of the Jiminez girls' daughters being there, but she couldn't recollect where all those girls had ended up after they were married. Seemed as though one of them was out in California and one of them in Mexico City.

The next month he went to Oklahoma when his aunt called. He'd worked hard at the ranch and met Amanda.

She wasn't Amelia, but then maybe Amelia was a just a dream and the teardrop earring was left in the room by another woman. He really believed it until right now, when he opened one eye and there was Amelia bent over him, showing him the way to eternity. He closed his eyes and got ready for the trip.

Milli wiped the blood with the tail of her cotton shirt, then ran back to Wild Fire and grabbed a cell phone from the saddlebag.

"Granny, I need help fast," she said when her grandmother answered the phone. "Out in the east pasture. Right by the fence those silly kids cut last week. Where Beau keeps his bull. He's had an accident. Send in an ambulance. I'm afraid to move him."

"No, not the bull. It's Beau. He's turned over on one of those three-wheelers and hit a rock. His arm and leg are pinned. Call the closest hospital and send me an ambulance. He opened one eye but he's unconscious right now." She flipped the phone back together and tossed it back into the saddlebag.

It was the longest thirty minutes she'd ever spent in her life. Buster arrived first on a four-wheeler, leading the ambulance down the cow path to the scene of the accident.

"Ammmmm," Beau muttered when they lifted the machine off his arm and leg, and loaded him into the ambulance.

"I'll ride with him," she said. "Buster, will you see to it Wild Fire is taken back home?"

Buster nodded. "Yes, ma'am, Miss Milli. I'll be over to the hospital soon as we can. When he wakes up, tell him I'm on the way."

"Ammmm," he tried to say her name but his tongue was too thick. He felt a sharp prick in his arm and everything went dark again.

He was evidently trying to call for Amanda and Milli's heart was a heavy piece of lead. But why shouldn't he call out for Amanda? He had just asked the woman to marry him, and even if she was a purebred witch, evidently Beau loved her with all his heart.

They wheeled him into the emergency room and she answered questions while they took him straight back through a set of double doors. Then she sat down in the waiting room and wished she were anywhere in the whole world right then but where she was. Amanda would be coming through the doors any minute in one of her fancy little short-tailed suits and high-heeled shoes. Her blonde hair would be picture perfect and her big, blue eyes would be filled with tears. And Milli sat there looking like the last rose of summer. She'd lost the clip holding her hair back and it looked as if it hadn't been combed in weeks. Beau's blood stained the front of her shirt, and there were wet grass stains on the knees of her faded jeans.

She heard the whoosh of the doors as they opened and looked up, expecting to see Amanda with that smug, better-than-you look in her eyes she had in the restroom at the Spencers' barn dance. But it was Mary who rushed to her side. She took her granddaughter's hand in her wrinkled one.

"What happened?"

"Looked to me like he hit a rock with the front wheel of the three-wheeler and it threw him. Pinned his arm and leg when it rolled on him, and he hit his head on another rock when he tumbled. There's a gash on the back of his head, and the EMT said he could have a concussion. He kept trying to say Amanda's name. I guess somebody should call her."

"Well, I'm not calling her," Mary declared. "Buster or some of the ranch hands can take care of that. I'm not wasting my quarter."

"Granny!"

"Well, that's a fact, honey, and I ain't apologizing, either," Mary said bluntly.

Buster was the next one to arrive. He plopped down in a chair beside Mary. "How's he doing? Got him sewed up yet?"

"Don't know," Mary said.

"He tried to say Amanda's name. He said Ammmm, at least. I figure he was trying to say her name."

Buster rolled his eyes to the ceiling. "I ain't using my quarter to call that woman. I sure don't want to have to sit in this little room with her for very long."

Mary patted his shoulder. "My sentiments, exactly."

A doctor stuck his head through the doors. "Anyone out here by the name of Amelia Jiminez?"

"Amelia Jiminez?" Mary asked.

"Yes, Beau Luckadeau keeps demanding someone by that name come hold his hand. He's got a concussion and we can't quieten him…"

Someone said you are Amelia Jiminez.

"Maybe I can help." Milli stood up slowly. He must have only remembered Amelia… not Camillia… when he awoke the next day, and somewhere back in the dusty attic of his brain he remembered Amelia Jiminez and that night.

Both eyes were open and the blood had been washed from his face when she peeped through the curtain. "Amelia. I knew you was more than a dream." He held out his hand and she took it.

"We're going to put a few staples in the back of your head where you hit the rock. You are a lucky man that your arm and leg are just bruised and not broken," the doctor said.

He winced when the staples went through his skin. "Where did you go, Amelia?"

"Home," she said.

"Now we're going to get you settled into a room for tonight. You can probably go home tomorrow if everything looks good. You've got a concussion and you'll have a big headache. Head wounds bleed a lot, but I don't think you need blood." The doctor filled a hypodermic with clear liquid. "This is going to make you sleep for a while."

He searched the room frantically until he brought her back into focus. "Amelia. Don't go home again. Stay with me this time. They said you were a dream, but I kept the earring. It's on my key chain in my pocket."

She patted his arm and touched his unshaven cheek "Just shut your eyes and go to sleep. It'll be all right. When you wake up everything will be fine."

"You'll be right here?"

"Just shut your eyes," she said again.

He awoke late that afternoon, to the tune of a bass drum doing double time behind his eyes and a whole orchestra playing some kind of horrid rock music—off key, and out of tune. Amelia was gone and some brassy woman with blonde hair sat in a chair next to his bed. She was using an emery board to file her long nails, which looked like hawk talons. The grating sound raked across every nerve in his ears.

"Who are you?"

"I'm Amanda. Your future wife."

"Where is Amelia?"

Her eyes narrowed down to slits as she eyed him, lying there with bruises and scrapes all over his arm and face. "Who is Amelia?"

"My dark-eyed lady. Where is she?"

She opened her purse and put her emery board away before she stood up. "That two-bit, wet-back hussy from the dance? Is that who you're talking about? The hired hand from over at the Lazy Z who found you and brought you in this place?"

"That's not Amelia... that's Milli, Jim's grand-daughter," he argued.

"Well, that's who found you and called the ambu-lance. She was still sitting here when I arrived, but I informed her that she could leave and never come back."

He turned his head toward the windows. "Go away."

Amanda suddenly saw a secure financial future slip-ping from her hands. "Oh, darling, I was so worried, and so angry with all those people for not calling me sooner." She willed a trained tear to escape from under her heavily made up eyelashes.

A tall, dark-haired doctor breezed into the room. "And how is our patient? Looks like he's awake and talking, at least. Getting hungry? Supper trays should arrive soon, and since you've not had nausea, you can go ahead and eat real food."

Amanda quickly faced the windows and dabbed the tear off her cheek, and by the time she turned back to face the good-looking doctor she had a sweet smile plastered on her face. "Doctor, he doesn't know me."

"That's not a surprise. He's had a concussion. But if I had a girlfriend as pretty as you are, I think I'd remember you in a hurry."

She opened her blue eyes even bigger and tucked her chin in a bashful pose. "Well, thank you. But I'm not his girlfriend. I'm just a caring friend."

"Well, now, that's interesting."

Amanda checked his finger for a wedding band and seeing not even a line where one once was, she carefully removed her engagement ring and dropped it in her pocket. "Are you new in Ardmore?"

"Yes, I am. Did my internship at Baptist just last year and started as an ER doctor here last month. Ardmore is a nice little town, but quite a social change from the big cities."

"I'm sure. Well, I'm glad you're taking care of my friend, Anthony."

"I didn't catch your name," the doctor said.

"Amanda… Amanda Whitman… like the writer."

"And *you're* from Ardmore?"

"Oh, yes. I teach school in Wilson. But I could never live in a town that small permanently," she told him.

Beau was tired of the games the two people played. It was evident they were flirting, but who cared. He didn't even know the tall blonde in the room with him. Maybe she was one of those women from the office who took down his medical history. The man seemed to be a doctor and said he could go home tomorrow. Home. That's where Amelia said she went. He distinctly remembered her saying she was going home. And tomorrow he was going home... and she would be there.

"Where is Amelia?" he asked.

"Your lady friend left a while ago. She stayed with you until your friend arrived," the doctor said.

"Okay," he nodded and shut his eyes. Home where he was going tomorrow.

Amanda walked to the door with the doctor.

"So Amanda Whitman, are you listed in the phone book?"

"Yes, I am," she flirted. A doctor! That meant social standing and as much or more money than the Bar M, without black cows and stupid barn dances.

"And would Amanda Whitman care if Dr. Jason Orbach called her sometime this week?"

"She would love for you to call," Amanda blushed again. She couldn't believe Anthony was snoring. Evidently, he really was out in a foggy land somewhere and didn't know who she was. If he'd been awake, he would have been standing in the middle of the bed with his fists up like a boxer, ready to duel with the doctor for her.

"Well, then, I'll hope to talk to you later tonight." The doctor went on to the next room.

She picked up her purse and started to kiss Anthony on the forehead. But why waste the energy and lipstick? And who was Amelia, anyway? Some past love he'd never mentioned? The woman who brought him in was Milli, evidently Milli Torres, if she was Jim's granddaughter. He just thought she was someone named Amelia. Maybe Amelia was his mother. She'd heard that often a concussion sends a person back in time, so perhaps he was calling out for his mother.

She shut her eyes dramatically and whispered, "It really doesn't matter. Because I think I've found someone who can appreciate all I can bring into a relationship so much more than you. Of course, you need me more, but this is not about what you need. So get well and we'll talk later, after I get to know this doctor a little better this week. I hate to break your heart, darling, I really do. I didn't set out to cause you grief and sorrow. But now I really must go and wait for his call. I cannot compete with your mother. Because it is her you beg for, not your only true love, Amanda." She sighed deeply and rushed out of the room, hoping to catch one more glimpse of the handsome doctor as she left the hospital.

Beau opened an eye to see if she'd gone yet.

Holy smoke, who is that woman? And what was all that about anyway? She sounded like she was deranged. I'm glad she left. What was she talking about my mother for anyway? I didn't ask for Momma.

At midnight he sat straight up in bed and looked around the room. Everything was as clear as a summer sky without a cloud in it. He'd topped the hill and hit a rock with the front wheel of his vehicle. He remembered it flipping over and something about a buzzard, then a dark-haired woman was bending over him. He knew this was a hospital room. He found the right button on the side of his bed and pushed it.

A nurse poked her head in the door in just moments. "Yes, sir. Oh, Mr. Luckadeau, I believe you're awake."

"Yes, ma'am, I am. What did I break?" He looked at both his legs and checked his arms.

"Nothing, lucky for you. You've got sutures in the top of your head. Had a lot of blood on you when the lady brought you in, but head wounds bleed quite profusely."

He felt the top of his head and winced when his hand found the staples. "How many?"

"Seven, I think. The doctor will remove them in a few days, and your pretty blond hair will grow back soon."

"I've had a few stitches before. Milli brought me in?"

"No, I think her name was Amelia. That's what you kept calling her, anyway. Amelia Jiminez. I had just come on the shift, so I might be wrong. I wasn't in the emergency room. The other nurse just told me about it."

"It was Milli Torres. Amelia isn't a real person. She's just a dream I have sometimes."

"Can I get you anything?" the nurse asked.

"Just Amelia," he said. He could have sworn she was a real person, but then two years ago he had thought she was real, too.

Chapter 7

BEAU WALKED THROUGH THE LIVING ROOM OF THE long, rambling ranch house and back down the hall toward his bedroom. The house was built the same year Alice Luckadeau married Tony Martin, in 1955. Both of them were thirty years old and expected to fill the four extra bedrooms with lots of children. But the bedrooms waited in vain because children never came to the marriage. Tony was killed when a horse threw him and several years later Alice was diagnosed with Alzheimer's. Beau had been named Anthony Beau Luckadeau—the Anthony for her late husband—and was her favorite nephew. When the doctor told her she had Alzheimer's, she called Louisiana and told Beau that she was deeding everything to him, then she checked herself into a nursing home.

Beau emptied his pockets on the oversized oak dresser, bent down, and rolled his eyes upward to check the staples on top of his head. The doctor said he would take them out in a few days, and they weren't really sore, but Amanda was going to cringe when she saw the shaved spot on the top of his head.

"That's why Milli looked so familiar. She reminds me of Amelia. Same long, dark hair. Same big brown eyes. But that's where the resemblance ends. Amelia was soft spoken, a woman built to love and be loved. Milli is as mean as a constipated cougar with a toothache."

Beau sighed. He loved a phantom; was engaged to a shrew. He had talked to Amanda on the phone the past two days, but something was missing even in conversation. Tonight was his engagement celebration and he didn't give a damn if Amanda was beside him or not. Surely it was the by-product of the accident. He loved the woman. He'd asked her to marry him. What in the devil was wrong with him?

He was tired of pampering her twenty-four hours a day, and the comments about ruining her figure with a baby weighed heavy on his mind. But more than anything else, he was tired of that recurring dream about a dark-haired lady. He wouldn't break the engagement because a man was judged by his word, and he'd keep it, but he'd always wonder if Amelia was more than just a dream.

He opened the closet door and took out a pair of starched Wranglers with a perfect crease. Then he picked out a white western shirt and a bolo tie with a silver slide in the shape of a steer's head. Maybe he'd feel better when everyone arrived and the band started playing. Maybe he'd dance with Milli again and everyone would make a circle around them and applaud... but he shouldn't be thinking about Milli Torres, no matter how well she fit into his arms. This was a party to celebrate his engagement to Amanda, and in spite of all she'd done to aggravate him recently, he had proposed to her and she'd accepted. All he could do was hope that she would change once they were married.

Milli shucked out of her work jeans and boots and slung open the closet doors. God, but she hated the idea of watching Beau dance with Amanda. No, Beau wouldn't dance with that bitch. Anthony would. That was the difference. Amanda was going to marry Anthony. A husband with a name like Beau would never do for her.

Milli all but snorted as she flipped through hangers. If that snooty blonde-haired witch looked down her skinny nose at her one more time, she was going to have to pick herself up off the ground, and Milli hoped she fell in a nice fresh cow pile… face first.

The next hanger held the off-white lace dress she had worn to the wedding where she met Beau. She wouldn't have brought the dress, but it was hanging in a garment bag with several shirts and she had picked up the whole thing without realizing it was there. Now wouldn't that be a hoot. See if it could jar his memory into remembering that's where he met her. Be good enough for him on the night of his engagement party, and after the way Amanda had ordered her out of the hospital.

He'd finally remember and know she was just an easy one-night stand, and then he could get right on with his life with his precious snotty Amanda. She hoped Amanda was as warm in bed as a well-digger's brass buckle in Anchorage in the middle of a winter blizzard. There was no way a woman with that much ice dripping off her could ever enjoy a rousting night of pure old unadulterated sex. Not like she and Beau had shared on a steamy Louisiana August night.

She hugged the dress close to her heart. "Stop it, Camillia Torres! Maybe she's a different woman when she shucks out of those clothes and takes him to bed. She probably knows a whole hell of a lot more than I did—or do. I'd be willing to bet dollars to donuts, she's been around the block more than one time. The only experience I've got is a single time in the back of a trailer, and Beau was drunk."

She took the dress from the bag, slipped it off the hanger, and put it on, with a pair of light tan kid sandals that laced up to mid-calf.

Granny already knows, but she won't say anything. I can tell by the way she keeps bringing up his name and insisting I go places where he'll be... just like tonight. I don't want to be at that party. But then, what the hell. Maybe that good-looking, dark-haired man will be there again. The one who looks like Matthew and probably is about as trustworthy as a tornado. At least I can dance with him, flirt a little, if I still remember how.

Katy held up her hands to be picked up. "Mommy."

She kissed the baby all over her face, relishing in the innocent giggles. "I'm going to do it. And before the night is over I'm telling him I was the girl... Camillia... not Amelia. He's already engaged to Amanda, anyway, and it won't matter. At least he won't keep asking me where it was he met me. But he won't ever know you belong to him, my precious baby."

Amanda threw her suit and panty hose on the floor of her room in her father's house. Pauline, the maid, would send them to the cleaners tomorrow. She chose a black column dress with gold buttons down the front and a pair of black high-heeled shoes for the party. Tonight she would break Anthony's heart into a million pieces and leave him an emotional wreck when she told him she didn't want to marry him, so black seemed appropriate.

She and the handsome doctor had driven to Dallas for supper on the top floor of the Loews hotel. He'd asked if he could see her again and she'd agreed. Now the next job was to get rid of excess baggage—called Anthony Luckadeau. By Christmas she intended to be Mrs. Dr. Jason Orbach.

She prowled through a jewelry case of earrings. "Just gold studs. And maybe a herringbone bracelet. That's enough for a funeral."

Her heels made a rat-a-tat-tat down the hardwood staircase and her father looked up from his paper when she reached the huge living room at the end of the stairs. "My, oh, my, don't you look classy this evening. You look more like your mother every day."

She kissed him on the forehead. "Thank you, father. I'm driving the Lincoln tonight. I won't be late, though. This is the last time I'm seeing Anthony Luckadeau."

"Didn't he ask you to marry him?"

"Yes, he did, but he's not the first one, is he? Daddy, he is a good man. He is absolutely boring. No imagination: dinner at a steak house and a movie a couple of times a week. I think I deserve a little more than that, don't you? I've got someone I really think you'll enjoy meeting next week. I'm not going to tell you about him. I want it to be a surprise. Ta-ta." She waved goodbye from the door.

Beau waited on the porch, hoping it was the effects of the concussion causing the heavy feeling in his chest. The lawyer waited in the study and as soon as Amanda arrived, they'd review the conditions of a prenuptial arrangement set down in writing before Alice went to the nursing home.

He watched the big Lincoln pull up in the circular driveway. The weight in his soul didn't disappear when Amanda waved. He crossed the porch and opened the door for her.

"Hello, Anthony. I think we better have a talk before everyone arrives for the party."

"Yes, we are going to. Aunt Alice's lawyer is waiting in the study, and we've got to talk about the way she set up this ranch. Just keep an open mind, Amanda, and remember that it's just an agreement. We won't ever need to think about it, anyway, because we aren't going into this marriage with a divorce looming at the end. We're going into it with thoughts of celebrating our fiftieth wedding anniversary right here on the Bar M. Maybe we'll even have the band play our song again and you'll knock everyone dead with your good looks even when you are near eighty. You look beautiful tonight, darlin'." He tried to convince himself with words.

Her lips made a firm red line as she jerked her head around to face him. "What are you talking about?"

He kissed her cheek and she saw the staples on top of his head. "Haven't seen you in a week."

She shivered. "Don't bend down and show me those horrid things on your head."

Nothing had changed. He was making the biggest mistake in his whole life and there wasn't a single thing he could do about it. Like a little boy with his feelings hurt, he wanted to go out behind the barn and cry. But even that wouldn't fix the problem. He'd given his word; he'd stand by it.

"Sorry. Let's go talk to the lawyer. Folks will be arriving soon."

Beau sat down in a burgundy leather chair on one side of the desk where the lawyer had strung papers in several piles. Amanda perched on the edge of a matching chair and wondered how in the world she was going to get out of this gracefully. If she could get it taken care of before long, maybe she could drive by the hospital and say hello to her doctor before she went home.

The lawyer turned the papers around so she could see them. "This is really very simple. Alice Martin deeded everything she had to Anthony Beau Luckadeau, but with the stipulation that if he ever married, the bride must sign an agreement that the ranch would not be part of the marital properties. In other words, if the marriage ends in a divorce, the ranch remains solely the property of Anthony Beau Luckadeau and his descendants, and can never be sold. It must pass from generation to generation. I have the papers right here…"

Rage boiled up out of Amanda like smoke and fire from the center of an active volcano. She'd already spent her half of the ranch sale proceeds in a thousand imaginary ways, and now this pompous, bald-headed lawyer was telling her she would have to sign a prenuptial agreement. "Do you mean that if we divorced I could not have my part of this ranch?"

Beau patted her hand. "Now Amelia, it's just paper. We won't ever get a divorce."

"Don't you dare call me by your mother's name, you idiot! You knew about this all along, didn't you?"

He looked at her incredulously. "My mother? I'm sorry I called you Amelia. But that's not my mother's name. Momma is Joann. Why did you think Amelia was her name?"

She pointed her finger at his nose. "Do you mean to tell me there's another woman in your life whose name is Amelia? You've got a woman you whine for when you're sick and you expect me to sign an asinine agreement like this? You are crazy, Anthony Luckadeau. Just plain crazy."

"Amanda, darlin'…" he stopped mid-sentence, his eyes fixed on the apparition getting out of a red and white pickup truck. She wore the same lace dress and her hair was piled high on her head, just like that night. He remembered taking the pins out one by one until her hair cascaded down her back.

Amanda wrenched off her engagement ring in a dramatic movement, and threw it on the floor at the toes of his boots. "I wouldn't marry you if you promised me this whole ranch on a silver platter. You can take this ring, and go straight to hell with it. I'm the best thing that ever happened to you, and you're too damned stupid to know it. So don't be calling me and begging me to come back to you when you finally wake up and realize what you've lost. Good-bye."

He didn't hear a word she said as he continued to look past her. Buster was talking to the ghost-lady as if it was a real person, but Beau knew she would fade in a vapor in a few minutes. Sometimes when he was in the barn she would appear for a few seconds, but then, poof, the vision was gone. Once when he was driving to town she had appeared on the highway right in front of his truck and he'd slammed on the brakes so fast he left a trail of black skid marks a quarter of a mile long, but she disappeared then, too.

"My God, Anthony, I didn't mean to affect you so badly. You look like you just saw a ghost," Amanda said.

His voice was scarcely more than a faint whisper. Too much noise and the lady would disappear in a wisp of fog, smoke, or dust. "Go on, Amanda. I don't really give a damn right now what you do. I'm sick of your whining ways and listening to you. Just get out of here."

"Whining ways! You're a pitiful excuse for a man. God, what I saw in you, I'll never know. Good-bye. I hope you rot in hell." She flipped her blonde hair over her shoulder and stuck her nose in the air with a sniff of disgust. She stomped her right foot so hard it broke the heel off her shoe.

Beau never took his eyes from the window. Any minute he was going to start slobbering if he didn't shut his mouth. If she didn't know better, she'd think he was drunk, but he didn't touch liquor of any kind. He wouldn't even have a glass of wine with her when they went out to dinner. It must be the accident. It really had affected something in his brain. Suddenly she could see a lifetime taking care of a man in a wheelchair with a bib around his neck and a blank look in his eyes. The mental vision caused her to run from the room and leave nothing but a streak of dust in her wake as she and the Lincoln left the Bar M.

The lawyer turned to see what was capturing Beau's attention. "Pretty woman."

"You can see her?" Beau bent down to pick up the ring at his feet but didn't dare blink.

The man laughed. "Sure, I can see her. I'm not blind, son. The one who just stormed out of here wasn't bad looking, either. But that one out there would make a man do a double take. I guess the engagement is off. Don't worry, though. I don't think I could stand bein' married to someone that hot tempered, so maybe this prenuptial thing of Alice's is a blessing. Evidently, she wasn't the right one for you after all. I'll gather up my things and get on back home."

"Stay around," Beau said absently. "We're having a party here tonight. With or without Amanda. There's enough food to feed an army of hungry men, and you're more than welcome. Call your wife and tell her to come on out, too."

The lawyer reached for the phone. "Well, that's mighty fine of you. Maybe I will do just that."

Beau laid the ring on the desk and started toward the door. "Excuse me."

The band struck up the first notes of "A Picture of Me Without You," by Lorrie Morgan, as Milli entered the barn to find only a few people already at the party. Granny and Poppy had laid claim to a table on the edge of the circular dance floor. The lady singing for the band did a pretty good imitation of Lorrie as she crooned into the microphone, expecting to see Beau and his fiancée enter the barn any minute, and then she was supposed to break into a very different song. They were going to dance a slow waltz and then Beau was going to take the microphone and make a speech. Then the real dance would start up.

Jim Torres wiped his brow in mock shock. "Whooo! What happened to my country granddaughter? You look like one of them city women or one of them models."

Milli tried to smile but couldn't. "Thank you, Poppy, but you are looking at me through those grandfather's rose-colored glasses. I feel out of place without my jeans and boots. I don't know whatever made me put this on to begin with."

Beau was suddenly so close to her that she could smell his aftershave and feel his breath on her bare neck. "Amelia? Amelia Jiminez?" He held his breath, fully well expecting the girl to turn around and tell him to drop dead.

Jim laughed. "No, not Amelia Jiminez. Just Milli. Camillia Torres. Her mother was a Jiminez... Angelina Jiminez from down in the valley, before she married my son."

The pieces fit snugly into place and he swallowed three times before he could speak. She'd been right next door all that time and she must have known from the first day who he was, and yet she hadn't said a word. He should wring her neck, but if he put his hands on her slender neck it wouldn't be to hurt her. His heart told him he was looking at a woman who just fell into bed with him on a whim, then ran away before he awoke. His body said it wanted more of what it remembered from that night in Texarkana.

Milli turned slowly to face him. "Hello, Beau. I think we met a long time ago, didn't we? Only a few people call me Camillia. I guess it does sound like Amelia, doesn't it?"

He was afraid to blink. "You're real. You're not a dream?"

"I'm real. I'm Milli Torres, your neighbor's granddaughter. Small world, ain't it? Where is your fiancée?"

"She broke up with me. Refused to sign the agreement about the ranch and... why didn't you tell me you were...?"

"Well, praise the lord!" Mary exclaimed. "That girl wasn't the right woman for you Beau. I don't mean to be ugly, but she was bad news."

"It don't matter," Beau tried to drink in every detail of Milli's face.

"I'm sorry about your engagement," Milli lied.

"I'm not. Could I have this dance, Milli?" He touched her hand and sparks flew.

"Well, would you look at that?" Mary said. "You know, I believe that boy is thunderstruck. I guess they've met somewhere before and he just now realized it."

"And I think I smell a rat," Jim said. "You've known all along, haven't you? And… oh, my lord, that's who it is? Now why didn't this old monkey-assed, mindless fool see it before? That boy is Katy's daddy, ain't he? You figured it out the first day and that's what you was talking about."

Mary put her fingers over his mouth. "Shhhh, he don't know about Katy yet. We'll have to be very quiet and let them work it all out. They don't need a couple of old meddling fools like us to help them. They've found each other. Lord, Jim, look at the way they dance together. Like they was made for each other. And just think about all the fun we'll have with Katy right next door."

"Don't count your chickens before they're hatched," Jim said with a grin.

"Why didn't you tell me the first day?" Beau whispered in her ear.

"Because you were screaming and cussing, and besides, I was shocked out of my mind about how in the hell you got from Louisiana to southern Oklahoma on the farm right next to my Poppa's," she whispered back.

"But what about at the Spencers' barn dance when we danced?"

"You were going to propose to Amanda, remember?"

The song ended and another began. "Don't go. Dance with me again."

She nodded and he drew her even closer.

"What happened to you? I got out of bed and you were gone. They told me I'd just dreamed you and you were never there," he asked.

"And I shouldn't have been. It was a mistake from the beginning. I was mad at my boyfriend and I was out to get even, so I used you."

"Did you go home and make up with your boyfriend?" He held his breath as he waited for an answer.

"No, I did not. I guess we just used each other. I knew your girlfriend had just broken up with you."

"What did happen, then?"

She leaned back and smiled, lighting up his whole world. "The whole thing backfired. How's your head?"

"You are changing the subject, but that's all right. I've got all summer to show you just how it did backfire. My head is still stitched—or rather, stapled. Was it you at the hospital with me?"

She stepped back and pulled his shoulders down so she could see the top of his head. "Yes—bend down here and let me see. They look pretty clean. Here I'll kiss them and make it all better."

Buster wandered into the barn, a hangdog look on his face and a shuffle to his walk. Lord, but he hated that uppity Amanda, and to think he might even have to take orders from her was enough to make his butt want a dip of snuff. He was too damned old to quit the Bar M and find another job and besides, this was home. It was where he and Rosa came with their three children when they were in their early twenties to work for Tony and Alice. And the ranch had been good to them. To leave would wrench his heart right out of his chest. To stay would drive him smack dab crazy.

He stopped dead in his tracks as Milli kissed the top of Beau's head and then put both her arms around his neck as they continued with the dance. He shook his head violently. Surely he wasn't seeing what he thought he was. "What the hell?"

Jim motioned toward a chair. "Engagement's off, praise the good lord above. I 'spect Beau will make an announcement when everyone arrives. Seems like he ain't too broke up over it. He waltzed right in here and saw Milli, and was as thunderstruck as any man I've ever seen. They've been out there dancin' ever since. Guess he met her a long time ago somewhere. We'll find out the whole story later."

Buster threw his straw hat into the air and caught it when it floated back down. "Well, hallelujah. There is a God up there after all. I'd begun to think maybe He had turned off His hearing aid when I prayed. Miss Milli, huh? Well, ain't the whole evenin' lookin' a lot brighter now! Wait 'til I tell Rosa. She's going to pass little green apples, she'll be so excited. This is goin' to be a good party, after all!"

"Yep, it is," Jim nodded and grinned from one ear to the other. Just wait 'til Buster found out about Katy. He'd really be dancing around on the clouds. Come to think of it, Buster hadn't ever even seen Katy. Maybe Jim would just make a point to invite him over one day next week. He'd see just what kind of expression Buster had on his face when he looked at the spitting image of Beau.

Beau kept Milli's hand in his as he approached the bandstand and reached for the microphone. "Folks. This was supposed to be a party to celebrate my engagement tonight. But things took a strange turn and Amanda and I decided we weren't cut out from the same bolt of cloth. So she's gone her way and I'm finding a new way, so we'll celebrate that instead of an engagement. The tables are ready for supper and the band will keep playing. Those of you who haven't met Milli Torres, please come around and I'll introduce you, but don't any of you fellers ask for a dance. She already promised them all to me tonight."

She raised an eyebrow. "Oh, did I?"

"Yes, ma'am." He took her in his arms and they waltzed out into the middle of the floor to "It's Your Love," by Faith Hill and Tim McGraw.

The black brooding feeling of something very wrong evaporated through the wooden rafters of the barn and a lighter mood of something entirely right replaced it. Smiles replaced grimaces, and the band members brightened up with a livelier crowd to play to.

Milli felt as though she was sitting on a keg of dynamite and the fuse was getting shorter and shorter. Any minute her whole world was going to go up in an explosion big enough to rock the whole state of Texas—and Oklahoma, too. But until the blast she was going to enjoy dancing around this big barn in the arms of the only man who'd ever made her soul complete.

"Now, let's talk about the past two years," Beau said. "Are you for real? Am I going to wake up in a little while and this will be a dream, too?"

She pinched his arm solidly.

"Ouch," he looked at her, disbelief on his face. Could this really be the woman who had kissed his head so gently just minutes before?

"Did that hurt?"

"Hell, yes, it hurt," he said.

"Good. I'm not an angel. I'm a real woman and you're not dreaming. This is a real night and it was a real night two years ago. I shouldn't have let things go as far as they did, but that's water under the bridge. I can't undo it now. But, rest assured, I'm not an angel. I'm full of spit and vinegar. Wasn't it you who asked me just this week why I was grouchy early in the morning, and who accused me of being a bossy bitch? After tonight, you'll probably be glad I was gone when you woke up that morning."

"Ain't damn likely."

"You've had two years to make me into a perfect woman. Now I've got a summer to show you I'm not perfect. I've got a hellacious temper. I can be as hard-headed as a holiness preacher at a revival meeting, and you can tell me to back off anytime you want to."

"Like I said, it ain't damn likely. Was it your earring that got lost in the bedroom that night? I found a silver teardrop on the floor next to my boot."

She stopped and pulled back her dark hair to reveal the match to his earring. "I figured I lost it in the bedroom."

He reached in his pocket and drew out the match,

hanging on his key chain. "You didn't lose it. You just left it for me to find you with."

"Can I have it back now?"

"What are they doing?" Jim asked Buster. "Looks like they're comparing her earring to his key chain."

Buster was so excited he all but shouted. "Well, I'll be damned. She's Amelia! That boy's carried that earring in his pocket for two years. Said when he was down at his cousin's wedding in Texarkana he met this woman and she lost her earring. Said all the boys thought he just dreamed her up and he kept saying her name was Amelia."

"Camillia," Mary told him. "He misunderstood. Milli's full name is Camillia."

Buster slapped his knee. "Well, hot damn! He's been in love with her for two years and now we find out it's our Milli."

Beau put the earring back in his pocket. "No. It's mine. It's all I've had for two years of a dream I'd begun to think couldn't be real, and I'll just keep it."

Chapter 8

MARY TOSSED HER WESTERN STRAW HAT ON THE burgundy leather sofa in the den and plopped down without any trace of the grace she usually displayed. Jim crutched into the living room and eased down into his chair. Milli stood in the doorway with a grin on her face even sucking a lemon wouldn't erase.

Mary spoke first. "I sure didn't want to go, but I wouldn't have missed that party for all the dirt in Texas and half the tea in China. It's been the most wonderful night we've had in so long I can't remember. Wait 'til I tell you about it, Hilda. You wouldn't believe what happened in your wildest dreams."

Hilda put her magazine in the rack. "Did the witch fall in a cow patty? Baby's been sleeping for hours. Didn't even know you were gone. Think we might talk Milli into leaving her here when she goes back? Sure does spice up this quiet old house. I can see you all three are bustin' at the seams to tell me a story and you better start talkin' before I lay down and die of curiosity."

Milli tugged her boots off and rubbed her tired feet. "Amanda didn't fall in a cow patty. It was even better than that. I don't think I've danced so much since before Katy was born."

"Well, somebody spit it out," Hilda demanded. "Just what did happen over there at the big engagement party?"

Jim cleared his throat and spoke up. "Hilda, you'll never believe what happened. That Amanda girl got mad over the way Alice set up the ranch and she just called off the whole engagement."

Hilda rolled her eyes toward the ceiling. "Well, praise the lord. Even if Beau's heart is broke right now, in a few months he'll figure out he's been saved from worse than hellfire."

"Oh, he wasn't too broke up. He waltzed into the barn, took one look at Milli, and got a case of thunderstruck love. They danced together all night. Wouldn't be surprised if something don't become of it," Mary said.

"Oh, hush, Granny," Milli said. "He just used me so everyone wouldn't think he was tore up with her acting like that. I'm going to bed. Tomorrow is church and it's already past midnight."

"Me, too," Hilda said with a broad wink at Mary. Tomorrow she'd find out every single little detail, such as the way Beau got thunderstruck, but Mary wouldn't part with the good stuff until Milli wasn't listening. "Better all of us attend in the morning and give thanks for answered prayers. I'll even make Slim crawl out and go, and when he finds out why, betcha he don't even carry on about having to get dressed up. Good night, y'all."

"Good night," Milli headed toward the stairs.

"Just a minute, young lady. I think it's time we talked, don't you?" Mary said.

Milli sat down on the floor in front of them. The time had come and there was no way around it, over it, or even through it. Granny had known for weeks and probably by now she'd told Poppy, so she might just as well face the fiddler and tell the truth—or as much of it as she could get away with. Maybe she could just tell them that she and Beau met at a wedding.

"So, what do you want to know?" She tried to keep her face passive.

"Let's start with the time you met Beau," Jim said. "Something about you going to a friend's wedding, was it? And he was there?"

"Yes, in Texarkana, a couple of years ago. We were friends in high school and she went out there to college, then her folks moved away from Hereford, but we kept in touch. She went to college on one side of the state and I went to West Texas over in the panhandle. Anyway, she invited me and it was just about the time I'd broke up with Matthew, and I went." She squirmed in her chair.

"And Beau was at the wedding?" Mary asked.

"Yes, he was. His girlfriend had just thrown him over. And he was pretty drunk when I met him. He didn't remember who I was until tonight. Guess someone told him I was Camillia and he thought they said Amelia since he'd had too much liquor. Then I flew home the next day and forgot all about him until he came charging across the pasture ranting and raving about me cutting the fence on my first day to go out and check the cows." She hoped that was enough to appease them for one night.

"So how come he didn't recognize you until tonight?" Jim asked. "You been together more than once and Buster says he's been talking about Amelia ever since he got to the ranch. So why didn't he know you? And why didn't you tell us you recognized him that day?"

She stifled a real yawn. "When I met Beau he was very drunk. And he didn't hold his liquor so well. He was all shook up because his sweetheart just dumped him and his mind wasn't any too clear. I guess that's why he didn't remember. Can we talk about this tomorrow? I'm tired, Poppy." She started to get up.

He shook his head. "Nope, I think we'd better get it all took care of now. I don't think I can sleep for thinking about this whole thing, so we'll just talk tonight."

She rubbed her eyes with the back of her fist, wishing they'd tell her to go on to bed and they'd finish tomorrow. "Okay, then what else do you want to know?"

"I want to know just what happened that night. Did you dance with him?"

"No, I didn't. Like I said, he was drinking pretty heavy and that's probably why he couldn't really remember me so well. We sat in the corner and talked for a while. He went to get another glass of champagne and I asked an older fellow about him and he said he was one of those Luckadeaus from down in Shreveport. Told me about the family and said Beau was lucky in everything but love. Said his girlfriend had just dumped him."

"Evidently he asked someone about you, too. Because Buster said he knew your mother was one of the Jiminez girls from down in the valley. Guess him drinking too much is the reason he thought your name was Amelia instead of Camillia. But he must have remembered Amelia all this time, because he asked about you in the emergency room last week," Mary said.

"Well, that's that. If you want to know anything more it's going to have to wait until morning or the only answers you're going to get is snores. I'm beat, Granny. And Poppy, I should have owned up to having met him. Good night."

She made it to the door and thought she was home free.

"Want to tell us about Katy and what went on after the wedding party? Or did you fly back out there later on?" Mary asked.

She turned around and sat down in the floor right in the doorway. The words wouldn't come. Her hands were clammy but her backbone was as straight as a rod. Tears welled up in the back of her eyes, but they wouldn't spill, either.

"I don't know if I can talk about it," she whispered. "It was all such a terrible mistake. I was still hurting and angry from the way Matthew had treated me. Telling me he loved me and treating me like some kind of porcelain doll while he was taking women to the motel right under my nose. Then not even calling to apologize or explain why he did what he did. I don't think he ever really loved me. I was just a good girl from a good family and his father wanted him to marry me for that. He wanted someone who was a virgin, who hadn't been around and wouldn't bring shame on his family name. It didn't matter that he had a different woman in bed with him every night. Just that I was a good girl."

"And Beau was there and drunk," Mary nodded.

"Yes, and he said why didn't we get away from the noise and confusion and go to his cousin's trailer where it was quieter. I was playing with fire but I didn't care. I'd been good my whole life. Saving myself for marriage so my husband could be a proud man. And what did that get me? A heartache bigger than Dallas. I'd had a couple of glasses of champagne, but I wasn't drunk and I knew what I was doing. You can't blame Beau. I was just available after his girlfriend dumped him. Kind of like tonight. I was there and he needed someone. And I…"

"And when you found out Katy was on the way?" Jim asked softly. "Why didn't you get in touch with him? Beau is a good man. He would have done the right thing."

"Poppy! It was a consenting one-night stand. How do I call someone in Shreveport and ask for Beau Luckadeau and say, 'Hey do you remember the woman you slept with a couple of months ago? Well, guess what? There's a baby on the way and what do you want to do about it?' It was my problem. I was naive enough to think I wouldn't get pregnant the first time and I did. Besides I had precious little pride left after Matthew and my own stupid mistakes. I didn't think I could stand another rejection. I didn't know anything about the man. But I did know that if I'd been in his shoes I damn sure wouldn't have hopped on the next airplane and rushed out to marry some girl who'd fallen into bed on a whim. He probably thought I was just a loose-legged woman out on the prowl at her friend's wedding."

Jim shook his head. "Beau is a decent fellow."

"I know that now. But I didn't know anything about him then, except he drank too much. Besides, I don't want a man to marry me just because he's decent and I'm pregnant. I acted cheap and he… well, Poppy, he doesn't know Katy belongs to him. And I'd just as soon leave it that way."

Jim Torres couldn't refuse her anything when she was a child. She'd looked at him like that when she was three and her father wouldn't buy her a pony so she could ride with her brothers. Jim bought one at the next sale. But this was a whole lot different than buying a pony. Katy's future was at stake. And Beau had every right to know that he had a daughter.

"I don't know, Milli. You need to think about Katy growing up. Someday she's going to ask questions. It wouldn't be right to deprive Beau of knowing his child until she's eighteen and demands an answer. I'm not sure I could keep him in the dark."

"And I'll answer her honestly when she asks. But until then, let's don't tell. At least give me a few weeks to get all this sorted out. There are emotions, anger, relief, so many things jumping around inside of me right now I can't even think straight. Can you just give me a little while to get my own mind straight? Lord, if I'd known Beau was living next door to you, I'd never have set foot in this state again."

"Okay," Mary said brightly. "We won't tell. But you won't throw ice water on Beau if he comes around askin' to take you out to dinner or something? You will get to know him better? From the way he looked at you tonight, I think he'll be around in a day or two. And I don't want that Torres temper of yours to run him off."

"Torres?" Jim snorted. "That Jiminez temper can out shout the Torres anytime of the week. Angelina might look like a cream puff, but she's tough as nails, and Milli gets her temper from her mother. We won't open our mouths, child, if you won't be ugly to Beau."

"That's blackmail."

"Temper, temper," Jim chided. "Jiminez coming out."

Mary looked at her granddaughter from the corner of her brown eyes. "Don't matter if she got it from the devil himself. What we're doing here is making a deal, isn't it?"

"Deal," Milli nodded. "You don't blow the whistle on me—that's not to Hilda or Slim or Buster, and *especially* not to Momma or Daddy—and I'll give Beau a fair shake. But he probably won't come around at all. Tonight was a special set of circumstances. He would have been poor old Beau, lucky in everything but love, if he hadn't remembered me at just the right time. But I promise if you don't tell him about Katy, and if he comes around, I'll be gracious."

"Good enough," Mary said. "Now give us a kiss, girl, and get on to bed. Church in the morning, and that old sun don't set still for nobody. Not even those who've danced all night and been forced to bare their souls. We love you, child, and we ain't judgin'."

"Thanks, Granny." She blew them both a kiss.

"Now why'd you go and promise not to tell a single soul?" Jim fussed when Milli's bedroom door at the top of the stairs was shut.

"Why not? We don't have to run an ad in the *Ardmoreite* and publish what we know, Jim. And we don't have to tell Beau. He's not totally stupid, you know. Someday he's going to look at that child and know where she got that dimple in her cheek and those big blue eyes. Or else he's going to look in the mirror and suddenly see something in his face that reminds him of her. Or maybe he'll go home for the holidays and see a picture of himself as a baby and make the connection. It will take care of itself. Now, let's go to bed and go to sleep. Like I said, the sun will come peeking over the horizon in a few hours."

"Wisdom of the sages, woman. I knew when I married you I'd gotten a prize."

"Oh, shush that sweet talk and come on." She slapped his arm playfully.

Milli pulled the straps down from her lace dress and let it fall in a puddle around her feet. So much for wearing the dress and surprising Beau at his engagement party. Fate sure had a strange sense of humor. Poppa and Granny knew all about Katy. Thank goodness Hilda didn't know. She'd bust a seam if she knew something like that and couldn't even tell Beau.

She took a quick shower, dried off, and slipped into a pair of white cotton bikini underpants and a nightshirt with two holes in the sleeve. But it was soft and old and comforting. She pulled the crib sheet back from Katy's legs and stared at her for a long time. Her blonde curls could get darker as she got older and her eyes might not stay that strange shade of pale blue. No one in Hereford knew about Beau and no one ever would. And after this summer, she would go home and he would forget her. Another big, blonde woman like Amanda would come along and take his eye and before long the Bar M would be overrun with tow-headed Luckadeau boys.

She leaned down and pushed the curls back from her precious daughter's forehead and kissed her lightly. At least tonight the baby wasn't old enough to ask questions about her parentage, and for that Milli was grateful. She'd answered enough questions in the past half hour to last for ten years.

She turned out the light and fluffed up her pillow. Sleep would come soon, as tired as she was. She shut her eyes and a vision of the singer's voice singing, "A Picture of Me Without You," appeared. She felt Beau's presence behind her before he even spoke her name. Her heart threw in an extra beat; her mouth was as dry as if it had been swabbed out with a cotton ball; her insides went all oozy, and the world stood still as she waited on him to speak.

She jerked her eyelids open, half expecting him to be standing beside the bed with that look of incredulous wonder in his big blue eyes. But he wasn't, and she shut them again; but it was a long time before she fell asleep.

Chapter 9

Hilda had breakfast on the buffet in the dining room when Jim, Mary, and Milli, carrying Katy on her hip, all arrived at nearly the same time. "Now I want to hear more about this business of the dance last night. I was too tired to ask questions, but me and Slim got so excited this morning, why, we was like a couple of kids. Did Amanda leave before the dance or in the middle or what happened? I bet she just about went into a rigor when she heard about the way Alice set things up."

Mary heaped her plate high with hotcakes and grabbed a cup of coffee. "Never came to the dance. The lawyer told her the conditions and she called it quits right then. Lawyer's wife said Beau saw Milli out the window and muttered some things to Amanda that set her off in a tizzy. She threw his ring on the floor at his feet and stormed out. Said she was the best thing that ever happened to him. The lawyer called his wife to come on to the party and she told Ilene Spencer, since they're friends, and then Ilene told me."

"I told you she wouldn't sign a paper like that. Be cuttin' her own throat," Hilda declared.

Milli yawned and wished for just one day she didn't have to listen to Beau this, Beau that, and Beau everything. It was hard enough to get off an emotional roller coaster without hearing his name every five minutes from daybreak until dark.

Jim winked at Milli. "I do believe that Beau was struck with old cupid's bow last night. He didn't let you out of his sight but twice, and that's only because you had to go to the little girl's room."

"Oh, Poppy, Amanda had just broken their engagement and he only needed someone to dance with so everybody there wouldn't be feeling sorry for him."

Jim chuckled. "Sure, darlin'. You don't believe that lie and neither do I. When's he coming over here to see you? I didn't think he was even goin' to let you drive away last night. Began to think we was going to have to send for a preacher right then and there."

"Beau isn't coming over here today. If he's not going to church, he's got work to do. And after church I'm taking Katy for a long walk around the ranch," she declared.

The words were scarcely out of her mouth when Beau knocked on the sliding glass patio doors out onto the balcony. He slid the door open when Jim motioned to him to come on inside.

"Mornin' folks. Thought I might talk Hilda out of a biscuit this morning."

Hilda pointed toward the buffet. "Help yourself. Biscuits, sausage, gravy, and pancakes. Take your choice. And just to clear the air right now, I'm not sorry that hateful woman broke off your engagement. Even if you think it's the end of the world today, you'll see better in a few weeks. Just count your lucky stars and realize there's an angel on your side."

He nodded, picked up a plate and helped himself, and pulled up a chair beside Milli. "Yes, ma'am, I can sure believe there is an angel taking care of old Beau. I was wondering if it would be all right if I kidnapped your granddaughter this fine Sunday morning after church services. Thought we might take a little picnic lunch over to the park in Sulphur and get our feet wet in the water at Little Niagara. It's colder'n snow, even at this time of year, but…"

"Don't ask me," Jim grinned. "Milli's free, part white, and well past twenty-one. I think she can make up her own mind about spending the afternoon with you, so ask her, not me, son."

He turned his head so he could see her and his heart skipped two beats. She was beautiful in a faded T-shirt and a pair of cutoff jean shorts with frayed edges. He didn't intend to ever let her out of his sight again, at least not for more than a few days. "What do you say, Milli?"

"Sorry, Beau. I'm in and out all week with the ranching business. Sundays I devote entirely to Katy. We go to church, and afterwards I play with her all afternoon."

"I was plannin' on takin' Miss Katy with us to the park. She'll love the Nature Center. There's bugs and snakes and all kinds of things. And we can take a blanket for when she runs her little legs off and gets sleepy. Maybe we'll forget Little Niagara and take her to the creek that runs through the park. The water is shallow there and the sun warms it up so she won't freeze." He slathered butter on the biscuit and popped a crusty chunk into his mouth.

"Oh, all right. But she's demanding, and you'll probably be ready to throw us both in the river before the day's out."

"Wonder where she gets that demanding business?" Mary teased.

Beau finished the last of his breakfast. "Fine breakfast, Hilda. Pick you up here in about an hour, Milli, and we'll go to church with Jim and Mary. Rosa's fixing lunch at the ranch for us and a picnic supper to carry along to the park, so you could bring a change of clothes and we can go from the Bar M to the park. See y'all later." He planted a kiss on Milli's cheek and was out of the door before she could disagree with him.

Hilda plopped down in the chair he'd just vacated. "Well, did you ever? I ain't never seen that boy's eyes that blue. He's just plumb in love with you, girl."

Milli fought back the urge to hold the kiss safely on her flaming red cheek. "Oh, posh. A person don't fall in love with someone in a single night. He's just on the rebound from a bad affair with Amanda. Come on, baby girl; let's go get you ready for church." She gave a small prayer of gratitude that Katy had been sitting in her lap and Beau couldn't really see her.

Beau drove up in the yard at 10:15 in his shiny black, club cab pickup truck. From the window in her bedroom, Milli watched him crawl out and shake the legs of his freshly-starched black Wranglers down over the tops of his spit-shined black eel boots. His broad shoulders and big upper arms stretched the fabric of a white western-cut shirt. She wanted to meet him halfway to the house and drag him upstairs to her bedroom.

"Stop it," she commanded her sinful thoughts and checked herself in the cheval mirror one more time. She was as nervous as a long-tailed cat in a room full of rocking chairs. Anyone would swear she was a teenager and this was her first date. She dabbed a bead of sweat from the top of her upper lip and reapplied powder.

"Milli, we're going to be late," her grandmother called from the bottom of the staircase. "Beau is here and we need to be going."

She rolled her eyes to the ceiling. *Lord, I know he's here. Every fiber in my body knows he just arrived.*

She picked Katy up out of the crib. "Let's just hope he can't see past the end of his nose when he looks at you, girl. There's got to be at least a gazillion blond-haired, blue-eyed men in this part of the country so... stop it right now, Katy Scarlett Torres. Don't you dare smile like that. When you do, you've got dimples as deep as his," she scolded but Katy kept smiling.

He looked up and didn't take his eyes from Milli as she carried Katy down the stairs. Milli wore a red and white gingham-checked sun dress with thin straps and white kid sandals. A gold chain around her neck held the Lazy T diamond charm her father had given her for graduation from high school and gold stud earrings glittered when her long hair bounced. Katy peeped out from the brim of a blue and white checked bonnet that matched her romper, and Beau could see blonde curls wiggling out from the back of the bonnet.

"Don't you ladies look beautiful. Hello, Katy. My, you've got the bluest eyes in the whole world." He opened his arms and to Milli's surprise, Katy reached for him. "Now, if your momma will get your car seat from her truck, I'm sure we can get you fixed right up in old Beau's truck."

Milli looked over her shoulder to find Mary and Jim

looking like two Cheshire cats who'd dined on sautéed canary in wine sauce. Well, she hoped it didn't give them a case of indigestion when they figured out everything wasn't going to go just as they planned. She and Beau were as suited to each other as a church deacon and a two-bit harlot. Every time they were together—except at the dance just last night and the disastrous time when Katy was conceived—all they did was fight. And after today, Beau would bring her home and scuttle his tight-fitting Wranglers right back to the Bar M, never to return again. When Katy slobbered all over his freshly starched white shirt or used that big silver arrowhead slide on his bolo tie for a teething ring, he'd be ready to haul her back to Jim and forget all about the drunken night of ecstasy. By the end of the day, Milli wouldn't be his angel or lady or anything else: her halo would be replaced with a set of horns and a pitchfork. He might even consider dropping down on his knees and begging Amanda for a second chance when Katy got through initiating him into the ways of a fourteen-month-old baby.

He held the door open with one hand and cradled Katy next to his shoulder with the other one. "And here comes Katy's saddle for this bronc. Put it right back there in the back seat, Mommy, and we'll rope her in. And now, Miz Milli, let me help you in, and we'll be off to church. Katy, you got to sit right beside me and promise to keep me awake in church. Sometimes those preacher men get to droning on and on and I kinda fall asleep."

"You're pretty good with kids for a bachelor," Milli said as they drove toward Ringling to the little Methodist church her grandparents had attended forever.

"I like kids. Got a whole passel of nieces and nephews

and I'm their favorite uncle. I'm the baby of six kids… all boys. We haven't got any nieces. Us Luckadeaus have big families and we don't throw very many girls. Six boys and twice that many grandsons. Momma keeps praying for a girl, but so far her prayers haven't made it past the ceiling. Guess someday I'll have a whole backyard of boys, too."

She looked out the window to hide the grin twitching the edges of her mouth. "I see. That's a lovely belt buckle. You ride bulls?"

"Yep," he nodded. "Do a little bull riding and bronc busting. You barrel race?"

"Yes, and also a little bull riding."

"You're shi… kidding me." He cleared his throat. "You really ride?"

"Did before Katy was born. Haven't since then. Picked up a few bucks and a lot of bruises. Eight seconds is a long time to sit on the back of a ton of pure mean hell, ain't it?"

"It sure is. Don't know many women who'll try it."

"Probably not many out there with two older brothers and who has got a chip on her shoulder trying to prove she is just as mean and tough as the boys."

When they reached the church, Milli tried to start for the nursery with Katy, and Beau balked.

"But why does she have to go to the nursery?" He argued as he held the baby close to his chest. "She's plenty old enough to sit beside me, and I'll take her out if she gets fussy."

"Oh, Beau, it's for her own good. She can play in the nursery and she'll be bored to tears up here," Mary agreed with Milli.

He might have lost the battle but he didn't have to

concede the whole war. "Then can I go to the nursery? Sometimes I get bored, too. And I'd rather play with the baby. Oh, all right. Don't look at me like that. If she can't stay in the sanctuary to keep me awake, then I get to carry her down to the nursery."

"Deal," Milli agreed.

During the Sunday sermon, he draped his arm over the back of the pew and thought about Milli. Buster had been fairly well floating around on a cloud all morning long. The rest of the ranch hands kept coming around to congratulate him on roping that filly from the next ranch. Mercy, but not a one of them had made this much to-do over Amanda. As a matter of fact, he couldn't remember even one of them congratulating him with a smile on his face after he'd proposed to the girl. Mostly it was a serious handshake and a wish for happiness... kind of like what he did that time when his cousin was about to mess up really bad and marry that horrible woman.

Milli fought back one of those delicious shivers when his hand touched her bare arm. No one had ever affected her the way he did. She could sit on the hard, wooden pew for hours and smell that wonderful aroma that was Beau: a strange mixture of a woodsy shaving lotion, freshly laundered and ironed shirt, and peppermint gum. She thought about taking his hand and leading him back to the Sunday school room, but she didn't know how good she was at dodging lightning bolts—or seducing a sober man, either, for that matter. He'd been drunker than a cooter's owl the night she'd spent in his arms in the back bedroom of a trailer. She fanned herself with the church program just thinking about those kisses that had turned her knees to jelly and caused her to drop her dress to the floor. The preacher said something about forgiving and forgetting, but she didn't want to forget one moment of that night.

Finally services were over and Milly and Mary went to the nursery.

"Mommy, mommy, look at the kitty," Katy sing-songed and pointed toward a stuffed black and white cat she had put into a toy cradle and covered with a blanket.

"Lovely child," the nursery attendant said. "And she's the absolute spitting image of her father. All those blonde curls and blue eyes. I know he must be really proud of her."

Milli almost swallowed her tongue. She tried to deny the statement but she couldn't stand right there after Sunday services in a church house and lie any more than she could have seduced Beau in the Sunday school room.

"Oh, hello, Sarah," Mary smiled brightly. "I see you've met my granddaughter, Milli, and her daughter, Katy. They're staying with us this summer while Jim is recuperating from surgery."

Sarah nodded her head until all three of her chins wobbled up and down. "Lovely child. I was just telling Milli that Katy looks just like her father. When he carried her in here, I thought to myself, 'Sarah, there's one man who couldn't deny his daughter,' and he's such a good daddy. Stayed here with Milli and Katy until the child was comfortable with me. Most fathers just let the mothers bring them down here and drop them off. Some of them I'm not sure who they belong to, but this baby sure is like her daddy."

"Well, she may look like her father, but she's got her mother's temper," Mary winked mischievously at Milli.

Milli finally exhaled as she carried Katy down the hall, with Mary right behind her. "That was scary."

Mary shook her head. "She's not blind, and there will be others who say the same thing when they see the two of them together. Just what do you intend to do about this lovely child looking so much like her father? It's not a matter of me or your Poppa telling it, either."

Milli stopped dead in her tracks. "Whatever are you talking about?"

"You know what I'm talking about. Sarah saw him with her for a few minutes and she knew. And someday soon, Beau's going to see it, too. So you better think about just how you're going to handle that. Sarah's liable to be the very one to tell him next week if you let him back in the nursery," Mary said.

"I think maybe the thing for me and Katy to do is forget about a picnic in the park this afternoon. We need to just pack our bags and go on back to west Texas."

"Can't run from it. Beau would search the ends of the earth for you now, girl. Besides, you're a Torres and you don't run from your problems. You stand up and face them. Grab them by the horns just like they was a charging bull, stare them right in the eye, and spit on them if you have to. But you damned sure don't run from them. Now get on out there and have a wonderful afternoon. Beau ain't stupid and he ain't blind. He's a good man, and evidently you saw something good in him at least one time. But I expect he's going to be pretty upset when he finds out he's got a daughter and you didn't tell him a thing about her," Mary said bluntly.

Milli stopped in the hall. She wanted to cut and run to the farthest corner of the earth. Somewhere no one knew her or Katy and had never heard the name Luckadeau. She could always make a living for the two of them on a ranch, and there were lots of ranches scattered over the United States.

She finally kissed her grandmother's cheek. "I love you, Granny. But I'm not about to tell him about Katy just yet. This whole thing is so new it's got me baffled and I need to sort out my feelings before I confront him with a thing this big."

Beau was waiting right outside the church door. "Hey, I thought you ran off to the Land of Oz with Miz Katy. Come here, baby, and let old Beau carry you out to the bronc and put you in the saddle. We'll go find us some lunch and play all afternoon. Do you like minnows? We're going to find a creek bed with water so shallow you can play with the minnows." He took Katy from her mother, propping her up on his hip with one hand as he reached down and took Milli's hand in his other one.

Milli put the diaper bag in the back seat and looked around hopelessly. "Oh, no! I've left my purse in the church. I'll be right back."

He nodded and finished strapping the baby into the seat as Milli headed back into the church. "Katy and I'll put on some music and we'll be fine, won't we baby? Now, what do you want to hear? Are you a Clint Black fan or do you like Miss Reba better?"

"Twinkle star," Katy said.

"So you like twinkle star, do you?" he asked and was thumbing through CDs when an old man knocked on the window of his truck. Beau rolled down the window and raised an eyebrow.

"Mornin', son. I'm Tommy Rogers. Been goin' to church here with Jim and Mary for a hun'erd years, give or take a few. Just wanted to tell you that you and your little family is welcome here. We need you young folks in our church, and any kinfolks of Jim's is friends of ours. One thing's for sure, you sure got a pretty wife and little baby girl."

"Thank you, but…" Beau tried to set him straight but it was like pouring water on a duck's back, and the old fellow kept talking.

"Little baby girl is the spittin' image of you. Even got your dimple on the right side there when she smiles. Maybe the next one will look like her momma. Pretty woman, that wife of yours. Bet she can put you around the corner. Them brown eyes look like they… oh, here she comes right now. Just come on back with Jim and Mary any time and we'll make you feel right at home."

"Yes, sir." Beau rolled the window back up.

Milli hopped up into the truck and threw her purse on the back seat. "I'd forget my head if it wasn't glued on right tight. Did you know that fellow?"

Beau's eyebrows drew down in a fine line. "Nope. He was inviting us back to church anytime we want to come."

"Oh, you don't come to this church all the time? Guess I just thought because Granny and Poppy and the Spencers come over here, y'all did, too."

A cold shiver of reality climbed up his backbone and made the blond hair on his neck prickle. "Buster and

Rosa go to the Catholic church over in Ardmore. I was going with Amanda to the Baptist church in Ardmore 'til last week. Aunt Alice went to one in Lone Grove. Never been over here before, but I sure do like these people and the atmosphere."

"They are sweet folks. I'm starving. I think I could eat a whole Angus steer—hoofs, horns and all."

"Calf fries?"

"My favorite. Rolled in beer batter and deep fat fried. Served up with pinto beans and fried potatoes."

He started the engine and eased out on the road, heading south until he reached the highway taking them back east to the ranch. "You're a girl after my own heart. How 'bout you, Katy? When you get to be a year old, you goin' to like calf fries?"

"Katy is fourteen months old already. And honey, she can eat her weight in calf fries if I cut them up in little pieces. She quit eating baby food months ago and started eating whatever I am."

Beau did the math in his head. "Birthday in April? What day?"

Milli turned the music down low. "April 20."

Beau had always been good with figures, and it didn't take a rocket scientist to figure out how long it was from the last of week of July to April 20, and it didn't take a physics major to know what had been evident to the old man at the church was the pure truth. He peeped up in the rearview mirror at the baby sitting in the car seat, reality hitting him in the chest like a tornado ripping up a one-hole outhouse. He remembered the copy of his own baby picture his mother kept on the mantle in the den. Take off the blue-checked bonnet and put on a little baseball cap and it was Beau all over again, except for that lightly tanned skin.

"You're pretty quiet. Hungry?" She asked when they were nearly back to the Bar M where Rosa was supposed to have lunch ready. She had packed a small duffel bag with shorts and a top, along with a two-piece bathing suit—if she had the nerve to wear it in front of him. Her stretch marks were still visible across her tummy, even if they were fading away slowly. Katy's diaper bag was stuffed with everything she needed plus a few of her favorite stuffed toys.

Oh, rot, I forgot her little plastic pail and shovel.

"Yep, I am," he said icily. "But more than hungry, I'm madder than pure hell, right now."

He pulled the pickup off the road and faced her. His eyes were slits behind long lashes, and his nostrils flared. There wasn't even a single sign of a dimple in his cheek, and his eyebrows were one straight line. It was beginning to look as if she'd been right all along. They couldn't breathe the same air for more than a couple of hours without one of them getting angry.

"Well, what in the world got your dander up?"

She hadn't done a single thing to rile him. Just like she'd promised her grandparents; if they didn't tell her secret, she wouldn't give him the cold shoulder. It looked as though he was about as stable as water. One minute leaning close to her in the church services and making her fairly well swoon with lusty desire right there in front of the preacher and the Almighty, and the next, jerking the truck to a standstill. Jim and Mary Torres could forget about happy endings. It wasn't happening with Beau and Milli.

He touched her cheek with his hand and turned her

face toward the back of the pickup truck. "Look in the back seat and tell me what you see."

She slapped his hand away from her face. "My purse? Are you mad because I forgot my purse? Well, that's a stupid, ignorant thing to get so worked up over. I forgot Katy's plastic pail and shovel, too. Good grief, Beau, haven't you ever forgotten anything before?"

"It's not your damned purse, Milli. It's Katy."

"Why are you mad about Katy? She didn't puke on you or leave a wet spot on your jeans…"

"Twinkle star," Katy said.

"She calls all music twinkle star. She wants me to turn up the volume," Milli said.

He clenched his teeth and slapped the steering wheel. "Why in the hell didn't you tell me Katy was my daughter? Why didn't you at least make an effort to get in touch with me when you found out you were having my child?"

She exhaled so long her lungs ached. "Oh."

"That all you got to say, just, 'oh'? I think we've got a lot to talk about. And all you can say is 'oh.' I want some answers."

Her eyes narrowed and steam could practically be seen coming out the top of her head. "Don't you talk to me in that tone. And don't you ever raise your voice like that in front of my daughter again."

"She's mine, too, damn it," he whispered loudly. "And just how long did you think you'd wait before you told me? Until she was grown?"

"Hey, you were the dumb jackass who was fixing to marry Amanda. What was I supposed to do? Come waltzing in with a baby daughter and say, 'Oh, Amanda, meet your new stepdaughter'? Hellfire, Beau, I damn sure didn't know you was going to show up across a cut fence from me, yelling and shouting about an Angus bull. When I found out I was pregnant, was I supposed to put out a bulletin with your picture on it and say, 'I slept with this man one night and he's the father of my baby. Can you help me find him? He doesn't hold his liquor well and he'll go to bed with any woman who's willing.' I didn't know anything but your name and that your family was from Shreveport."

"There's a whole page of Luckadeaus in the phone book in Shreveport. All you had to do was call anyone and ask for Beau and they would have told you how to get in touch with me, since I'm the only one named Beau. Besides, we're all related. Luckadeau is not such a common name."

She raised her voice almost as high as her eyebrows. "Sure, I could call anyone of them. Can you please tell me where Beau Luckadeau is so I can tell him I'm pregnant from a one-night stand? And what would you have done? Crawled up on your fancy little tricycle, put on your shining armor, and ridden all the way to west Texas to rescue the loose-legged woman who said the baby she carried was yours? Get real. Even you wouldn't have believed a story like that."

Beau fumed. He wanted to turn around and stare at his daughter until his eyes memorized every detail from her unruly blonde curls to her toenails peaking out from the ends of white leather sandals. With one breath he wanted to slap thunder out of Milli for depriving him of his daughter for a whole year, not to mention the joy and anticipation of waiting for her for nine months. With the next breath he wanted to reach across the seat and draw her close to his side and make her vow never to leave him again.

"Why don't you just take us to the Lazy Z? I don't think this is a good day for a picnic after all. As a matter of fact, it might be a good day for me and Katy to go back to Hereford. I think both of us need a lot of space to get this worked out. It's pretty damned evident that the lady you kept talking about last night was a figment of your imagination. And darlin', I never did think you were such a great knight-in-shining-damn-armor."

"Well, it might not be a good day, but I promised my daughter a picnic and by damn she's having a picnic. I don't make promises I don't intend to keep," he declared.

"Beau, be realistic. You didn't even know until a few minutes ago that you had a child. When the newness wears off and the air clears, your common sense will tell you there's more to a baby than just picnics and…"

"And what, Milli? I'm thirty years old. I think I know what there is to a child. And today we're going to the ranch for dinner and to the park for the afternoon. Lord, wait until Buster sees Katy. If I hadn't found out this morning, I would have known before the day was out, because Buster knows about the dream I had about you, even though he doesn't know just how far things went that night. He knows you ran away and I found your earring. And besides, he knew me when I was a little kid. One look at Katy and he'd have been telling me how stupid I was. Guess what they say about me is true. I'm lucky—in everything but love."

"That's the gospel truth. And it don't look like it's going to get a whole a lot better in the near future. I told you last night you'd be kicking me across the state line when you got to know me. Like I said, you can just take me to Granny and Poppy's right now. At the end of the summer, Katy and I will go back home, and you can forget you figured it all out this fine June morning."

"Huh," he snorted. "Miss Katy, I think your pretty momma has got cow chips for brains. Let's go see your daddy's ranch. Betcha it's bigger and better than your Poppy's, and I bet you like Angus cows better, too."

"When cows fly…" she snorted right back at him. "No Torres in the world would pick a fool Angus cow over a white-face."

He started the engine and pulled back out onto the highway, bound for the Bar M. "But a Luckadeau would, and Katy is a Luckadeau—or haven't you noticed that dimple in her cheek?"

"But the part that has bovine sense is Torres, and don't you forget it."

Beau just grinned real big.

Chapter 10

MILLI WATCHED THE GREEN OKLAHOMA COUNTRYSIDE speed past at sixty-five miles an hour and wished her heart was going that slow. She wondered if Beau could see it pumping faster than a gushing oil well when he stole glances toward her. Every time his eyes traveled from her sandals to her forehead she felt as if a red hot iron had touched her bare skin. Why in the hell did he affect her like this? She dealt with cattle buyers, farmers, ranchers, bankers, and hundreds of other men on a daily basis, so why did this one long, tall cool drink of southern water have her panting like she'd just spent eight seconds on the back of a mean bull?

Probably because he was the only man she'd ever known sexually and she didn't have anyone else to compare him with. What she needed to do was get the hell out of Dodge—or Oklahoma, as the case may be—and find a lover. One who would kiss her until her knees were weak and all she wanted to do was fall backwards and pull him down with her. Someone who would take Beau's face from her mind and send it back to the Texas–Louisiana border where it belonged. Someone who would erase the indelible mark he'd left on her heart. Where could she find a man like that? She didn't know right then, but she wasn't going to find him until she started looking, and that would be tomorrow morning. In Hereford, Texas. Not in southern

Oklahoma where she would run into Beau every time she turned around.

Beau glanced up in the rearview mirror to make sure his daughter was still there and hadn't faded like a dream, and kept a watch on Milli for the same reason. This was sure enough a twenty-four hours to remember. Yesterday at this time he was thinking about his engagement party with Amanda and wishing he hadn't been so hasty about buying that big diamond for her. Today he was sitting in close quarters with the woman he'd begun to believe was just a crazy piece of his imagination. Last night he really thought he had an angel in his arms while they danced. He breathed in the essence of Milli and wanted more and more and more. Today she was more than a puff of angel dust. She was a real woman, full of spit and vinegar, and she'd have him toeing the line if they ever did get into a relationship.

And he had a child. Wait until his parents got wind of this whole thing. His mother would probably be so upset with him she wouldn't even talk to him. Not for having a child out of wedlock; Luckadeau men weren't perfect, by any means. But for not taking time to make sure there wasn't one on the way after that night. But she'd damn sure forgive him the minute she found out she had a granddaughter. A girl baby in the Luckadeau family—now that was a pure miracle.

It wasn't his fault. He'd tried to find Amelia and had even called information for several towns in the Rio Grande Valley and in Brownsville, too. There were lots of Jiminez folks down in that part of the world. It was like looking for a Smith in downtown Dallas. If Joann Luckadeau wanted proof that he had tried, he still had an enormous telephone bill in his file cabinet.

After a houseful of sons and several grandsons, Katy just might be the very thing that got him out of hot water over this to-do. It didn't matter that he was thirty years old, had his own ranch, and ran it well. There were some things that were unforgivable. And this was number one on the list. His father didn't care how modern the world was; could care less that lots of men and women chose to have children without the sacrament of marriage. The old standard was upheld in the Luckadeau family and there wasn't a lot of room for argument about it.

His mind ran in circles so fast it made him dizzy. Milli was so blessed straightforward and bossy, he didn't know if he could ever live with her every day. They couldn't even keep company for a few hours without making each other mad enough to chew up railroad spikes and spit out thumbtacks. It'd be a topsy-turvy world and they'd argue so much they'd end up spending half their time making up. A shock went through him from the ends of his boots all the way to the stitches on the top of his head when he remembered her snuggled up beside him in the bedroom the night Katy was conceived. Now, wouldn't that be just like dying and going to heaven, to have to make up with her like that on a regular basis?

No matter what they decided to do about their own violent tempers, he fully well intended that the whole world know from this moment on that Katy was his daughter. If Milli didn't feel that same magic he did every time their hands brushed together, then he'd just have to live with her decision. But Katy was his, the next in line for the ranch, and even if he lived to be an old bachelor and his luck never did change when it came to women, she was going to grow up knowing him. They'd just have to come to some understanding about child support and visitation rights.

Milli bit the inside of her lip until she could taste blood. That fool man, anyway. They could no more be a family than she could sprout wings and sit on the clouds with a golden harp. Just because she was physically attracted to him didn't mean they could run a ranch and ever make a marriage. But then, he hadn't mentioned anything like that, had he? Well, he had fertilizer for brains if he thought for one minute he was going to step in and take Katy Scarlett away from her even for one week out of the summer. Katy was her daughter and she wasn't sharing her with him. Not even if he offered to pay child support and acknowledged her and the whole nine yards. Not even if he hired the best lawyer in the state and the judge said she had to let him have her so many weeks out of the month. Milli could disappear so fast it would make his old head swim, and by golly she'd do it.

Despite the vibrations and thoughts bouncing around like feisty, hyperactive two-year-olds in the cab of the pickup, neither said a word from the time he drove back out onto the highway until they pulled into the circle drive in front of the ranch house on the Bar M.

He gently put his hands on her shoulders and made her look at him. "Milli, the way Aunt Alice set up her will means that when I'm dead, everything on this place will belong to Katy someday. She's my firstborn…"

She stared him right in the eyes without blinking. "Not necessarily. If you just back off and forget all about today, you can marry later on and have a son. I won't ever come back to haunt you, I promise—well, I'll be damned."

He followed her gaze to the porch. "Well, I'll be damned, too."

Amanda wore a long denim prairie skirt with a western-cut lace blouse and actually had a pair of brand new Roper boots on her feet. A turquoise and silver necklace hung around her neck and a wide bracelet of silver with accents of turquoise jingled on her arm as she walked. She looked like she was playing dress up in someone else's clothing as she sashayed off the porch and toward the truck. She put on a big smile and Milli just sat there in silent awe.

About the time Amanda reached the driver's side of the truck, Milli finally found her tongue and whispered, "Whatever is she trying to prove?"

Amanda opened Beau's door. "Hello, darling. I think you and I better have a little talk. I was too rash." She stopped and glared at Milli. "What the hell are you doing in his truck? You're that bitch from the next farm over, aren't you? The one who Anthony felt sorry for and danced with because your grandfather lives on the next ranch. The one who took him to the hospital but looked like hell. I told you at the hospital you aren't welcome around him."

Beau set his jaw. "I don't have anything to say to you, Amanda. It's finished, but you do owe Milli an apology. I might have died if she hadn't found me and took care of things. Besides, you've no right to call her names."

"Oh, shut up. And besides, darling, it's not finished. I'm ready to sign that little piece of paper. You know I was just angry last night, and now I realize how much I love you. So let's go in the house and I'll sign the papers and set a date for the wedding and I'll put my ring back on. How about the end of July? We won't have to wait until fall after all. Who knows, we might even get a jump start on that son you were talking about."

Beau stepped out of the pickup. "Too late."

When Amanda put her hand out to touch his arm, he sidestepped and she let her hand fall limply in the folds of her skirt. "I don't love you, Amanda. I'm not sure I ever did. You were there and I was in love with the idea of being in love. Besides, you made the choice last night and now you can just live with it. I probably wouldn't ever have broken up with you since I'd given you my word and a Luckadeau's word is gold, but you broke it off when you threw my ring on the floor, remember?"

Amanda put her hands on her hips and planted her boots in the dirt in front of him. "I suppose that bitch in the car has something to do with this? Tell her we're going in the house to talk and she can call her grandfather to come get her. God, Alice Martin would rise up and pitch a fit if she knew you were bringing a low-class Mexican bitch like that on her property."

He stepped around Amanda and the pickup, and opened the door for Milli. "I'll get the baby, sweetheart. She's been asleep for the past ten minutes. I hate to wake her, but…"

Amanda stepped between him and Milli and glared down at Milli like she was a fresh cow patty on a hot day. Her nose curled and her upper lip sneered. "Get out of here. You're nothing but a cheap Mexican bitch. Alice would never want the likes of you on this ranch."

Milli took a deep breath and tried to will the red-hot blur of rage from her eyes. But it didn't work. She tried to think about Katy waking up and the fresh look on her face, but all she saw was Amanda's sneer and mocking eyes. Finally, she gave in to her own anger and rocked the woman's jaw with a hard right hook, then slapped her on the other cheek as she fell backwards to sit down in the dry dirt.

"Don't you ever call me a bitch again. You don't even know me, but I know you and I heard what you said about divorcing Beau in a year if he didn't do just what you wanted. Remember what you said to your little friend in the bathroom the night he asked you to marry him? And remember what you told Granny and me at the mall just a few days ago?"

Amanda just sat there bewildered and confused. She was right about the dark-haired, low-class woman. She didn't have an ounce of dignity. Not a single lady she knew would have done something as base as actually hitting another woman. They might try to kill each other with barbs, but to actually double up her fist like a man? It just wasn't done in polite circles.

"Now crawl your sorry old scraggly ass out of here, and don't come back. This ranch is my daughter's inheritance, and if I ever catch you looking at Beau again, I'll break that expensive nose job. Now get out," Milli said between clenched teeth.

Amanda popped back up to a standing position and wiped at a big brown stain across the front of her lace blouse. "I'll have an assault suit filed on you by tomorrow morning. You could have broken my jaw. My lawyer will be at the courthouse when the doors open in the morning. You ever hit me again and I'll…"

Milli turned around to find a wide-eyed, grinning man holding her child. "Be careful and don't wake her up, honey. I damned sure don't want her tender little eyes to look upon such filth as this."

She turned back to Amanda. "You'll what? Darlin' if you think you can whup me, you better run along home and get your supper and maybe even bring your red-haired friend. You'll need the help and food because it will be an all-day job. If I wanted to break your jaw, it would be flapping like a pair of underwear on a clothes-line. And if you don't get off the Bar M, I'm going to do more than slap fire out of you, honey. I'm going to beat you until your body is as cold as your heart. That is not a threat. It's a solid promise. Torres women don't make promises they can't keep and when we make a promise, it's every bit as gold as the Luckadeau word."

Amanda stomped away hard enough to boil the dust up around her skirt tail. She opened the door to her big, gray car parked at the end of the house. What on earth had gone wrong? She'd intended to play up to Anthony and convince him she wasn't herself the night before when she got so angry. Things hadn't gone well when she stopped by the hospital and caught her doctor introducing his fiancée to the staff. When she realized she'd just been a passing fancy and not a long-term arrangement, she decided maybe Anthony wouldn't be such a bad catch after all. Good lord, what in the world had happened in less than twenty-four hours? It really had been just that long, hadn't it? She revved up the engine and left a dust cloud in the yard as she sped away.

"You got anything to say?" Milli asked Beau before they opened the front door.

"Nope. Guess you can take care of yourself. Remind me never to call you a bitch," he grinned.

One minute she was ready to find another lover to erase Beau from her mind, the next she was fighting for him like she was ready to put her brand on him for life. The whole situation was enough to make her want to crawl into a hole and pull the entrance inside with her so she could figure out just what she was going to do.

"That's right. Or you'll find yourself on the ground, even if I have to find a two-by-four to help me make up the difference in size. That's one thing I hate to be called. First time I got into trouble for fighting was over that. Girl kept saying I was a wet-back bitch and telling me to go back home to Mexico; that Texas didn't need any more of my kind in it. We were in the sixth grade and I whipped her soundly. I got a black eye and a bloody nose but she looked just as bad. I had to stay in from recess for three weeks for slapping her first, but it was worth it. Guess I should have given Amanda a fighting chance. I might have just warned her about my aversion to that word, if she'd have said it once and at least given me time to speak my mind."

Rosa opened the door before Beau could turn the knob. She wore a white, bibbed apron, her hair pulled back in a bun, and a smile so big a Cadillac could have driven through her mouth and not touched a single tooth. "Miss Milli, so glad to see you put that woman in her place. She got here about ten minutes ago and was sure ugly to Buster when he told her Beau went to church over at Ringling this mornin'. She told him he'd just as well start packing his sorry belongings because his days on this ranch was numbered. He told her that when Beau kicked him off the ranch he'd go without a word, but he wasn't listening to any of what she had to say. Buster didn't even mention you. Oh, look at that precious little baby!"

Beau took her bonnet off. "This is Miss Katy. Tell me, Rosa, what do you think? Does she look more like me or Milli?"

Rosa's grin faded. She'd heard about Katy from Jim and Mary, and she knew the child was fatherless, but standing on the floor looking up at her was the exact image of Beau. He and Milli only met two weeks ago, so that had to be impossible. Her head began to swim as she searched for words in her first-time-ever speechless mind. Katy couldn't have looked more like a Luckadeau if they'd cloned her, like Rosa had read about what they were doing with sheep.

Milli draped her arm around the woman's shoulder. "That's not a question you have to answer. Come on and let me help you put dinner on the table. We're so hungry we could eat the south end of a northbound heifer right now. And besides, Beau ought to be horsewhipped for putting you on the spot like that. Beau, take Katy out to the horse barn and show her the horses, and call Buster in to dinner. Be back here in ten minutes flat."

Beau and Katy smiled at the same time, showing off a deep dimple on the left side. "Yes, ma'am. Sorry I scared you like that, Rosa."

Rosa shook her head in disbelief. "Oh, my. It is really his baby, isn't it?"

"Of course, she's mine. And now we're going out to the barn and see if Buster can tell which one of us she looks like."

Rosa plopped down in a kitchen chair and looked up at her for answers. "What is going on, Miss Milli?"

Milli explained as briefly and honestly as she could in as few words as possible, then looked around at the dinner preparations. "I see you've got the table set. Can I help you put the food in serving bowls?"

Buster stood in the door of the horse barn where he'd been for the past fifteen minutes. Amanda had knocked on the door, all dolled up in a western get-up, looking like the cat what caught the sparrow. She had this smile on her face until Buster answered the door, then she sneered at him like she always did and rudely asked where Anthony was. The man had never gone by Anthony in his whole life. What was the matter with plain old Beau?

"Well, he's gone off to the church over in Ringling with the Torres family," he had answered.

"What in the hell is he doing going to that podunk place? He knows we attend church in Ardmore. What's the matter with that man?"

When Buster didn't offer any answers, she opened the screen door and stared at him with pure venom. "Old man, you better be putting out the word that you're looking for a job. I'm marrying him before the summer is out and the first change I'm making on this ranch is your removal. You and that wife of yours are going to be fired and gone before we even get back from our honeymoon. So start deciding what you're going to pack in your rattletrap truck, because your days are numbered."

"We'll see," was all he had said as he stepped out the door and around her.

She had eased herself down on the porch swing and glared at him as he went to the horse barn and watched her swing on the porch, wishing all the time he had the nerve to load a gun, shoot her between the eyes, and do the world a tremendous favor. The best thing she could ever do was lay down and die, but he couldn't help matters along no matter how much he disliked the crude woman. He couldn't disgrace his children and Rosa by committing murder, even if he might have to go to hell for just thinking about it. He'd have to go to confession next week for sure. Then Beau had driven up, and one minute Amanda was talking, and the next Milli had knocked the hell out of her and she was on her back on the ground. Buster was so excited he didn't know whether to wind his fanny or scratch his watch when he saw her spin out of the driveway.

Now, Beau was walking out across the lawn, carrying Milli's little girl he'd heard about from Slim over at the Lazy Z.

"Mornin'," Buster nodded. "Guess Miss Milli set that woman straight."

"Yep. Don't ever call Milli a bitch. She drew a gun on me when I called her a bitch, but man, she really gets hot under the collar when someone calls her that more than once. I guess Amanda won't be back around here. Miss Katy, I want you to meet Buster. He's my right hand around here, and you'll really like him when you get to know him."

Katy eyed Buster with the innocence of a baby, and Buster eyed her with the wisdom of the sages. Katy saw a nice man who could be trusted, and Buster's old brown eyes widened as he looked from Katy to Beau and back again. An eerie feeling crawled down his arms and made the gray hair on the back of his neck prickle. This was Milli's child and she had Beau's eyes, his hair, even his dimple when she smiled at the horses.

"Horsey. Ride, peas," she said.

"Cat got your tongue?" Beau teased.

Buster let a gush of air escape from his lungs. "Just how did this happen, son?"

"Way most babies happen, Buster. I met Milli at the wedding down in Texarkana two years ago this July. Remember the dream girl I've talked about ever since? Well, we weren't real careful, and I didn't know about Katy until today. Think she looks like me?"

"Lord, son, if you'd have cloned yourself and started all over as a baby girl, it wouldn't look as much like you as that child. Now, just what do you intend to do about all this?" Buster talked to him and continued to stare at Katy.

"Don't know, yet. Evidently what Milli and I do best is fight and make a beautiful baby girl. Don't know if the two of us could live together every day and not tear a ranch down around our ears. Lord, she's bullheaded," Beau said.

"And you're not?" Buster snapped. "Been tryin' to tell you about that Amanda for months, but would you listen? Noooo! Wouldn't hear a word I said."

Beau hugged Katy close to him, taking in the sweet smell of baby lotion. "I'm listening now. Think maybe we'd better go in for dinner. Milli was helping Rosa get it on the table, and we don't want them two women mad at us, do we?"

"You got that right."

Chapter 11

ROSA FINALLY FOUND HER TONGUE. "MY, OH, MY, DON'T the world look brighter this day. Does Hilda know? How about Slim?"

"I don't think so, and don't you dare tell them," Milli suddenly had a vision of all the people standing in a line she'd have to deal with and it made her weary just thinking about it. Hilda would give her a sound dressing-down and then she and Granny would be in the corner, their heads together making big plans about the future.

"Well, it does look brighter," Rosa declared. "Me and Buster were scared we'd be kicked off the ranch. That woman told Buster just a few minutes ago the first thing she was doing was getting rid of us. Would have been a hard choice for Beau, but if she was his wife, and all…"

"Oh, that's where Beau would have held the line, I'm sure. Besides I don't know if the world is all that much better today or not, Rosa. Seems to me like that the world has fallen down around my ears in the last twenty-four hours and I've completely lost control. I don't quite know what to do to put it back together again. One day it's just me and Katy on Poppy's ranch, checking cattle, living a normal life, and the next day Beau is no longer engaged, he finds out about Katy, and everything is wild and crazy."

Rosa scooped up fried potatoes into a bowl and set it on the table. "You did say that Mary and Jim know about all this?"

"I told them just last night. I tried to get out of it. If I'd just known about Alice—but Granny didn't ever mention it when we talked on the phone. Granny knew about Katy, or at least had some real strong ideas, a few weeks ago. I wasn't going to tell Beau. I'm still not sure how he figured it out. We went to church and I forgot my purse and when I got back to the truck, he'd put two and two together."

"Well, it's about time. He mentioned Katy when he came home the other night. Said he'd pushed her around in her stroller while you shopped and went on and on about her pretty eyes. Then Amanda said something about not wanting children about that time and me and Buster could tell it upset him. Seemed like he was worrying over things like a hound dog worries a ham bone, but he's a Luckadeau, and even if it meant living a miserable life, he wouldn't have gone back on his word."

The last sentence stuck in Milli's mind. The Luckadeau pride would have kept him in an engagement he wasn't sure about. The Luckadeau pride would have made him marry the woman even when he'd discovered what she really was. The Luckadeau pride would make him marry her so his child wouldn't be tagged a bastard. But Milli wanted a man to love her. Simply. Completely. For life. Not because of his inherited pride.

How would she ever know the difference?

"We're hungry," Beau called from the front door. "Katy says she wants a corn cob, Rosa. Buster, could you could find us that old high chair Aunt Alice had out on the back porch? The wood one I used to sit in when the folks brought us kids to visit."

Buster couldn't get that silly grin off his face no matter how hard he tried. "Reckon I could. Give me two minutes to fetch it and wipe the dust off, and we'll set right up at the table."

Rosa beamed as she stared unabashedly at Katy in Beau's arms. Not once had Amanda ever come in and helped Rosa put the dinner on the table. As a matter of fact, she'd never eaten in the ranch house before. Not that Beau hadn't invited her, but she always had an excuse. Suddenly, Rosa heard wedding bells and saw wedding dresses and bridal bouquets and she was happy instead of sad. Buster whistled as he used his red handkerchief to dust off the high chair. Beau looked as if he'd just caught cloud nine on its way to heaven.

Milli wanted to hit something or else sit down and cry. She didn't want Katy to sit in the family high chair that her daddy had used. Her daddy. She didn't want Katy to have a daddy. Not even if it was Beau, who was quite enamored with her. Milli didn't want to share her child. What she wanted to do was run and never look back until she was safely out of southern Oklahoma.

Milli looked around the bedroom where she and Katy were supposed to change into shorts and T-shirts. A king-sized four-poster bed made of burled oak took up most of the south wall and a matching dresser with a triple mirror the north one. The lone star handmade quilt done in shades of blue served as a bedspread. As a child, she remembered playing around on the floor at the ranch with fabric scraps while Alice and her grandmother lowered an old quilting frame from the ceiling and talked ranching business while their needles flew in and out. She wondered if this was one of the ones they had worked on back then.

Why hadn't she even asked about Alice in the past two years? If she would have simply asked how she was faring, then Granny would have told her all about the new owner at the Bar M and probably even mentioned his name. But hindsight is the only 20/20 vision and it was too late to go back now.

She removed Katy's Sunday romper and dressed her in shorts and a soft T-shirt. "Well, baby girl, this has already been a day. Next thing you know, he'll be wanting you to call him daddy, but that ain't happening today. I've had enough turmoil for one day."

"Daddy, daddy, daddy," Katy picked up on the word immediately.

A tear formed on Milli's lashes and traveled down her cheek, streaking her makeup. Then another one hung there a while and in seconds she was wiping away the streams as they dripped off her jawbone. "Why, oh why, didn't we stay in Hereford?"

Beau stopped long enough to look in the mirror to see if there was a change in his face since morning. Surely fatherhood would add a wrinkle around his eyes, but the grinning fool looking back at him didn't look so very different, except there was a glitter in his eyes that hadn't been there yesterday. Even if he and Milli couldn't ever get past the fighting stage and even if she didn't feel that prickly feeling in her heart like he did when their hands touched, at least he had a child to carry on the Luckadeau name. Someone to run the Bar M when his time on earth had ceased. It didn't matter now if he was always unlucky in love. Women could come and go in his life and he wouldn't have to put up with one whining moment just to get an heir.

He brushed his hair back one more time. *But oh, how wonderful it would be if Milli could be as attracted to me as I am to her.*

The sun was high in the sky and the bank thermometer said it was a hundred degrees when they went through downtown Sulphur. He chose a spot close to the shallow part of the creek running through Chickasaw National Recreation Area, formerly known as Platt National Park.

"We'll spread the blanket right here to stake out our claim. We'll put the chairs right out in the middle of the water where Mommy and Daddy will sit with their feet in the water and watch Katy play," Beau said.

Milli's eyebrows shot up. "Daddy?"

"And what else should I call myself? I'm not Uncle Beau. I'm Daddy, and she can start learning that today."

He jerked his T-shirt over his head, picked up two folding lawn chairs from the back of the truck, and set them in the middle of the shallow creek. "Would you please put her little bathing suit on her? That diaper is going to draw up enough water to make her bottom heavy. And take your sandals off. Wade right out here when you get her ready. The water isn't cold. Before we leave, I'll take you over to little Niagara. Now, that's too cold for our baby to play in, but it's a pretty sight."

Milli peeled off her shirt and shorts, leaving them in a heap on the blanket. She tugged at the bottom of her bright red, two-piece bathing suit, trying to pull it up above the faint white lines left from stretch marks. She frowned when Beau whistled appreciatively and shot him a hateful look. So he thought he could just pop right into this fatherhood role and be "Daddy," did he? Well, Katy Scarlett was her daughter. Rosa and Granny already had wedding bells in their eyes, but Milli damn sure didn't see anything but arguments in the future. The biggest one yet was probably coming on in the next five minutes.

She undressed Katy and put a pink and white polka-dotted swimsuit on her while she squealed and pointed toward the water. When Milli dipped her toes in the water, Katy shrieked and wanted more.

"Put her down and give her that plastic cup. She'll entertain herself for hours with it."

She held the baby close to her heart. "Don't be telling me what to do,"

"What got in your craw? For cryin' out loud, Milli. The baby wants down. Don't hold her so tight. Let her play. That's the whole reason we're out here."

"Of course it is," Milli shot right back. "So Beau can be a daddy."

"Is that what your problem is? Got a little green jealousy sticking in your craw?"

"A lot of it."

She eased Katy into the water and handed her a cup. Katy filled it with water and threw it on Beau's bare legs and he yelped, pretending to be freezing. She giggled and threw more and the game was on. The dimple in her cheek deepened and so did his. Her blue eyes twinkled and so did his. Milli was losing control faster than a shooting star and it scared her senseless.

"I'm not ready to share her, Beau. I'm not ready for you to tell me what to do. I'm not ready for a relationship like everyone is throwing me into. I feel like Daniel in the lion's den. I'm independent and I intend to stay this way. It's what has kept me going during rough times and the whole bunch of you are going to have to back down and let me have some breathing room. I know how to take care of her. I've been doing it for over a year now, and I've managed fairly well without any input from you."

"Hey, don't be selfish. I'm not going to grab her up and run off with her. I just want to be part of her life, too. Now look at the fishes, Katy. See the little minnows. Here, baby, set the bucket right here and Daddy will show you how to put gravel in it."

"I mean it, Beau," Milli's tone caused him to leave Katy to her own games and look into Milli's eyes.

"Want to talk about it?"

"Sharing Katy isn't something I want to do right now. I think what we better do is fly back home and forget about the rest of the summer. Slim can do the chores and Poppy is getting along pretty well."

"It isn't going to be any easier in six months or a year or even ten years, Milli. I'm her father. I'm willing and eager to acknowledge that, even if we have to go our separate ways. She will always be mine and I want her birth certificate amended with my name on it. She's going to inherit the Bar M someday and—"

"But like I told you. She doesn't have to. What if I don't want her to be a Luckadeau? She's done just fine as a Torres this long. What if I don't want her to inherit the ranch? Did I lose all my rights this morning when you realized she was your child?"

"No, matter of fact you didn't lose any of your rights, Milli. But I have rights, too. She's mine as well as yours. And I want to share in her life. I want her to have her rightful inheritance. I want her to know the Bar M and learn to run it just like you can run Jim's ranch without even thinking about it. I want her to know the joy of seeing a newborn calf or even pulling one like you do so expertly. There's things I want, too, and I'm entitled to them because I'm her father."

"But can't we just ease into it?"

He cocked his head off to one side. She was as beautiful in her red two-piece bathing suit as she'd been in the off-white lace dress. He could see a couple of faint stretch marks peeping out over the top of the bottoms and wished he could have been there through the pregnancy. She'd never been just a one-night stand to him. Not in the beginning. Not one day since. He'd looked across a crowded room and found an angel. His aching heart had been soothed when they'd made love. His soul had found its mate that night, and he'd been in love with her for two years.

"No, I don't think we can. We might try to ease into a relationship between the two of us, but Katy is something different. She's yours and mine and we'll just have to get used to the fact that we both have to share. I'm damn sure not looking forward to the end of summer when you take her back to Texas, and I've only known her a few hours. I can't imagine the way this old cowboy's heart will break when I have to watch her leave with you. And it'll break every time I have to give her back, but at least I'll have her for a little while each year."

"I can't think about that right now. It scares the hell

out of me that someday she'll call me from the Bar M and tell me she wants to live with you and not come home. And that's only the thoughts I've got now. I can't imagine how many more will come plaguing me by the time we get home tonight. Beau, what are we going to do?"

"We're going to play right here until Katy gets bored, then we'll go find something else to entertain her, because today we've both got her and we'll think about that and not tomorrow."

"Not about today or even Katy. About us."

"I've been in love with you for two years, and I fell in love with Katy this morning before I even realized she was mine. I know what I'd like to do about us. Now what would you like to do?"

"Beau, you've been in love with a woman you created out of the ashes of a disastrous night. You could make her think or say or do anything you dreamed, because she wasn't there. I'm stubborn. I say what I think and I'm not some sweet little angel on a puff of smoke who sugar coats everything. I don't know if I love you. I don't even know if I like you. We've got a child and yet you've never even courted me, except last night at a dance. And then you were evidently upset because you'd just been ditched by Amanda and needed someone to help you make it through the night."

"Give me the summer, Milli. I'll court you, if that's what you want, and at the end of the summer we'll talk about what kind of plans we can make as far as Katy is concerned. That fair enough?"

She thought about it for a while. A whole summer to worry with the issue, when she usually didn't think about anything more than thirty minutes, sometimes not even thirty seconds. Like the issue with Amanda—she'd settled it right then and there beside the truck. If Beau hadn't liked the way she took care of it, she would have taken Katy and walked back to the Lazy Z. How could she spend a whole summer worrying about the outcome, and yet, what a summer it would be. The thought of Beau actually courting her took her breath away. What other choice did she have? He knew about Katy now and so did lots of other people, and he did have his rights as a father, whether it broke her heart or not. But would he be courting Milli Torres as a woman, or Milli Torres as the mother of his child?

"Fair enough," she nodded.

Chapter 12

MILLI FILLED THE DROPPER WITH MEDICINE AND SHOT it into Katy's mouth. It made her drowsy after the first fifteen minutes, but at least it kept her from throwing up. Who would have ever thought Milli Torres' daughter would get nauseous when she flew? It probably came from the Luckadeau blood lines. Not that she could ever see Beau afraid of anything. He'd fight a forest fire with a cupful of water and expect not only to put it out but have a long drink afterwards. Surely he wasn't afraid of flying. Not Beau.

Mary hugged both of them and helped get Katy buckled into her car seat. "You be careful, now. Give your folks a big kiss for me, and don't get any wild notions about not coming back. Your grandfather would be disappointed. Not to mention the cowboy over on the Bar M who—"

"That's enough, Granny," Milli shook her head.

Milli buckled her own seat belt, gave her grandmother the thumbs up sign, and fired up the engines to her plane. It was one of those old Russian war buzzards, a Yak-52, which had been customized with room for the pilot, co-pilot, and enough room to put the baby's car seat behind the pilot. She'd flown a Cessna 172 at first and she loved that little bitty plane, but this old bird had taken her eye at an air show when she was in college and she decided on the spot she had to have one like it. So she sold her Cessna and with the money she'd saved from stunt shows and a season of crop dusting, she bought the Yak-52. She loved the bubble of glass over her head and felt like the Red Baron every time she flew.

It was a far cry from the camouflaged plane she bought three years ago. She'd had it painted candy apple red with thin yellow pinstripes and viewers often said it looked like a ball of fire when she danced it through the acrobatics in a show. That's exactly what she wanted it to look like. Just like she felt when she was doing dives and rolls. Like she was riding a piece of the sun. Like she was fully in control.

She talked to Katy. "Well, we'll be there in an hour, give or take a few minutes. Maybe someday you won't be sick and you can enjoy the whole trip without having to sleep away part of it."

When they had gotten home from the park, Beau had told her that he had a cattle sale in Kansas City to attend on Monday and Tuesday and would be home on Wednesday. Could they go to dinner Wednesday evening?

"With or without Katy?"

"With, of course. There's no reason she can't sit in a high chair at the restaurant. Besides, it'll be two whole days since I've seen her, so I'd like for her to come with us. Now Friday night is a different matter. That night, if Hilda and Mary don't mind, I would like for them to keep her while we go out to dinner and a movie."

She had agreed. He'd be gone for two days and she needed to take the truth to her folks. They needed to hear it from her mouth and not the family gossip vine. When she got back, they'd sit down with a couple of lawyers and figure out Katy's future and she could get on with her life.

Butterflies the size of gypsies danced in her stomach as she landed the plane on the little strip at the backside of the Lazy T ranch west of Hereford. A Yak was made to be landed on a dime and it didn't care if the takeoff-landing strip was dirt or concrete. Her mother was leaning against her dad's old work truck and scarcely waited for the plane to stop before she started waving and running toward it with her hands outstretched to take Katy.

Milli hopped down. "Well, well, seems to me like I should get a little attention. I *am* the daughter."

Angelina nuzzled her face down into the soft curls on the baby's sleeping head. "Oh, hush, you had all the attention for years. We've missed this baby so much. I don't even care why you came home for two days. I'm just glad to see this critter."

Angelina Jiminez Torres was of half-Mexican descent and half pure-bred English. It was a strange combination producing a lovely woman with a soft Texas drawl. Her chestnut brown hair had red highlights, and flecks of gold floated in her pecan-colored eyes. Her face was a work of art, permanently and perfectly tanned, with a small, thin nose, soft, sensual lips, and a ready smile. But her looks were as deceiving as her ultrafeminine name, because Angelina took sass from no one. She would mourn for her husband, John, if he died tomorrow and might never look at another man even though she was only fifty years old. But she could take up the reins and run the Lazy T as well as he could, and she ruled her household even yet with an iron hand.

She'd raised Milli to be exactly like her. When Milli stood her ground where Matthew was concerned, and later when Katy was born, Angelina was proud of her independence and glad she'd raised a daughter who could think for herself and take care of herself in the bargain.

"So what is this big secret you called about?" she asked as they drove back to the ranch house.

"Is Daddy home yet?"

"No, he's off to see about a bull, but I phoned him and he said he'd be back in the middle of the afternoon. There's not something wrong with Poppy Torres and no one wanted to tell us on the phone, is there? Don't tell me he's not ever going to be able to ride again. He'll swivel up and die if he can't sit a horse."

"No, Poppy is fine. You'd be amazed how well he gets along. He's already refused the wheelchair and only uses the walker when he goes outside. I caught him getting in the pickup by himself yesterday morning before church, and he said he was just sitting in the seat for a little while. He swears by the end of summer, he will be two-stepping with Granny at the barn dances."

Angelina let out a whoosh of air. "That's good news. I've been worried about him. Then when you called this morning and said you wanted to talk… can't you even give me a clue?"

"No, Momma. It's not something I want to tell two times. We'll eat lunch and then maybe Daddy will be home and…"

"Okay," Angelina parked in front of a rambling ranch house, which had never looked so good to Milli. She carried the sleeping baby into the house and laid her gently on the sofa in the great room: enormous living room, dining room, and kitchen all one open area, the furniture in soft, supple leather and weathered wood. Lemon candles burned on the square coffee table and a pot of coffee gurgled in the kitchen. Milli sank down on the end of the other end of the sofa and leaned her head back, taking in the smell that was home. Angelina always had coffee brewing. She poured two cups and took them to the living room.

"Something to sip on while lunch finishes. There's lasagna in the oven and a salad in the refrigerator. Now tell me all about what's been going on at the Lazy Z. Your father and I are kicking around the idea of flying out there in August and driving your rig home. We could send one of the boys, or Jim said one of his crew could drive it home and then fly back on the commercial plane, but it would be fun for us to get away for a few days. Your grandparents whine that we don't visit often enough as it is. So we might even go down to the valley and visit your other grandparents instead of coming right home. They have a place for Wild Fire, so you wouldn't have to worry about her. I'm glad you decided to take the plane so you could scoot in and out for a visit."

John's big booming voice filled the room when he opened the door. "Where's my baby girl? Don't tell me she's asleep. And I finished my business early so I could play with her. Oh, well, I guess I'll have to do with a hug from my daughter, then."

Milli crossed the room and he wrapped her up in a bear hug, which was exactly what she needed right then.

He pushed her away without letting go of her shoulders. Something was drastically wrong. Fear was clouding Milli's eyes, and she had never been afraid of anything in her entire life. Not from the time she was born. She could whomp a rope around her hand and set the meanest bull in the rodeo for eight seconds. She could do stunts in that funny-looking airplane of hers that even made his hair stand on end when it looked like a red ball of pure fiery hell coming down for a crash and then whoosh, up it went again. She'd stood in front of them, declared she was pregnant and would not talk about who the father was, and she didn't bat an eye. In the worst of situations there had never been fear, only solid determination. Chill bumps danced down his arms when he thought about what could scare Milli. John wasn't sure if he really wanted an answer to that question, or if he would rather let well enough alone.

"So, is that lasagna I smell in the oven?" he finally asked.

"Yes, it is," Angelina said.

The doorbell rang.

Milli stepped back.

John answered it.

"Roses for Miss Milli and balloons and a bear for Miss Katy," a feminine voice said.

Angelina carried the huge bouquet of roses and balloons attached to a teddy bear to the living area. "My, oh my, maybe you do have something to tell us. Have you been keeping company with an oil baron or something?"

Milli unpinned the card from the front of the red satin bow and opened the envelope. "Just part of the courting process. I already miss you. See you and Katy Wednesday."

A warm feeling like the start of a sunburn crept up the back of her neck and into her cheeks. She removed the card from the bow around the teddy bear's neck. "Daddy loves his baby girl."

The blush deepened and she rolled her eyes. He must have phoned this morning before he left for Dallas to board his plane and Granny gave him her address in Hereford. If she hadn't been coming to explain the situation, he wouldn't have left her any other choice. He probably hadn't even thought about the consequences of his impetuosity. She wondered if he'd telephoned his parents and told them all about her and Katy! Damn his sorry old scraggly hide anyway. If he was close enough, she'd start a shouting match that could be heard all the way to the valley in south Texas. She tried to frown—but it wouldn't come out past the silly grin on her face.

"You going to tell us about this? Or has the cat plumb eaten your tongue off, girl?" her mother asked.

Milli buried her face in the bouquet. They even smelled like roses. Most hothouse flowers had no odor, but her roses smelled just like roses. The baby's breath and soft fern fronds tickled her nose, but none of it gave her the courage she needed to tell her folks the tale of Katy's conception. She'd have to find that on her own. "I'll tell you."

"Thank goodness!" Angelina said when she'd finished her story.

"Amen!" John nodded in agreement.

Milli could scarcely believe her ears. "What?"

"I've been worried all this time that Katy's father was a married professor at the university and someday he would find out about her. I knew you were in pain when that rascal, Matthew, did what he did. And I figured you went to college and some slick-talking professor seduced you. But he was married and that was the problem and the reason you wouldn't talk about it. At least this Beau is a decent fellow. Poppy Torres talks about him on the phone all the time. So, he wants to do the right thing by our Katy and make sure she has her inheritance. He's got enough money to support her and from the looks of that bouquet in there, he's pretty took with you, too."

"But Momma, I was…"

"So?" Angelina said. "You were young and in pain and… that's water under the bridge and in the past. What happened, happened. And now the baby's father wants to acknowledge her. I think that's in his favor. Besides, if some good-looking fellow sent me half the roses in Texas, I'd think maybe he was interested in me as much as Katy."

"What does this Beau Luckadeau look like?"

Milli threw up her hands. She sure wasn't expecting a reception like this. "Just like Katy. Same blue eyes, same hair, only his is a little lighter from being out in the sun so much. Same demanding streak. Same awful temper."

Angelina shook her finger. "Oh, come on Camillia Kathryn Torres. You're not about to pawn all of Katy's temper off on someone else. If this Beau fellow has a temper, that's good. You could never live with someone who's mealy-mouthed and wimpy."

"Momma, I'm not going to live with him!"

"I should hope not," John declared. "But don't be throwing ice water on the young man. He sounds like a good man and it's pretty plain he must like you, even if you two did get off to a bad start."

Milli still couldn't believe the way they'd taken the news. "That's what Granny said. Something about throwing ice water on him—"

The phone rang and Milli jumped up to answer it. Probably was one of her two brothers calling to see if she'd made it home. Neither was especially fond of her flying and they were extremely negative about her taking Katy up in the plane. They'd be ready to form a posse and go to southern Oklahoma with a new rope when they found out about Beau. She'd have to do some tall talking and fancy explaining to make them understand it was as much her fault as his.

"Hello."

"Milli?" Beau's soft Louisiana accent questioned.

"Beau?"

"Just calling to make sure you arrived safely," he was glad to hear her voice, even if it was just one word.

Milli turned her back so she wouldn't have to look at her parents. "Thank you for the flowers and balloons. Katy is still asleep, but she'll squeal when she sees the balloons and bear. She'll think she's been to the circus."

"You are very welcome. You must have made really good time, or at least left earlier than I thought," he sounded stilted. What he wanted to tell her was how much he already missed her, that he'd dreamed about her last night, and he was holding the silver earring in his hand.

"Oh, we did all right."

"Sounds like you flew. You need to watch that speed, lady," he admonished in a teasing tone. "Did you buckle her up good?"

"Yes, sir. How was your flight?"

"Great. No air pockets. I hate flying. Makes me about half queasy to think about being up that far in the sky crammed in a tube with all those other people. It's unnatural, if you ask me. I'd rather drive any day, but sometimes it just takes too much time. Gotta run now. My car is here to take me to the sale. I'm thinkin' of you and Katy."

"Thank you." She wished she had the courage to say she'd thought about him every minute since he kissed her on the forehead last night when he brought her and Katy home to the Lazy Z, but saying the words wouldn't be easy, even without an audience of two behind her and a baby who was crawling off the couch in the living room, eyes all aglitter as she reached for John and said, "Poppy. My Poppy. Ride, peas."

"Can I call later tonight? Might be around ten-thirty or eleven?"

"That would be nice," she said.

"Then it's good-bye until then. Have a nice day."

Nice day. He didn't have two sane brain cells to rub together. She'd gotten past her parents with the story, but she still had to face her brothers and that wasn't going to be easy.

"Well, I'd say he does have some kind of feeling for you. Roses and phone calls," Angelina said.

"Oh, Momma, he just wanted to be sure I hadn't driven too fast and put his daughter's life in jeopardy," Milli sighed.

"Didn't you tell him you flew? Doesn't he know that you do stunts in competition?" John asked. "Katy Scarlett wants me to take her to the barn and put her on a horse for a ride. I've missed her something awful."

Milli actually blushed. "I told him I rode bulls and that was about all he could take in at one time. Most of the time, we argue a lot. I really don't think we could ever agree on anything, except maybe Katy's welfare."

Chapter 13

MILLI WORRIED WITH HER HAIR FOR TEN MINUTES while Katy played on the floor at her feet. Finally, in exasperation she twisted the back up and held it with a clasp. She checked her makeup again and reapplied a tawny lipstick. It had literally been years since she'd been out on a date. Not since Matthew. Not since the night before she had found him in the motel room and swore that she'd never trust another man. If he could look deeply into her eyes and tell her how much he loved her without blinking, and go straight into the arms of another woman, then how could she trust anyone else not to do the same thing?

She adjusted her bra strap so it didn't show under the sleeveless dress she'd chosen to wear. It was just a simple, bright floral rayon, flowing in soft gathers from a fitted waistline to the edge of her anklebone. She slipped her feet into a pair of red leather sandals, the same color as the predominant flower in the fabric. "Do I look like someone set me down in the bougainvillea?"

She picked up the newest perfume she'd bought at the mall the previous week—something called Green Tea—then, with a mischievous grin, she set it back down and picked up a half-used bottle of Taboo and dabbed a little behind her ears. She seldom ever used that fragrance anymore, not since the wedding in Texarkana. Matthew hated it and in defiance she'd picked it up and taken it with her when she went to east Texas. After she'd found out she was pregnant, she put the perfume aside as a bad luck omen and hadn't worn it since.

"We'll see how good his memory really is, or how drunk he really was," she said nervously.

Just like always, Beau shook the legs of his jeans down over his boot tops when he got out of the truck. It hadn't been so very long since he'd dated Amanda and called her every night during the week, so why did he feel like a fifteen-year-old out on his first date? If he hadn't sworn completely off liquor when he awoke in the back room of that trailer almost two years ago, he would have poured himself a healthy shot of Jack Daniels just to get rid of the jitters.

"Hello," Jim said from the shadows in the corner of the porch. "See you're right on time, son. Have a seat here and talk to me. How'd the cattle sale go?"

"Fine. Bought a bull and two calves. One of the boys over at the Bar M left this morning with the trailer to go bring them home. Saw some fine white-faced cattle and missed you being there with me. Might have bought a cow, but I wasn't quite sure. Remembered you saying once something about when in doubt, back out. Maybe you can go with me next year?"

"I damn sure hope so," Jim said. "I could've gone this year, but I'd have had to fight Mary and it wasn't worth the trouble. The ranch don't need any new bloodlines right now. But I sure missed the steaks and good times and I just flat pouted around here a couple of days when I thought about the poker games. I think them women is about ready in there. Funny how things turns out sometimes, ain't it?"

Milli opened the door.

"Katy. Come here to Daddy, baby." He turned quickly to see how Jim would take the idea of him calling himself daddy to Katy and only caught a wink and a nod. "I missed you so much these past two days. Look here what I brought you." He held his hands out and she reached for him. He put a stuffed Angus bull in her chubby little hands.

She stuck the ear in her mouth. "Kitter," she said.

He looked at Milli.

"Kitter. It means critter. That's what my dad calls the cows to her."

"Kitter it is, then. She's after my heart," Jim laughed. "She knows those critters are made to feast upon."

Beau held up a long, thin white box with a bright red ribbon around it. "And for you, Milli. Just something I found and thought you'd like."

Milli loved presents. Her brown eyes sparkled, but she would have gladly handed it back to him for just one long, drawn out kiss, complete with her tongue sliding across his lower lip to taste the remnants of peppermint gum.

"Thank you."

He'd have to remember the sweetness in her face when he gave her a present. It might come in handy one of these days after one of the fights they were bound to have.

Opening the box, she found a tooled-leather hatband with bead work in the middle and beads entwined in the thongs falling off the back of the brim. She held it up under the porch light and examined the intricate work. Hours and hours of someone's precious time had gone into the making of the thin strip. Red beads were mixed with tiny chunks of real turquoise and silver, and she could already picture it on the brim of her red hat, which she wore when she barrel raced.

"Thank you so much, Beau. I love it, and it's so nice of you to remember us."

"At least Katy gave me a hug." he pouted.

Jim chuckled.

"Oh, all right." She hugged him, then quickly backed away when she realized the effect his long, lean, muscular body had on hers.

"You are very welcome, Miss Milli."

The vibes passing between them were enough to make his voice catch like it did when he was going through puberty. But it was not supposed to reappear when he was thirty years old and a father.

Milli headed toward her truck. "I need to get her car seat."

"Nope, I bought her a new one. Saves a lot of bother." He opened the back door of the club cab truck and sat the baby in the seat.

He opened the passenger door for Milli and waved good-bye to Jim as he shut it behind her.

"You look lovely tonight. That perfume"—he inhaled deeply and dramatically—"it's what you wore to the wedding. I'll never forget that wonderful smell. I took the pillowcase off the bed the next morning and slept with it until it didn't smell anymore. Even when the boys told me you were never there, I hung on to hope because of that very smell, and the earring I found on the floor."

"You did what?"

"Well, they kept telling me you were just a figment of my imagination." He braked at a stop sign and turned to really look at her in the moonlight streaming through the truck window. Her mouth was full and sensuous and her skin a permanent tan. Jet-black eyebrows and lashes framed the softest brown eyes in the whole world. At least they were soft until she got angry, then a whole bevy of icicles or sparks could come shooting out of them. "But I found the earring, and the perfume was there. The same kind you've got on tonight. Wear it forever, Milli. It brings back some beautiful memories."

"But it's an old fragrance." She shifted nervously closer to the door. Another backfire. She'd only worn it to torment him, and now she was the one with an itch down so deep she could never scratch it.

"I don't care if it's a buck a gallon and worn by women my grandmother's age. It's heady and wonderful."

Boy, did Amanda throw away more than just the diamond on her finger. If he's this romantic all the time, then she's the grand chump fool of the century. I can understand now why she came back in her new western finery to try to make up with him. I would have changed my tune, too, once I thought about it.

"Burger King?" she asked incredulously when he pulled into the parking lot.

"Sure, this is for Katy. We'll have burgers and fries and ice cream and then we'll play in the jungle gym stuff with her. And after that we'll go to the Wal-Mart store out on Commerce and let her look at all the toys. She can take all the time she wants, since they stay open twenty-four hours. Friday night is our night. Just me and you night. I hope it can always be that way."

Always be that way? What about the other five nights? she thought. Are those the nights when we fight to the draw and try to bring blood with our anger? "O…kay," she finally said.

So much for romance and perfume and worrying about which shoes to wear with her dress. But Burger King?

It seemed as if they really were a little family of three by the time Beau strapped Katy into the car seat and they started home. He tucked a new stuffed bear—this time it was honey brown—into her arms and she was sleeping before the lights of Ardmore had faded away. He put on a Vince Gill CD and kept time with his fingers on the steering wheel as he drove.

Milli listened to the music with one ear and to her heart with the other. Every fiber in her body longed to be brazen enough to slide across the wide seat and kiss him on the earlobe. She'd like to put Katy to bed, pick up a blanket, and take it and him to the woods between his ranch and hers and simply make love with him all night. But she had played the wanton hussy once and what a mess it had made. She should build a relationship before she toppled into bed with Beau again. And yet, other than a few pleasant moments, it seemed as though building a relationship might be more difficult than staking claim to one of those bright stars up in the sky. She'd gotten past the place where she didn't want to share Katy, and overcome the hurdle of telling her folks… and her brothers, who surprised her by wanting to meet Beau rather than kill him. But she still didn't trust her own judgment. She'd done so once and it had failed her miserably. She knew about those women who were drawn to the same type of men over and over again, and she didn't think she was so very different from all the female population. There was a flaw in Beau somewhere or they wouldn't say he was lucky in everything but not so lucky in love. She didn't know if her heart could stand the agony of being broken in a million pieces the second time.

"Think she had a good time?" Beau asked.

"I think you will spoil her. She doesn't need something every time you arrive at the door or take her out. What are you going to do for birthdays and Christmas if you keep buying like this?"

"Those holidays are for really big things. Like ponies and three-wheelers when she's older. A playhouse with all the trimmings when she's four or five and a swimming pool in the backyard when she's a teenager. I can't spoil her with too much love, Milli."

"Love, no. Material possessions, yes. From now on, it's one toy a month and then something big for holidays."

"Okay, it's a deal. Does that mean I can only bring you one thing a month, too?"

"Of course not."

"But I might spoil you."

She smiled and used his favorite phrase. "Ain't damn likely."

He carried Katy through the front door and shook his head when Milli reached out for her. "Shhh. I'll take her on up."

He laid her gently on the bed, fought with his imagination as he thought about Milli sleeping here every night, let his eyes take in the room in a sweeping glance, and eased Katy's sandals off her feet. "Where's her little gown?"

"Right here. And you don't need to whisper. Once she's asleep, a tornado could sweep through her crib and she'd never know it. She sleeps like you do," she finished without looking at him.

He raised an eyebrow. "Oh, really?" So she did remember things about that night, too. He did sleep like the dead, and even more so after drinking too much.

"Yes, thank goodness she doesn't snore."

"Neither do I."

"Oh, yes you do. Very loud."

"Are we arguing again?" he asked as she slipped Katy's red-checked sun dress over her head and put a cotton gown on her. "Now, Daddy will tuck you in," he whispered softly as he carried her to the crib beside the bed.

Once he had her covered and had given her at least a dozen kisses, Milli followed him downstairs to the door.

"Thank you," she said.

He wrapped his arm around her shoulder and pulled her along with him. "What? You weren't going to walk me to the truck?"

"Beau, you don't have to do this. I won't stand in your way with Katy. I promise I'll share. I won't lie and say it'll be easy, but it's what is best for her. You don't have to take the cow with the calf."

He tilted her chin back and was mesmerized. "Milli, I happen to like the cow. I happen to have liked the cow very much from the first time I saw her and even liked her before I knew there was a calf. The cow was the best thing that ever happened to me. Why are you so defensive?"

"What we did... I'm not that kind of woman. I don't just fall into bed with a man because he's good-looking—"

"Oh, you think I'm handsome."

"Beau!"

"Okay, this isn't the time to make jokes. I know you're not that kind of woman. I knew it that night, too, even as drunk and irresponsible as I was. I wasn't so drunk that I didn't know it was your first time. It surprised me, but we were both so... involved... so hot. I couldn't have stopped if there had been a pistol stuck in my ear. I'd just have said for them to go ahead and blow my brains out, but to please wait until I finished the best night of my life. Katy is important to me. But so are you, and I think this is part of the courting process." He leaned forward until his lips met hers.

The impact went from her lips to the pit of her stomach and down her jelly-filled legs to the Oklahoma dirt where she stood. She had the urge to reach out and hold on to his pickup fender just to keep from swooning. And that was crazier than a cross-eyed chicken at a coyote match. Because Milli Torres didn't swoon for anyone. She was as independent as hell on wheels and no one ever touched her heart so deep that she saw stars. At least not until right now... and one other time a couple of years ago. But she'd just thought that was because it was the first time, and all women felt that way their first time.

He pulled her closer and closer to him until she was pressed against his chest so tightly she could hear the steady rhythm of his heartbeat, but he didn't stop kissing her mouth, running his tongue deftly over her lips, tasting the last bits of Coke and dill pickles. Her tongue met his in playful battle and she tasted the sweet peppermint gum he'd been chewing while the woodsy aftershave he wore filled her nostrils. She wished this part of the courting process could go on forever.

His hand fell down to cup one hip and pull her even closer yet.

"Mmmmm," she groaned.

He broke the kiss but kept her in his arms. "Well, we seem to do that part of courting pretty good together. Good night, my Milli. I'll call tomorrow, and remember, we've got a date Friday night. This time we'll eat Italian or Mexican or whatever you like."

She didn't care if they ate frog legs from a boiling cauldron on the banks of the Red River. For a few more of those earth-shattering kisses, she'd forsake supper altogether. For a trip to the nearest motel she'd even give up breakfast, too. But that was all in the future. Build a relationship first, her mind had said, and it seemed like good advice even if it didn't satisfy the craving in the pits of her soul.

"Italian. Nobody can cook Mexican like Momma and I'm spoiled to the good stuff."

"Then Luigi's, here we come." He kissed her one more time, this time sweet and brief on the lips. "I'm looking forward to it."

"Are we still talking about food?"

"I think we better be or Jim might fill my sorry old hide with buckshot. We did it, Milli. We said good night without a fight."

She hurried across the wide verandah. "Then you better leave and we'll call it a miracle."

Chapter 14

BEAU PULLED THE TRUCK SEAT FORWARD AND REMOVED an old quilt. He carried it to the edge of the lake, straightened it on the grassy beach, and motioned for Milli to join him. A warm breeze promised a hot wind on the morrow. Stars twinkled in the dark sky surrounding the half moon like subjects around a king.

She sat down stiffly, leaving two feet of space between them. How many times had he brought Amanda to this very spot on Lake Murray and flipped out the same quilt? How many more before that? Was she simply the next in line to be seduced on his quilt?

The day might come when they would have a big fight and he would walk out the door and into the barn right into someone else's arms. Her breath caught. Beau seemed like a good man. So did Matthew in the beginning. He was good-looking beyond words. So was Matthew. He thought he was in love with her. So did Matthew.

He patted the place closer to his side. "Come closer so I can smell that perfume. Look at the stars. Aren't they beautiful? I love them in the summertime but even more in the winter. When it's so cold you can see your breath every time you exhale and you need to wrap up in the quilt rather than lie on it, that's my kind of weather."

She scooted over a foot, drew her knees up under her chin, and wrapped her arms around them tightly. "So how many other women have sat on this quilt with you and how many others did you tell about the stars?"

He touched her arm.

She drew back.

"Listen to me. I've been on the ranch almost two years. Aunt Alice called me a couple of weeks after Darrin's wedding and told me what the doctor said. She hung on for another month until I could get things arranged and get here, then she checked herself into the nursing home. I didn't date anyone for several months and then a friend introduced me to Amanda, and you know the rest. You also know Amanda. Can you see her out here swatting mosquitoes and sitting on a quilt watching the moon come up? I wouldn't have even gotten the quilt out of the truck before she'd have been whining to get back home. Now let's don't spoil a wonderful evening."

He was damn sure right about that. Amanda didn't even like two-stepping in a nice clean barn, and her idea of fun was a golf match or something a lot more social than watching the stars twinkle. "Okay. Guess a little jealousy sprouted up there."

"And I'm a little flattered that you're a little jealous. But you don't have to be. You can work out things in your own time and your own way. I've already faced my demons. Slide on over here. I want to feel your body next to mine."

She did, and he draped his arm loosely around her shoulders. He wanted to make love to her right there. To kiss every part of her body at least once and some parts numerous times. But she had a few issues of her own to exorcise before then. When they made love again it would be in the perfect place, the perfect time, and she'd never look back on it with worry again.

"Can we trust our bodies?" she asked.

"Probably not." He tipped her chin back and kissed her, which is exactly what he had wanted to do all evening. He ran his tongue over her lips, pleased she'd eaten off her lipstick with supper. He hated kissing a woman with a greasy mouth. It always felt like he was about to make love to a slab of cold bacon. He toyed with her upper arms, feeling the soft skin, and deepened the kiss.

"Mmmm," she moaned appreciatively. "Don't stop. Kiss me again just like that. I hear bells in the distance and I get this oozy kind of soft feeling in my stomach that tells me it doesn't give a damn about anything but kissing."

"Yep, it sure has a similar effect on me. What are we going to do about us, Milli?" he said hoarsely.

"Kiss some more?"

"Want to take a chance on where it might lead?"

She straightened up and wrapped her arms around her legs again. "No, I don't."

He sat up and watched the moonbeams flicker on the lake water. This was absolutely sophomoric. They were two grown adults and they'd acted more like that two years ago than they had recently. She wanted him as badly as he did her, so why was she willing to play at kissing and then call it quits?

"Want to talk about it?" Beau asked.

"Nope, I just want to watch the moon and stars and be quiet while I get my heart to stop pumping like crazy and my stupid hormones to be still."

He didn't answer. They'd done better on Wednesday night when Katy was with them. Maybe Katy's presence was going to be like pulling calves and making hay. Something to talk about without discussing their feelings. Such heat would be disastrous, anyway. When it tuckered out there would be nothing left but a lifetime of fighting and disagreement.

She wanted to go farther than a few kisses, to feel the tautness of his body touching hers even through their clothing, but she didn't trust herself. Look what happened the last time she'd let her heart rule her better sense. She still wasn't on any form of birth control, so another baby could easily be on the way if she threw common sense in the lake water. She'd proven she was indeed a fertile myrtle the first time around. The way her luck would run, Katy would have a brother or sister in nine months if she played with fire again.

"Look at the moon on the water. Ever wonder how many women used water for a looking glass long before mirrors were invented? Bet you'd look just beautiful in the water. Go down to the edge and lean way over and let me see you, both in the reflection and for real. Two beauties at one time."

"You'd push me in."

He fell backwards on the quilt and laced his arms under his neck. "Oh, ye of little faith. Well, then, lie down here beside me and tell me about yourself."

She was careful to keep a few inches between her and Beau when she unfolded her legs and stretched out beside him. "What do you want to know?"

"Oh, what you liked when you were growing up? Did you really ride bulls, or were you just joshing me?"

"I did ride bulls. Never did get a trophy, but did stay on one for eight seconds a few times. Just didn't get the job done in real competition. I've got two brothers and I had to keep up with them. I started out barrel racing, but they laughed and called it a sissy sport, so I just figured I'd show them and I did."

"What're their names?"

"The bulls? Lord, I don't remember. Seems like one was Speedo and another was Diablo."

"No, not the bulls. Your brothers. And your folks. What're their names? I've heard Jim talk about his son, John, and I know he's an only child, so I guess that's your father. Who's your mother?"

"Angelina. And my brothers are Andy and James."

"They going to string me up by my toenails when I meet them?"

"Why would they? Besides, I haven't decided whether I'm inviting them to our steak cook-off. They'd probably win by beginner's luck and then strut around telling me they could cook better than me for the rest of my life. They're egotistical males. Just like you. One egotistical male does not string another up by his toenails. They just tolerate each other. So why would you even worry about them?"

He was next to her in one roll and gathered her into his arms for another passionate kiss. "Because, I did not do my gentlemanly duty by you or Katy. Never mind that I didn't know. I should have at least made you give me a phone number so I could call later. My intentions were not so honorable that night, and the next morning you were gone. And honey, my intentions are not honorable right now, either. I want to hold you and kiss you until you are breathless. I still have trouble believing that you are here and I am here and—"

A star shot through the sky in a final blaze of glory. "Did you see that? It's our lucky night."

"I saw it. You really didn't bring Amanda here?"

"No, I really did not. I've never brought anyone here, ever. This is my own special spot, Milli. It's where I straighten out my problems. Sometimes I just sit here on the blanket for hours. And I wanted to see what your reaction was to this place tonight. I wanted to see if you'd be bored to tears or if you'd like the moon and stars. If you'd like the cricket and frog concert."

"I love it. And now I'm going to take off my shoes, tie up my skirt tails, and wade in that water. Something is going to have to cool me off after those kisses or I'm not going to be responsible for my actions."

"Oh, did they make you a little warm?"

"No, they made me damn hot!" She tossed her sandals behind her, knotted up both sides of her skirt until there was a healthy length of thigh exposed, and swatted a mosquito off her upper arm.

He shucked out of his boots and socks and was rolling up his jean legs when she stepped off the quilt. "Beat you to the water."

She was in the lake before he could blink twice. "No, you won't."

"Ohhh, this is heaven. I love water. I love swimming and wading and skiing."

"Then let's get rid of these clothes and swim."

"Not on your life!"

Skinny dipping did sound wonderful, and where it would lead sounded even better. She'd never even thought about making love in the water. But what a sexy thought. Hot kisses. Cool water.

"Do you really love swimming and skiing?"

"Adore the water. All of it."

"Then I shall buy you a ski boat next week."

"No, you won't."

"Then I'll call a real estate agent and see if I can purchase this whole lake."

"Beau, you are incorrigible."

"Nope, I'm a Cajun. Who happens to love a black-haired woman with doe-colored eyes."

"Don't say that."

"What—that I'll buy you the lake, or that I love you?" he asked.

She splashed water up on her arms and then flicked her wrist, spraying his face with a fine mist. "The latter. Don't ever say those words lightly. If you loved me so much, then why did you propose to Amanda?"

"Because my Amelia was hiding in the panhandle of Texas and wouldn't come to me, no matter how hard I tried to get her to reappear. And now remember…" He took a step toward her. "Paybacks are hell."

She backed away from him until she was at the edge of the bank. "Don't you dare get me any wetter than I am. Poppa and Granny will…"

He swept her up in his arms and carried her back to the quilt. "I'm not going to get you wet. I'm going to kiss you until your knees are jelly and…"

Just your touch turns my knees to jelly.

Chapter 15

"I'VE GOT A CATTLE SALE TODAY AND TOMORROW. IT'S only up in Oklahoma City, but it'd be a booger to drive back that late every night so I've got reservations at a hotel. I'll be gone until Wednesday afternoon. Tell Katy her daddy will miss her. And tell Katy's mother he'll really miss her," Beau said into the phone. "I forgot all about the sale until I looked on the calendar yesterday. Seems like this raven-haired woman has me bewitched these days."

"Well, I expect me and Katy both can survive two days without you. And no prizes this time."

"We'll see. I'll miss you. How about a picnic at the lake on Wednesday? We can play with Katy in the shallow water..."

"I'll miss you, too," Milli said honestly. "You may be worn to a frazzle by the time you get home."

"I'll call tonight." He hated to hang up the phone. There was always the fear in the back side of his mind that she wouldn't be there. She would disappear like she did that other time, and after knowing her and Katy, his heart would stop beating if they weren't there any more.

Milli sighed and leaned against the wall. This was exactly what she needed. Her heart was split in two separate pieces. One faction had the good solid notion that fairy tales were only in storybooks, and this wasn't Prince Charming and Cinderella. The earring he carried in his pocket could scarcely be classified as a glass slipper, and it most certainly would fit into any pierced ear on any woman. Only characters in hot, steamy romance books rode off into the sunset on the last page and lived happily ever after. If she and Beau ever really did think about a long-term relationship—she shuddered when she even thought about the "M" word—it sure wouldn't be a perfect little world where she smiled all the time and agreed with every word he said. She might not be a first-class bitch like Amanda, but she damned sure wasn't about to be one of those submissive little women who walked two feet behind her husband and lived and breathed just to make his world perfect. She fully well intended to have a marriage like her own parents had, like Poppy and Granny, too. Like a business relationship on the ranch, each one pulled their own weight and took care of their responsibilities. A business relationship with hot steamy nights; she moaned just thinking about it.

The other part of her heart sighed and pouted about Beau being gone for two whole days.

Granny and Hilda talked non-stop about Beau. She didn't need to be convinced he was a good man or that she was attracted to him in a very real way. What she needed to build was trust and that was very difficult. Did she really trust Beau to stay alone in his hotel room at the cattle sale? A seed of doubt wiggled its way into her mind and stuck there. If she called his number at midnight tonight, would he answer, or would there be another woman in his bed?

"Stop it!" She looked at her reflection in the rough cedar-framed mirror hanging above the antique credenza beside the front door in the foyer. "Young lady, you've got two hard day's work and you haven't got time to see him anyway, so there. And if you don't trust him, then put an end to it right now."

She saddled Wild Fire and rode out into the pasture to check on the barns at the back of the ranch where the hay baling crew had worked until midnight the night before. She found them stacking square bales at the back of the barn, so she pulled on her leather work gloves and helped them until lunchtime. In the afternoon she crawled up on a bright green John Deere tractor and plowed the field where the alfalfa had been harvested the day before. Then she hooked up a disc and covered the ground again. By suppertime, the pouting half of her heart was so tired it didn't even mention Beau's name.

Tuesday morning found her in the same place doing the same things. She grabbed a set of hay hooks and stacked hay until lunch, then ate with the men in the field instead of going back to the house. Cold sandwiches, ice-cold tea, and donuts Hilda had fried that morning had never tasted so good. She found a shade tree and used it for a backrest while she crammed the food in her mouth and washed it down with sweet tea.

One of the men took up a position a quarter of the way around the big pecan tree. "Beau still gone? You two gettin' pretty thick?"

"He'll be back tomorrow and I don't know how thick we are," she answered.

The tall, dark man looked down at her with brooding green eyes. "Well, if he don't do things to suit you, just remember old Bob is waiting on the sidelines. I wouldn't knock a man out of the saddle, but I'm here if he takes himself out."

"Bob, you better keep your thoughts to yourself or you'll be hangin' from the first branch of that tree come tomorrow evenin'," Slim said from behind the tree. "Beau Luckadeau has staked a claim and you better just back off."

"Beau hasn't staked anything," Milli snorted. "But I'm not interested right now, in you or anyone else, Bob. We'd better all get back to work or else Poppy Torres will hang us all from the tree."

The next morning she saddled Wild Fire again and went to the eastern field to see how many round bales the crew had harvested. Bales were lined up end to end like giant worms along the edge of the fence. What could be stored in pole barns had already been taken out of the field. It had been a good year and Poppy wouldn't be buying hay this winter. That always pleased him and her father. They liked the idea that their ranches supported themselves and no outside feed or hay had to be purchased.

After an exact bale count, she was back in the saddle and headed back to the house. After lunch she planned to play with Katy until nap time and then treat herself to a few hours of reading before supper and seeing Beau again.

She rode through the creek that flowed through her grandfather's ranch and drew the reins up. The cool water rippled over a gravelly bottom and practically sang her name as it flowed gently along. It was barely deep enough to wade much less to swim but perhaps she could float downstream a little way before it was too shallow for even that.

No, it was insane to even think of skinny dipping. What on earth would she do if one of the ranch hands saw her there and reported it to Poppy? Maybe she'd just wade like she had at the lake.

That reminded her of Beau and she'd sworn she wouldn't think of him for two whole days. It hadn't worked. Everything out of Hilda's mouth started with Beau and ended with the same. Poppy and Granny were nearly as bad. Milli didn't fare much better when she was out working. Memories of the good times they shared kept popping up at any old time.

For the past few weeks they'd had a Friday night ritual. Dinner at a nice restaurant. Talk of ranching and then a steamy kissing session at the lake. If the latter affected Beau the way it did her, he went home and stood under a cold shower for thirty minutes before he could go to bed. Even then it took a long time to fall asleep.

It was going to lead to something, and Milli still wasn't trusting him with her whole heart. She sighed one more time and rode Wild Fire across the creek. A thirsty old cow or horse can smell water a quarter of a mile away. She knew just how they felt when it splashed high enough and she caught a whiff. When she reached the other side of the creek bed, she pulled back on the reins and stopped Wild Fire. She stepped out of the stirrups, looped the reins around a scrub oak tree, and sat down beside the stream.

She laid back in the shade of an old willow tree and watched two mockingbirds flirting and flitting in the drooping branches. She dropped her hand into the ripples, the cool water tantalizing her hand. A little minnow darted in and nibbled at her finger, but she swished her hand and it swam away. She thought about how nice it would feel to put her whole sweaty body in the water.

She let her mind go as blank as she could, and just like it did every time she tried to erase all her thoughts, it threw up a Technicolor screen and provided her with a slide show of Beau. There he was, drunk at the wedding… in the bedroom at that trailer house… behind her at the dance on Saturday night… lying in the dirt with a three-wheeler on top of him and blood everywhere. At the hospital with Amanda pointing at the door and telling her to get out and not come back. And most recently, across the table from her on Friday nights, flirting and edging closer and closer to a physical relationship. But would that be all they had? Because if it was, she didn't even want to start it, no matter how badly she craved his hands on her body and his lips claiming hers for his own.

She ran her fingers through her tangled black hair, drawing it up into a ponytail and wrapping a rubber band from her shirt pocket around it to keep it off her neck. She pulled off her brown work boots and socks and stood up. She unzipped her jeans and shucked out of them. Her underpants and bra she hung on her saddle horn. She stepped into the water and gasped for just a minute when the chilly spring-fed creek water hit her sweaty skin. She waded out to the middle and laid down in one fell swoop. A minute later she floated on her back with her eyes shut, letting the ripples flow over her naked body.

She hadn't been skinny dipping since she was thirteen and then it was right here in this same creek, only a mile or so upstream. The stream carried her a few yards down away from her horse and clothes.

Although she could easily have spent the rest of the afternoon right there, duties called and if she didn't report back in, Poppy would send someone to find her. But it had been absolutely delightful. Besides, Beau would be arriving soon. With a sigh she stretched her arms out and gracefully back stroked back to where her horse was tethered.

She heard his whinny and opened her eyes to see Beau sitting on the biggest, blackest horse she'd ever seen.

He tipped his hat and cocked a leg up over the saddle horn. "Afternoon."

She scooted out far enough that all he could see was her bare shoulders and face, but the look on his face said he'd already seen much more than that. "Good grief, you scared the liver out of me. Where's your tricycle?"

"At home. Thought I'd give Brassy a run today. I've neglected him lately. You come here often and skinny dip? Or did it just look inviting today?"

"Neither one is any of your business."

"I'm making it my business, Milli. I want to know everything there is to know about you. And I mean everything."

"In your dreams."

So be it, he thought, mischievously. There was no way he'd lose this battle. Not in a million years. He had the sassy Miss Torres right where he wanted her and she could concede his victory.

"Turn around so I can get out of here. We've got

a family date, remember? And I'm supposed to be at home getting ready."

"Nope. I ain't turning around."

"Beau, I mean it. Pick up those reins and turn Mr. Brassy around. I've got to get home."

"Brassy says he don't want to turn around."

"I'm not joking," she said.

"Me, neither. But if I was invited, I might join you. Water looks cool and it's hotter'n seven kinds of hell today."

"You're not invited. And you're on Lazy Z ground so get your sorry—"

"Scraggly ass off it," he finished for her. "Nope, I don't think so. Jim lets me ride anywhere I want on his property. I do the same for him. We're good neighbors. Me and Brassy are just going to sit here for a spell and enjoy the sights. Right nice day, ain't it? Not too bad here under the shade of the willow trees."

She found her footing on the gravel bottom of the creek, and duck walked slowly backwards until she was only a few feet from her horse and clothing. "All right, if you can't lick 'em, join 'em. Come on in with me, Beau. The water feels wonderful."

"You mean it?"

"Sure. Tether Brassy up to that bush and dive right in, honey. Like they say, 'The water is fine.' And I do mean fine, sweetheart."

He didn't need a second invitation. He threw his long, lanky leg back over the horse and stepped out of the stirrups with the ease of a man born and raised on a ranch. He unsnapped his chambray shirt by tugging at the snap closest to his neck and tearing it off in one motion. He sat down on the grassy bank and took off his boots and socks while she continued to dog paddle in the middle of the creek. Then a sudden bout of modesty overtook him and he turned around to peel out of his jeans. He did just what she hoped—turned around to undress—just like he did that night in the trailer before they fell into the bed. Those few seconds gave her enough time to scramble out of the water, jump into her bikini panties and shirt, swoop up her other clothes in a hurry, and mount Wild Fire from a dead run. By the time he'd splashed out into the middle of the shallow creek and blinked the creek water out of his eyes, she had Brassy's reins and was galloping off toward the Lazy Z with his horse running beside her.

"Well, damn it all!"

"See you later, Beau," she called from several yards away and let Brassy's reins drop.

Beau slapped the water again and whistled shrilly. The horse picked up the sound and came back to the edge of the creek. "Rotten, damn spit-fire woman, anyway! I couldn't live with her five minutes without shooting her or knocking the hell right out of her. And then my daddy would kill me for hitting a woman. Damn it all anyway, Brassy, if I ain't the unluckiest feller when it comes to love. Just when I think maybe we might be made for each other, she…"

Outwits you. Admit it, you're just mad because she got the best of you, and you wouldn't like the game nearly so well if she let you win every battle. She's a pretty smart girl and faster than greased lightning to be able to throw on a shirt, mount that horse, and steal yours while you were diving into the water.

"Oh shut up. I'll make her pay for this. I swear I will."

Milli reined in Wild Fire when she reached the pecan grove on the top of a rise a quarter of a mile from the creek. She had the rest of her clothes on before Beau crawled up out of the creek.

She fished around in the saddlebags until her hands found the little square case her mother had given her several years ago.

"A woman's hands are small and you need glasses you can hold a long time without getting tired," Angelina had said when she gave them to her. "If you're watching rustlers or a mean bull, you might have to be still a long time."

She zeroed in on him as he stood up at the shallow edge of the water, rising up like a blond Greek god from the creek. "I ain't watching a thief or a bull, but that sure undoes the effects of the swim! That is one fine hunk of man out there. And I didn't just imagine that mole on the left side of his bottom, either. It's still there, and all that soft hair on his chest. I'd better put these glasses away and cool myself down. Betcha my blood pressure is higher than Poppy's at a cattle sale." She put her hand over her mouth, hoping the sound of her giggles didn't carry with the Oklahoma breeze to where he was zipping up his jeans.

Chapter 16

SHE PULLED THE RUBBER BAND OUT OF HER HAIR AND ran her fingers through the wet tangles. It would be dry by the time she reached the ranch and no one would ever know she got caught with her underwear down around her ankles. Quite literally.

Well, almost. Actually I got caught with my bra on the saddle horn and my underwear hugging up next to a willow tree.

Beau wouldn't dare mention it because he'd look like a fool, and she'd be hanged from the nearest pecan tree by a brand new rope before she'd tell a soul that she'd been caught floating down the creek in her birthday suit.

Just as she reached to open the back door, Hilda opened it from the inside. "You look a little flushed, sweetie. Them boots is muddy. You get them off right there. I just mopped this kitchen floor and your granny would have your hide if you traipsed mud on her pretty blue carpet. Katy is in the den with Jim. They've been playing with that stacking toy thing all morning. I don't know if she likes her toys best or if her Poppa Jim does. What on earth have you been doin', girl? Your shirt is as wet as if you'd gone swimming in it."

"I did. It was hot, so I rode Wild Fire through the creek and splashed water all over us both."

"Girl, you're a grown woman now. You know better than to race a horse on a hot day and then get it all wet. Hummph."

She stuffed her socks into a clothes hamper and padded across the floor in her bare feet. "Oh, Hilda, quit your worryin'. I let him cool off. Matter of fact, I shucked my clothes, hung my bra on my saddle horn, and went skinny dipping. Felt real good."

"You did what? Girl, you ain't a kid. What would have happened if the hay haulers had come along and caught you out there without no clothes on your body? Grown woman with a baby of her own acting like that."

"Come on, Hilda. Didn't you and Slim ever go down to the creek at night, shuck out of your clothes, and let the minnows nibble on your little toes or whatever else they could find?"

A smile played at the corners of Hilda's mouth. "Get on out of here and play with Katy. And you be careful down around that creek, girl. Last time Slim and me—oh, never you mind. That ain't a story to be tellin' no young girl like you."

Milli giggled and disappeared into the den where she grabbed Katy and swung her around until both of them were breathless.

"Well, aren't you in a fine mood," Jim said. "I'll send you out to the hay fields again if it makes you that happy."

"Poppy, it's been a wonderful year. We won't be buying hay all winter. The Lazy Z is going to support the herd. There's the pole barn full of round bales and two barns full of square ones and the cows are going to be happy all winter. Wait until the first frost and we—" She stopped in the middle of her sentence. She wouldn't be here this winter to feed the fruits of her labors to the cows. She'd be in Hereford, Texas. No more battling with Beau. No more fussing with Hilda. Just back to Hereford and her routine.

"We what?"

"Oh, nothing, I was just thinking. I better get upstairs and get the creek water out of my hair."

"And how did creek water get in your hair?" Jim asked.

Hilda answered for her as she brought a tray laden with cookies and coffee into the room. "Oh, she's been out there skinny dippin' in the creek. Mary just drove up out front from the grocery store and she'll need something to keep her going until supper, so don't you two eat all the cookies up from her. I don't care if you do have an appetite from swimming in the creek water. Lord, the bailers would have gone stark ravin' mad if they'd come up on you out there without no clothes on. Or what if Mr. Beau had been riding by on one of his three-wheeler things and seen you? You better think about those things. And yes, girl, you better get that creek scum out of your hair. It'll make it dull and limp."

Jim cocked his head to one side. "Skinny dipping?"

"I told her she was too old for that kind of shenanigans. But does she ever listen to me? Nooo. Still sittin' there when I told her to get up there and get that junk out of her hair."

Milli giggled in spite of the sadness that nagged at her. Hilda would always be fussing about something, thank goodness.

At six o'clock sharp, Beau parked his pickup in the driveway. She watched him open the door and shake the legs of his crispy-creased blue jeans down to stack around his shiny boot tops. His hair was finally growing out around where the stitches had been. She could see the scar from her bedroom window as she looked at him. She couldn't keep the grin off her face when she thought about that scar, since it was the last thing she saw before she conned him into the creek.

"Milli, Beau is here," Jim called from the bottom of the stairs.

She opened the door and yelled back. "Be right down. Tell him I'm putting on Katy's sandals."

Beau's grin was extra big when she entered the room. "Well, now, don't the ladies look pretty tonight. I do believe your momma looks good in anything she wants to wear, Katy. I believe she'd even look good in a cloak of creek water."

"Daddy!" Katy Scarlett reached for him.

"What?" Mary asked. "What did you say?"

Jim Torres bit his tongue to keep from laughing out loud. Either Beau had found her and she knew it, or he'd been sly enough to hide and watch the show and she didn't know it. But she hadn't gone skinny dipping and gotten away with it Scot free after all.

"I said I love Milli in that shade of yellow."

"I thought you said something about creek water," Jim grinned.

Just wait until he told Mary about it later. They'd have a good laugh. Milli seemed bound, damned, and determined that she would be going back to Texas at the end of the summer. Nothing anyone said could make her change her mind and he was sure Beau had tried harder than any of them. He was sure going to miss the fun when she and Katy went back to Hereford.

Milli took Beau's arm and steered him toward the door.

He resisted. "Why are you in such an all-fired hurry? I'd like to hold my daughter before we go rushing off to put her in a car seat."

"I thought maybe you'd already been here this afternoon. Something about riding Brassy over to show her your horse." Milli kept a straight face but it wasn't easy.

"I thought about it but got distracted." He turned his attention to Katy. "Daddy missed you so much. Two days is way too long to be away from you."

He buried his face in soft blonde curls and a sweet baby lotion smell. "It's just not normal for a daddy not to love his baby girl in two whole days."

"Now can we go?"

"What's the big hurry?" Jim asked. "Ice cream place don't close 'til ten o'clock. Come on in the den and sit a spell with us. You can play with Katy better in the den than in the ice cream parlor, anyhow."

"Would you mind, Milli?" Beau whispered.

She couldn't refuse him. If he'd asked to go skinny dipping with her in that voice this morning instead of being so insolent, she would have waded through the water and helped him peel those skintight faded jeans down over his fine rear end with a freckle on the left cheek.

"That's fine. We can go for ice cream later, or not at all. You know we don't have to go somewhere every Wednesday night," she said.

"Thank you."

She felt as if she'd just handed him the winning ticket to a million dollar lottery.

He sat down in the middle of the floor and put Katy in front of him. "What shall we play with first? The stacking thing or the telephone?"

"Stack 'em up," Katy said, picking up the stacking toy she and her grandfather had played with all day. She pulled all the bright-colored plastic donuts from the stem and threw them all over the den floor. Then she put her hands on the floor, her bottom straight up in the air, and stood up as only an agile toddler can do, and tried to retrieve all the donuts at one time. She dropped one, then another as she tried to hold all five at one time, then she stomped her foot and drew her eyes down, just like Beau did when he was angry. She carefully picked up the yellow one in her right hand and the red one in her left hand and carried them to Beau. She went back to the green one and blue one and finally to the purple one. When they were all in front of Beau, she plopped down with a thud and began fitting them onto the rocking stem.

"Boy, she is one smart cookie, isn't she? Okay, put this orange one on first." He handed her the biggest ring and she slipped it on the yellow carrier and looked up.

Jim whispered, "Clap for her. Yeah, Katy! That's good."

Four adults clapped as if Katy had just scored the winning three-pointer in the last two seconds of a basketball game.

She smiled, showing off baby teeth and a deep dimple.

Beau's heart swelled so big he thought his chest was going to explode in tiny pieces all over the den.

He kissed her on the forehead. "You're daddy's girl."

"Daddy. Daddy. Daddy. Daddy. My daddy. My daddy." Katy chattered as she put the red ring on the holder.

"Did you hear that?" Beau said. "She said 'My daddy.' Did you hear her, Milli?"

Milli heard it loud and clear and her heavy heart fell past the floor and down into the dirt at least six feet. She saw the future in all its brilliant colors outlined in Beau's smile and eyes, but she didn't want to see it. She'd known today was coming way back when he told her to look in the back seat of the pickup and tell her what she saw, when he pitched a blue-blooded fit because she hadn't combed the woods of Louisiana to tell him she was having his child. But knowing it was coming wasn't facing it, and Katy had just brought reality to her on a silver platter. Katy had a father and she was recognizing him. She suddenly wanted to grab her child and run until she was out of breath.

"I heard her," she finally said.

"Bedtime," Milli said at eight thirty. "You want to help give her a bath?"

"You bet I do," he said.

Well, bath time isn't a whole lot different than splashing in the creek, and he might change his mind about his "pretty baby girl" by the time we got the job done.

He didn't. His freshly ironed jeans were splotched with as much water as the faded ones were at the creek that morning. His shirt was wet from picking Katy out of the tub for Milli to wrap the towel around her as she wiggled and giggled.

"Guess all you women like to play in the water," he said.

"That's Torres blood," Milli said smartly.

"Bet if I set her down she could jump on a horse before I could blink."

"Yes, she could. And take another horse with her while she was at it. She's going to be independent. Haven't you heard her say, 'ride, peas'? Those were her first words. My father put her on the horse with him before she cut her first teeth."

"Just like her mother, and as beautiful, with nothing but a soft shimmer of water floating over her beautiful body."

"And if you don't hush, Granny will hear you."

"You didn't tell her? I told everyone at the Bar M. Buster thought it was a hoot that you got the best of me again. Told me I'd better stay away from creeks and your rifle."

She felt the heat of a blush crawling up her neck. "You told Buster?"

He pointed his forefinger at her like the barrel of a pistol and fanned back his thumb like the hammer. "Bang. Gotcha."

"Oh, hush. You wouldn't tell or else you'd look silly."

"Yep, but you'd look worse. Now let's put our daughter to bed with her bottle. How old are they supposed to be when you take this thing away from them, anyway?"

"I don't give a damn if I have to pack it in her lunch box when she goes to kindergarten. I don't care if I have to go up to the school and wipe her fanny when she goes to the bathroom. I think everyone makes little kids grow up too fast anyway."

"Amen," he agreed. "Can I rock her to sleep? Or do you just put her in the bed when she doesn't fall asleep in the truck?"

"Oh, no, I rock her every night and I'm sure she'd love that." First Katy had called him daddy and now he was stepping into another place. It didn't settle well with Milli, but Katy loved him. It was evident from that first time he'd picked her up that she knew him. How was that possible? Genes must be one helluva a lot stronger than anyone realized.

He hummed a lullaby while Milli straightened the bathroom, picking up toys, drying the floor where Katy had splattered water, and wishing with all her might that she could trust Beau. In time she could overcome her issue with trusting him with Katy—it was trusting him with her heart that was so difficult.

Beau tiptoed to the edge of the crib and lifted the baby over the edge.

"I told you, she's a heavy sleeper like you," Milli reminded him. "You don't have to tiptoe or be quiet for that girl."

"But I like to. It makes me feel like I'm doing something right for once. Like maybe I'm not so unlucky after all. Now let's go see if the night air has got any cooler. Want some ice cream? We could still drive into Ardmore."

Milli reached down and flipped the switch on a white plastic box.

"What's that?" Beau asked.

"A monitor. I take this part with me downstairs, and I can hear her if she cries. Too late for ice cream. Wait for me on the porch swing and I'll get us a glass of iced tea. Sugar and lemon?"

"Both. Promise you won't ride away with my pickup while I'm sitting there waiting?"

"Promise."

When she crossed the porch, he stood up, stopped the swing and held it for her, then sat down beside her. She handed him his tea and sipped her own as he started a gentle swinging motion. They sat in silence for a while, each deep in thought. She liked the way he abandoned all inhibitions and played with Katy as though he'd really been there every day from the time she was conceived. He liked the look in her eyes when she looked at the baby. That's the way he wanted his wife to look at their children, and yet, even though he was helplessly in love with Milli, he wasn't sure they'd ever make it as a couple. It would be like putting two bulls in a china shop and expecting the china to be unbroken at the end of a week.

"Penny for your thoughts?" he said.

She set her empty glass on the rough wood cart beside the swing. "Cost you a lot more than that."

He brushed the back of his hand across her bare arm as he put his glass beside hers. The next second he gathered her into his arms and kissed her. No fanfare, no talk, no asking. Just a kiss that made both of them shudder like it always did.

"Could we try that one more time? I know one of these times it's going to lack pizzazz," she said.

"It's always the same. Always has pizzazz. Just like the first one at the trailer that night."

She pulled his mouth back down to hers for another kiss, amazed that even without the desire to get even with Matthew, without the liquor, the chemistry was still there. She tasted sweet lemon tea with just a faint tinge of the peppermint gum. Every bone in her body turned to jelly as she longed for more than just kisses and pressed herself against him so tightly she could hardly breathe. She'd be in the cold shower at least an hour after he left.

He slid his tongue over her bottom lip and savored bare lips with a touch of lemon on them. Desire surged through his body. He'd have to throw himself in a tub of ice cubes when he got home.

"I think we better stop that," she pulled away.

He kept his arm around her. "Why? I thought we were doing it just right."

"Too right. And besides, if you look to your right— don't turn your head, just your eyes—you'll see Granny and Poppy peeking through the curtain."

He tipped her chin back for another kiss.

She shook her head when the kiss ended. "I told you, we have an audience."

He kissed her again. "Then let's not disappoint them."

She saw stars exploding like a Fourth of July fireworks show.

"Think we'll survive this courtin' process?" He finally hugged her close, pulling her head down to rest on his shoulder.

"Ain't damn likely," she said with a sigh.

Chapter 17

MILLI AWOKE EARLY THE NEXT SATURDAY MORNING. It was barely dawn and for the first time in weeks, she could sleep late. With a moan, she slammed the pillow on top of her head and tried to will herself back to sleep, but it didn't work. She'd been out past midnight with Beau the night before and there was nothing pressing on the ranch to make her rise before daybreak. Finally, in exasperation, she sat up and looked out the window. The moon was disappearing and the sun was still just a sliver of orange in the eastern sky. She picked up the monitor so she could hear Katy and carried it to the kitchen, where she made herself a cup of strong, black coffee and carried it out to the deck to watch the birth of a new day. When she should have seen the rounded end of a bright ball coming up on the horizon, dark clouds scuttled around, covering what few rays there were.

Jim walked slowly out onto the deck. He set his coffee cup on a round table and eased down into a padded chaise lounge. "Mornin'. Doin' pretty good for an old man with a steel hip, now, ain't I? Don't tell Granny I left the walker in the living room. She's scared I'll fall."

She handed him the mug when he was settled. "Poppy, you ain't never going to be old."

A low rumble heralded the approach of a storm.

"We might get that summer rain we've all been praying for so hard these past weeks," she said.

Jim slapped the arm of the chair. "Well, damnation. Saddle up Wild Fire and run out to the north pasture before it hits and put that tractor in the barn. I told Slim there wasn't no way in hell we'd get a rain this early and not to worry about leaving it out. Guess it wouldn't hurt nothing for it to get wet, but I sure hate to see a rusty piece of machinery."

"Don't worry. I'll have it in the barn and be back by the time Hilda has the sausage fried for breakfast. You listen to this monitor. When Katy wakes up, tell Granny to change her diaper and bring her downstairs. If I'm not back by breakfast, save me a biscuit. I'll be waiting out the storm in the barn."

"Take your slicker," Jim said.

Milli was already on her way into the house and shoving her feet into dusty boots beside the back door. "Oh, I won't need it. Just a summer rain and it'll probably feel good, but if it's lightning, I won't bring Wild Fire back 'til it finishes. Don't want to take a chance of letting my favorite horse get hit."

She stuffed the tail of her nightshirt with a picture of Taz on the front into faded jeans with holes in the knees.

"Don't you take no chances, either, girl, and be damned sure you don't rein up under a tree. That's more dangerous than being right out in the lightning," Jim reminded her. "Barn is good and dry so stay there if it's a bad storm."

She kissed him on the forehead. "Yessir, and don't you try to get up out of that chair 'til Granny helps you." She jogged off toward the corrals.

❖ ❖ ❖

Buster shook Beau awake that morning. "Wake up, son, there's a storm brewing off in the southwest, and the television weather man says it's comin' this way at a fair speed. Your prize bull is out in the pasture where all those damned pecan trees are, and if it starts lightning it could kill him dead as a doorknob."

Beau was up like a shot. "Three-wheeler got gas?"

"Yep," Buster said. "Guess the fastest thing to do is to move that bull to the west pasture over there where the hay barn is and house him up 'til this has blown over. Who'd ever thought we'd have a storm like this in July? Lord only knows how bad the gardens need it, and the pastures, too, but that bull don't need to be out in it."

Beau dressed in the same clothes he'd dropped beside his bed the night before. "I should have already moved him. Thanks for waking me, Buster. Tell Rosa to save me some breakfast. I might have to ride out the storm in the barn with the bull." He combed his unruly blond curls with his fingers.

He found the bull hugged up to a tall pecan tree and rumbling thunder told him the storm was approaching fast. It wasn't an easy feat to convince him to abandon his security tree and be herded into an adjoining pasture with a nice big barn. With lots of creative cussing and just plain stubbornness, Beau finally got him inside the barn.

He could smell the rain, even if he didn't feel a single drop falling yet. He jumped on his three-wheeler making plans to call Milli as soon as he was back at the ranch. Rain would put the hired hands in the bunkhouse for the day. He could listen to them moan about how much work they were missing, how hot and muggy the rain was going to make the rest of the week, and how boring it was to be locked up inside. Or he could spend the day with Katy. The latter sounded much, much better.

He had just topped a rise when he spotted Milli riding Wild Fire like the devil was chasing her. Her ponytail was straight out behind her, just like the horse's tail. The way she sat a horse was as graceful as a ballet.

"Ballet, nothing. More like a sassy gypsy from a hellcat movie of some kind. Now just where do they think they're headed in this kind of weather?" Beau wondered aloud. Then he saw the tractor parked in the field.

It might not be brand new, but Jim didn't like his equipment left out in the rain. If it had a full tank of gas, it could be dangerous with lightning dancing around the country. He drove his three-wheeler back into the barn with the bull, slammed the door shut and bolted it with a cross bar, and then trotted over to the fence separating his land from the Lazy Z. He put the palm of his hand on the top of a post and hopped over the fence like a little boy playing leap frog with his father.

He got Milli's attention about the time she reached the tractor and the first giant rain drops fell behind a blinding flash of lightning and the roar of thunder. "Get Wild Fire inside. I'll drive the tractor in."

She nodded and raced the horse to shelter. She dismounted and swung the huge doors open, led her horse to the back of the hay barn, and tethered her to a support pole. She stripped off the saddle and her blanket, and rubbed her wet hide down with hands full of hay. By the time she finished, Beau had the tractor inside and the doors closed. A crash of thunder and a sudden downpour of rain sounded like bullets on the barn's tin roof. Milli shuddered even though she wasn't cold.

"Thanks. Guess we almost got caught," she said.

He shook his hair like a wet puppy and water sprayed in all directions. "Glad Buster heard an early report. I had my bull out in a pasture with a whole grove of pecan trees. When I went to check on him, the sorry sucker had hugged right up to one like it was his brother. Seen a lot of stupid cows die because they tried to hide under a tree."

She nodded. "We've lost a few, even though trees are few and far between out in my part of the world. They don't have much sense when it comes to finding a safe spot. Well, guess we might as well sit a spell. It don't look like it's going to wear itself out for a little while."

Beau grinned and started toward her with a mischievous look in his eye.

She backed up until she felt the ladder leading to the loft. "Don't look at me like that. It reminds me of the night in the trailer, and you're not drunk and I'm not getting over a broken engagement. So just sit down over there on that bale of hay and don't get closer than six feet to me. I don't trust me any more than I trust you."

He took two long strides and pinned her against the ladder. "I'm stone cold sober. But if I had one right now I'd drink a double just to loosen up a little." He inhaled deeply, taking in the clean smell of hay, rain, and the faint smell of Milli's perfume leftover from the night before.

She wrapped her arms around his neck. If he wanted to play games she'd sure give him a run for his money or hormones or whatever he was willing to put on the betting table. "Feeling a little tight, are you?"

"You'd never know just how tight. I'd be willing to fall off my wagon if you'd fall off yours."

"But I just don't like the stuff. I've never been blind drunk," she argued as he brushed kisses across her eyes, her cheeks, her ears and neck. "And I've never been on a wagon."

"Haven't you? I quit liquor and you quit men. You get off yours and I might get off mine for a shot of Jack Daniels every once in a while."

He picked her up and carried her to a mound of hay at the far side of the barn, kissing her all the way. He grabbed a horse blanket from a nail on a support beam and threw it on the hay, then laid her down gently. "Feeling like somebody upstairs must think you and I belong together. What's the odds of both of us getting cooped up in this barn all by ourselves? Not very good. But here we are."

"Not really. Wild Fire is here."

"Wild Fire don't tell secrets," he whispered. "She didn't tell about the day at the creek, did she? I bet she won't even watch us. We'd be boring to her."

"Ain't damn likely." She used his favorite phrase between fast heartbeats and quick short gasps as she tried to control her fevered body.

He covered her mouth with another kiss and both of them forgot about the horse on the other side of the barn. The rain played music on the tin roof, but they couldn't hear the thunder for the loud beating of their hearts. He removed her T-shirt as gently as if it were the silkiest lingerie. She moaned and for a fleeting moment knew she should put a stop to what they were about to do. She still hadn't gotten any form of birth control, but right that moment nothing seemed to matter except satisfying that dull, aching need filling her whole being.

He removed her jeans slowly from her hips, kissing her belly button above her cotton bikini underpants. Looking deep into her brown eyes, he pulled her down to a sitting position, facing him. Planting soft kisses on her eyelids, forehead, and the tip of her nose, he reached around behind her and unhooked her bra.

She flipped the bra away and leaned forward to undo the first button on his shirt. "It's my turn."

She'd envisioned several scenarios for that moment. A motel room with satin sheets and candles. A cabin on the banks of a river. Certainly not a hay barn with a raging storm outside. But what better place for two ranchers? The smell of fresh-cut hay and a raging thunderstorm only heightened desire as she buried her face in the soft hair on his chest.

Then fear grabbed her in a vice grip and for a fleeting moment she panicked and almost called a halt to the whole thing.

"I'm in love with you," he whispered into her hair as his hand caressed the soft feminine flesh on her bare back and she moaned.

Desire and fear fought for a few seconds. Desire won the battle. She unzipped his jeans and peeled them off his slender hips and gasped.

"Milli, we don't have to do this. We can wait," he whispered.

She put her finger on his mouth and kissed his eyelids. "Don't say anything. Just make love to me like you did before."

❖ ❖ ❖

Later, when the thunder ended and their hearts were beating normally, Beau propped up on an elbow. "I meant it. I do," he whispered as if Wild Fire might tell everything he knew.

"Shhh." She didn't know why she didn't want him to tell her that he loved her. Maybe it was because Matthew said those same words and that's all they were—just empty words.

Beau twirled a strand of her long, dark hair around his finger. "What are we going to do about us?"

Milli snuggled closer to him. "I don't want to talk about any of that right now. I just want to lie here beside you for five more minutes, then I have to go home and pretend this never happened."

"Why?"

"Because breakfast is ready."

"No, why pretend this didn't happen?"

"Beau, I'm still sorting things out. I've been trying, honest I have. But there's got to be more to it than just the physical part. Give me some time."

He stood up and began to dress. "It's yours, sweetheart. But I betcha Jim and Mary both can tell by that glow in your face that you didn't spend your whole morning watching a storm go by."

"And I suppose Buster is going to believe that you spent your morning talking to that stupid, ugly Angus bull?"

He knelt down beside her. "Hey, that bull made more than enough money last year to put Katy through her senior year of high school. By the time she's ready for college, the money will be ready for her. Where I come from, if you borrow a feller's knife and it's closed, you hand it back closed, but if you borrow it and it's open, then you hand it back opened."

"Or it'll bring bad luck."

"You unbuttoned this shirt, madam. I think maybe you better put it back the way you found it. I sure don't need to take any chances where love is concerned. You know what they say about me, and this is one time I want them to be wrong."

Her fingers fumbled with the buttons and it took every ounce of will power she had to keep from peeling the shirt from his wide chest and throwing it to the side. "There, even though that's the hardest job I've ever done we sure wouldn't want you to be unlucky in love, now would we?"

He bent forward from the waist and kissed her on the forehead, sending a new wave of hot chills down her body. "Thank you. I'll saddle up Wild Fire for you, and you can get on home to your breakfast. I'll see you tonight at the dance over at the Lazy Z. You wearin' that lace dress again?"

"No, I am not. Folks would think it's the only thing I own." She pulled on her boots as she watched him put the blanket and saddle on her horse. He wasted few motions and had led the horse out by the time she had her shirt tucked back inside her jeans.

He handed her the reins. "Have I told you today that you're beautiful, Milli Torres? And you can wear exactly what you have on to the dance tonight and you'll be the prettiest woman there."

"Bet you say that to all the girls."

He watched her sling a leg over Wild Fire's back. "Nope, just the ones who button my shirt back up. Hey, you ever think maybe that's why I'm not lucky in love? You didn't re-button my shirt two years ago? Seriously, I only say it to the one who has been my dream angel for two years. I'll open the door. See you tonight."

The creek was swollen to the top of its banks, so she spurred Wild Fire, dug her knees in, and the two of them jumped the raging water at the narrowest place. Even flying over the creek didn't lighten the tight feeling in her chest. Something was wrong. Now wouldn't that just be a hoot… if she'd gotten pregnant again on a one-time love affair. Surely the odds of that happening twice in a woman's lifetime were slim to none.

She should have been floating on a cloud by the time she got back to the ranch, but she was in the foulest, blackest mood she'd known in more than two years. The last time the whole world looked so damned dark was the night she'd given Matthew his engagement ring back. Beau hadn't been anything but attentive since the evening Amanda broke their engagement. He hadn't even looked at another woman in her presence, and everyone talked about him being thunderstruck, he was so in love. That meant the problem had to be inside Milli.

"You get the tractor in before all hell broke loose?" Jim asked when she led Wild Fire into the barn and started pulling off her saddle for the second time that day.

"Sure did. Quite a storm, wasn't it? Did Katy cry?" She kept her face turned so he couldn't see the glow in her cheeks or the anger in her eyes.

Jim shook his head. "No. Granny told her it was a man rolling taters down the mountains. I don't think she really cared what it was as long as it wasn't going to make her world crumble."

Well, it made mine crumble. Just when I knew I was ready for Beau to do more than kiss me good night. I'm so mad I could chew up nails and spit out staples. It was my idea to make love as much as his. I'm not a sixteen-year-old child and I can make up my own mind about sex without a guilt trip afterwards. So why do I feel like this?

"What's the matter, Milli?" Jim asked. "Something happen out there in the pasture to upset you?"

"No, not a thing. I'm starving to death, Poppa. You know how us Torres women get when we're hungry."

He shooed her away with his cane. "Then get in there and rustle up some breakfast. Slim is on his way back in here and he can rub Wild Fire down. You go eat, girl, and shake that mood out of you. We've got a party tonight in the sale barn, and I damn sure don't want you bringing a black look like that to our dance."

She stopped in the utility room long enough to take off her dirty boots. Hilda was folding towels and Katy was under her feet, playing with a toy vacuum cleaner that made a loud popping noise every time she pushed it.

"Get that tractor in? Crazy men folks," Hilda fussed. "Tractor wouldn't have been hurt a bit sittin' out in the rain. Send you out there in a blinding tornado, I guess, to keep a single bit of green paint from rusting. Don't make a lick of sense to me, but then, men folks don't usually make sense, do they? That's why they're men folks. They put stock in some of the craziest things. Got a dance tonight to fix for, and just what would have happened if lightning would have struck you dead? They damn sure don't think with the head on their shoulders. Kept you a sausage biscuit and eggs on the stove. Get on in there and eat. You Torres women get cranky when you don't eat and you look like you could whup a forest fire right now with a cup of water."

"Yes, ma'am," Milli said, but she couldn't even force a smile.

Jim and Mary insisted on taking Katy to the barn dance for the first part of the evening, and Beau was elated. "Come here, Miss Katy Scarlet Luck…" He cut off the last of the name when he saw the look on Milli's face. "Well, maybe before long it will be."

He carried her around, showing her off to all the neighbors and friends who hadn't seen her yet, and wallowed in the compliments when everyone realized she was his daughter. Milli smiled at the right times and when it was time for Katy to go to bed, she and Beau took her back to the house to Hilda, who was looking forward to rocking her to sleep.

"Now get on back to the party and dance until your feet hurt. Thank goodness you can do that. Those crazy fool men and savin' their tractor might have got you killed," Hilda fussed like she'd done all day.

Beau laughed and drew Milli closer to his side. They stopped along the way back to the barn for a few stolen kisses, but they didn't set Milli into the usual emotional tailspin.

She was tired, emotionally and physically. She just wanted to drop her jeans and western-styled blouse with cutouts on the shoulders and sleeves in a heap on the floor and fall into the four-poster bed in her room, curl up in a ball, and go to sleep forever. Deep, deep sleep where she didn't have to think about Beau or the future. About trusting him or not trusting him. About Katy leaving her someday to live with him. Or worse yet, about marrying the man and then finding she'd made another big mistake.

She couldn't express her feelings when there were no words. So when Beau put his arm around her and led her back to the party, she danced away the rest of the evening with a fake smile pasted on her face.

"I love you," he kissed her good night when the last two-step was finished, the band had packed up and gone home, and everyone else had long since left. He slid his tongue over her lips.

"I hate lipstick," he said.

Then, by damn, I'll go buy a truckload.

She opened her eyes and watched his eyebrows knit together as he enjoyed the sensations of kissing. But she didn't feel that sensuous tingle down inside her heart like she usually did when he kissed her. It was all over. Something wasn't there anymore.

Chapter 18

WHILE KATY SLEPT, MILLI PACKED, AND SOMETIME IN the wee hours of the morning, she loaded their suitcases into the back of her pickup truck. The moon was a big, full white ball in a bed of twinkling stars and she remembered waiting on the porch of the trailer for the taxi to arrive. But even memories couldn't make her stay. One did not ride a dead horse. When it died, they buried it and got on with life, and this relationship was dead. She didn't know if she'd killed it or if Beau's terrible luck really had murdered it. But something had done so, and by golly she was leaving.

With a long sigh, she hitched up the horse trailer and in the darkness put Wild Fire inside. She threw the saddle in the back of the truck beside the suitcases and then went back inside to pen a note to her grandparents asking them to forgive her for running out on them the rest of the summer, and propped it up on the kitchen table.

Her first idea was that she'd fly away in her airplane and never look back. But when she arrived at wherever she was going, she'd need something to drive. If she landed a job on a ranch, she'd need the horse.

She thought about writing a note to Beau and even had the pen in her hand, but she couldn't make her hands and mind work together to write the words that she knew would break his heart. She couldn't tell him why she was running away when she didn't know herself. He'd never made any bones about the way he felt, but then neither had Matthew. She didn't want to wake up someday and know she'd ruined his life, but she couldn't write it on paper. Sometimes words could not explain the heart or its reasoning.

What could she say? That he'd never hold his daughter again in his entire life, but that, too, was best for everyone? When he found out she was gone, he'd realize there really were no options and this was the only wise thing to do. In a few days he'd have another woman at the dances, maybe even Amanda, since she seemed eager to move back into his life a few weeks ago. She wiped away a tear as she thought about him making love with Amanda, but even that didn't change her mind.

She gathered Katy up in her arms, and carried her downstairs and across the backyard to the barn where the truck waited. Katy whimpered when she strapped her into the car seat, but she hushed quickly when Milli put the pacifier in her mouth. She fired up the engine but didn't turn on the headlights until she pulled out onto Highway 70 headed east.

"Well, Miss Katy," she whispered, "we've cut the strings now. You might be mad as hell at me in a few years because I didn't let you grow up with your daddy, but honey, it ain't goin' to work. Better to leave it now than have to hand him a divorce decree through a motel room door someday."

"Daddy with kitters?" Katy asked.

"That's right, honey. Daddy is with the critters," Milli turned on the radio and argued with herself.

I've got to listen to the voice inside me. The one tells me that something is not right with this. I knew it yesterday. Lord, it was pure ecstasy when he touched

*me, but there's more to a relationship than an hour in
the back bedroom of a trailer house or a romp in the
hay. I'm doing what is best for me and my child.*

She caught Interstate 35 north toward Kansas and
decided that when she reached the state line, she'd
decide whether she was going to Montana or Wyoming.
She had a little cash and lots of plastic in her purse and
it wouldn't take her long to find a job. In a week or two
she'd phone her parents and tell them she was alive and
well. Angels with golden halos were going to sell shares
for time-share condos on the back side of hell before she
ever looked at another man.

She caught a glimpse of a falling star somewhere
around the Purcell exit. She shut her eyes tightly for a
moment and wished desperately upon that star that she
had made the right decision. No matter if it was right
or wrong, it was over now. She'd seen Beau that fatal
Sunday when Amanda tried to inch back into his life.
Contempt was written in stone on his face when he
looked at the tall, blonde beauty on the porch. There
wasn't any doubt that she'd made her bed and now she'd
have to sleep in it. He didn't give second chances. By
the next barn dance at the Spencers' place, he'd be two-
stepping with another woman and declaring she was the
prettiest woman there and Milli had just been a fleeting
fancy in his unlucky days. She ached at the picture of
him holding someone else.

At daylight she passed the lights of Oklahoma City.
A hundred miles behind her and several more to go
before she stopped at some motel for a few hours of
sleep. Katy opened her eyes and spit out the pacifier.
"Daddy. Daddy. My daddy," she said.

"You won't remember that word for long," Milli said. "It'll fade like his memory and pretty soon it'll just be me and you, baby."

They stopped at a McDonald's. She changed Katy's diaper in the bathroom and changed her into a soft knit romper. She ordered the big country breakfast and fed Katy some hash browns, soft scrambled eggs, and sausage. She tried a bite of the biscuit, but it was too much trouble to swallow past the lump in her throat, so she wrapped it back up. Maybe later she'd be able to eat when there was more time and distance between her and the Bar M ranch.

At eight o'clock she passed the Perry exit. Granny and Poppy would have found her note by now. Beau might have slipped in the back door to beg a biscuit like he did most Sunday mornings. He probably would be angry, but then maybe he wouldn't be. He wasn't mad when Amanda broke off with him. He just walked up behind Milli in the barn and was instantly in love again. Perhaps he would go to church with Granny and Poppy and by now he'd be in love with someone else.

The DJ broke her thoughts. "And now here's the song that brought CMA awards to Trisha Yearwood a few years ago. It rode the top of the charts for several weeks. I knew she was going to bring home the glass first time I heard it. And if she's not in the running this year with her very newest one, then I'll eat my hat and have my dirty socks for dessert. Don't turn your dial, folks. Here is 'How Do I Live,' and then we'll hear from Shania and our own Garth after that."

One minute she was driving north with determination. The next her face was bathed in tears, dripping off her cheeks and soaking the front of her chambray shirt. She started to weave onto the shoulder and jerked the truck back onto the highway. Finally she pulled over to the side of the road and laid her head on the steering wheel as she listened to the haunting country singer put into words the feelings in her heart.

Her body was in a red and white pickup truck heading north to Montana or Wyoming or wherever the hell she could run to. But her soul had never left the southern part of the state and there was no way she could survive with the two factions split in half. It was one thing when her soul and body argued—when her body wanted Beau to touch her, kiss her, hug her, or just brush the back of his hand across her bare shoulder as he shooed away a mosquito, while her soul never wanted to trust a man again. But to leave one part on a ranch in Oklahoma and take the other to Montana was asking too much.

"What have I done? Lord, what have I done?" she sobbed. "Well, I know what I've got to at least try to do."

She fumbled in her purse for her cell phone and turned it on. It registered ten calls from her Poppy's number and six from Beau. She said a silent prayer as she dialed the familiar number and listened to it ring a dozen times. Evidently Granny and Poppy were still at church. She wiped at her eyes with her shirtsleeve and dialed the number to the Bar M.

"Please, God, let him be there," she whispered aloud as she listened to the buzz.

It rang once and she shut her eyes. She'd deserve it if he didn't ever want to see her or Katy again. The phone rang again and she prayed harder. Everyone always picked up the phone on the second ring. It was some kind of unwritten social rule. Never pick it up on the first ring, but always on the second. The third time she began to worry. They weren't home.

On the fifth ring she heard Rosa's familiar voice.

She fought the lump still in her throat. "Rosa, this is Milli. Is Beau there?"

"Where are you girl? Yes, he's here. He's out in the bunkhouse and won't even come in to eat. What did that boy do to make you so mad you run away? I'm ready to string him up and he won't say a word. Buster says he's just lyin' out there staring at the ceiling. Where are you, Milli? I called over and talked to your Granny and she said you'd left a note that you were on your way to find a job somewhere. Everyone is worried sick about you and that baby. Lord, we thought this was written in the stars."

"Just get him on the phone, please," Milli begged.

A moment later she heard the squeaky hinge on the front screen door when he opened it and the slam of the big, wooden door when he shut it behind him, and she could imagine him running his fingers through his blond hair as he picked up the phone, probably to tell her to go to hell on a silver poker and not to waste his time calling.

"Milli?

She could feel the pain in his voice.

"Please don't talk, Beau. Don't say a word. Just listen. I've made a big mistake. I got scared after yesterday. I thought…" she stammered.

"What, Milli? You thought what? Just tell me what in the hell did you think?" Raw pain was still there but so was that old edge she'd heard when he thought she'd cut the fence between their properties.

"I did something really stupid, Beau. I compared you to Matthew, and in my mind you were going to run out on me and hurt me. I'm so sorry. I just want you to know I was wrong. You are fine and decent and you're not Matthew."

There was a long silence and she prepared herself for the click of the phone as he hung it up.

"And what are you going to do now?"

"I'm coming home, Beau. I'll be back before suppertime. I've finally figured out that when it comes to you, I'm helpless. I'm hopelessly in love with you and I intend to fight for that love whether it takes standing up and fighting or dropping down on my knees and begging. I love you."

Her heart, mind, body, and soul were in agreement and that brought peace. Beau might throw it all back in her face, but at least Milli wasn't a disconnected being anymore.

"I'll be waiting at the bunkhouse for you. Come here. Don't go to the Lazy Z. I'll call Jim and Mary and tell them you're on your way back so they'll quit worrying. Drive careful and tell Katy her daddy is waiting," he said.

She heard a soft click as he hung up, without telling her he loved her.

She caught the southbound lane back out onto I-35 and headed back to face the music. Beau was going to look at her like so much trash beneath his feet, and tell her that they needed to talk about when he could see his daughter and what the visitation rights would be. Or he would tell her he was going to get on with his life, find a woman he could trust, and they'd have a house full of Luckadeau boys, and he didn't want to acknowledge Katy after all.

She stopped at a drive-by window for lunch and by mid-afternoon she was on Highway 70, the last leg of her journey back to the same place she couldn't wait to get away from only a few hours ago. By the time she pulled her truck into the circular driveway at the Bar M, her bones were aching from driving all day and her mind was numb from lack of sleep.

Beau stood up from the porch swing and walked slowly across the porch toward the truck. He opened the door and took Katy out of the car seat. "Come here to Daddy, baby. Been a long day for my little girl. Bet you've got saddle sores from sitting in that old seat so long. Meet me in the den, Milli."

He scarcely looked at her.

Her heart rose up to her throat and tried to strangle her to death.

The best scenario she imagined as she drove was the one where he threw open the pickup door and folded her into his arms, telling her she'd scared him to death and begging her to promise never to leave him again. But that wasn't Beau, and she knew it. If it had been, she probably wouldn't be in love with him, anyway. If he didn't challenge her every minute of every day, it wouldn't be long until their relationship, physical or otherwise, would be in shambles.

She opened the truck door for herself and stretched the kinks out of her back before she followed him through the screen door, through the foyer, across the huge living room decorated in an eclectic mixture of early American and country, and into the den where a strange man sat behind a big, oversized desk in front of massive bookcases.

Beau nodded toward the man, who stood up and extended his hand, "This is my lawyer, Mr. Anderson, and this is Milli. Camillia Torres. This is my daughter, Katy Scarlett." He turned Katy around so the lawyer could see her.

He motioned toward two dark green leather chairs that matched the one the lawyer was sitting in. Beau sat down in one, but he didn't wait for her to sit first, and he didn't let go of Katy.

She sat and waited for the explosion.

"As you know, Aunt Alice set things up kind of strangely. But she had her reasons, I'm sure. As a matter of fact, all Luckadeau property carries the same pre-nup agreement. It's not just this place. I cannot sell this ranch. It has to pass from me to my children and to their children, and if my wife ever leaves me, she cannot ask for one ten-penny nail from this ranch. Do you understand that?"

"Beau, this seems unimportant right now. I know about the way the ranch is set up. Granny and Hilda told me and I know that Amanda didn't like it."

His blue eyes snapped as they finally stared into her brown eyes. "You need to understand this."

"Why?" she asked.

"Because, Milli Torres, you have to sign that piece of paper, and you have to be fully aware of what is on it before you sign it. Everything I acquire other than this ranch, you could ask for if you ever leave me again, but this ranch is not up for grabs," he explained and she could see this wasn't easy for him either.

"But I told you, I won't hold Katy over you. I won't contest."

"It's not Katy we're talking about. It's us. I'm asking you to marry me, Milli. I love you with my whole heart and have for two years. I'm not going to leave you, not ever. But if you ever leave me again, you've got to know your rights."

"You are what?" She couldn't believe her ears. He hadn't touched her, hadn't kissed her or even hugged her, and he was proposing. There was something wrong with this whole picture.

Oh, yeah. And there was something wrong with the picture last night, too.

"I'm not going to give you an engagement ring, Milli. I don't want another engagement. I want a wife. I want you to be my wife, and I want my daughter on the Bar M where she belongs, learning to take care of the cattle, learning to love the land that's going to be hers when I'm dead and gone. I'm not going to leave you, Milli. I'm not going to hurt you like Matthew did. I love you. And you can trust me. You've got my word on that, and it's as good as a solid bar of gold. Maybe better. Matthew had gold but no integrity. Don't judge me by him ever again because I'm a different man. I love you. I said it before and I'll repeat it every day for the rest of my life. So if you want to marry me, just sign the papers and then we'll talk about the rest of the problems we are facing."

She stared at him sitting there with their daughter. He didn't move. Neither did Milli. They didn't reach across the span separating the two chairs and touch fingertips, or stand up and fall into each other's arms with Katy between them. The world did not stand still and the sun was still moving toward the west. The clocks didn't stop. It was just a normal day after all, except for the fact he'd asked her to marry him and made promises that she believed with her whole heart. She picked up the pen and signed her name right below the lawyer's finger.

"Now, what else do we need to talk about?" she asked.

"This." He set Katy on the floor and gathered her into his arms and hugged her so tightly she could hear his heart doing double time. He tipped her chin back and kissed her soundly. She shivered all the way to her toes.

"Now, sir, Milli and Katy and I are going to go down to the corrals and have a long talk. Thank you for coming out here on a Sunday, and next time we have a barn dance, bring your wife and join us."

Buster watched from the barn door as Beau opened the front door and the three of them walked slowly toward the barn. He smiled for the first time that day. Lord, he'd thought for sure Beau would die. He wouldn't talk all day long. He'd waited more than four hours on that swing, just sitting there like the weight of the world was on his shoulders. Seemed like they were doing fine at the dance and he saw Beau kiss her good-night beside the pickup, but evidently that crazy fool boy said something that upset her. Why else would she cut and run like a scalded hound? Hopefully, whatever that lawyer said had helped them to work through whatever the hell the fight was all about.

"Now, tell me again what you told me on the phone," he said softly.

She looked up into his eyes and didn't blink. "I said I love you. I'll stand and fight or I'll drop down on my knees and beg, but I love you, Beau Luckadeau, and I was wrong to judge you by Matthew's half bushel."

"Matthew's half bushel?"

"You know. I judged you by his standard and that wasn't fair. And I ran because I was scared of my own self, scared to trust you, scared of all these feelings you make in my body, scared that someday you'd leave and all I'd have left was a broken heart."

"I'm going to tell you one more time, Milli. I love you. I love this baby we've made and it don't matter if we make one more, six more, or no more, she's my firstborn. Now I want to marry you, and I don't want to wait forever to have you here where you belong. But I want things to be right there, too. I want you to go to Shreveport with me next weekend to meet my folks," he said.

"You're going to take me home to meet your momma? I'm the one-night stand from the wedding! She'll have your hide tacked to the smokehouse door if you come dragging someone like me into her house. And remember, I'm part Mexican. What's she going to do with that?"

"Love you just like I do. Momma ain't prejudiced. And she's going to fall in love with Katy, too. So is next weekend all right?"

"Only if you go to west Texas with me the weekend after that."

"Hey, you got two big brothers. I've seen pictures of them over at Jim's house. What do you reckon they'll do? Remember, I'm the sorry sucker who got you pregnant and didn't marry you. And I'm French and English.

Maybe those Mexicans want you to marry one of their kind and they'll hate my blue eyes and blond hair."

"They love Katy and she looks just like you."

"Guess we better make both trips to take care of things proper," he nodded. "Now, about a wedding date. What do you think about August first?"

"Less than a month? Momma will shoot me. I'm the only daughter and she'll want a big hoopla."

"Nope, just a simple ceremony right here at the Bar M. It's midway between the two families and seems only right that we start here."

"Sounds good to me. Momma can come stay with Poppy and Granny and make plans from the Lazy Z. She'll have to have flowers and a cake and a big reception, no matter if it harelips the governor of the great state of Texas, himself," she said.

"That's fine. Guess that's all settled now."

"Guess it is," she nodded.

But she didn't have that breathless, ecstatic feeling in her heart she had when he finally kissed her in the house. He'd proposed and they'd just discussed their wedding and she felt strangely as if they'd just talked about whether they were going to ride three-wheelers or horses out to check the pasture fence.

He set Katy on the ground and she toddled off to chase a passel of kittens scampering around the back porch steps. Then he carefully and deliberately took Milli back into his arms and kissed her and that terrible feeling in the middle of her chest dissolved. "And Milli, if you ever scare me like that again, I intend to turn you down over my knee and give you the whipping you were begging for."

"You and what army?" A secure feeling enveloped her entire being and she knew she'd just made the right choice.

"Don't ever do it again." He left no room for discussion. "We're not going to talk about this again. Just don't ever break my heart like that again. Promise?"

"I promise. I love you, Beau."

He hugged her close enough that she could hear the pounding of his heart. "I'm scared to let you drive out of here, but I've got to trust you just like you have to trust me. You'd better get on over to the Lazy Z. Jim and Mary are going to be sitting in hot water until you get home. Unless you want to take me to the barn before I go. Or you want to take a drive to the nearest motel."

"I'm so tired I couldn't hold my eyes open for another kiss," she whispered. "Good night, Beau."

Everything was perfect, or was it? So much could still go wrong. She hoped they were strong enough to face the hurdles and get on with their lives—together. But the thought of facing a whole tribe of Nordic-looking gods made her knees go weak.

Chapter 19

MILLI DRESSED IN A STRAIGHT DENIM SKIRT WITH A SLIT up the side, showing off a tanned, muscular leg. Then she picked out a sleeveless, light blue lace shirt from the closet and buttoned it up the front. She heard Beau's truck tires crunching the gravel in the driveway followed by Katy's squeals as Beau swung her around.

They're Katy's kin, so don't be so nervous. You'd think you were plain old white trash from the wrong side of the tracks the way you're acting.

"Milli, you're goin' to miss the plane," Jim called from the bottom of the steps. "They don't hold them big birds for women just because they can't figure out what to wear!"

"You are beautiful. I'll have trouble keeping you for my own when all my cousins see you," Beau said when she made it to the living room. "Especially Griffin. He's the only one of us who's not blond. His wife left him and he'd snatch you up in a minute to help him raise his daughter, Lizzy."

"What color is his hair?"

"Black with a white streak right in the front. Lizzy has it, too. It's a genetic thing from his momma, but the rest of us are all blonds. Just be careful one of them don't try to beat my time with you."

"One big old blond feller is enough for me," she said nervously.

"That's good news," he beamed.

They settled Katy into the car seat and drove south. Beau tapped out the rhythm to tunes from an Alabama CD, and she chewed on a thumbnail.

"They ain't goin' to bite you, so quit chewing your fingernails." He gently pulled her hand down and held it firmly in his.

"I had a hangnail. Besides, how do you know they won't bite? You're the fair-haired son. I'm the dark-haired witch who has caused a big family embarrassment."

"They'll love you because I do."

"We'll see who's biting their fingernails next week." She looked out the side window.

Mercy, what was she doing in this truck on the way to the airport, anyway? It was only four hours, but Beau said the baby didn't need that big of a trip plus a full weekend. So they would drive to Dallas and catch a 30-minute hop over to Shreveport. She should have offered to fly her plane, but she hadn't told him about that yet, and besides, she really needed the time to calm her frazzled nerves and get ready to meet the horde of Luckadeaus, who were planning a big hoedown party tonight, church tomorrow morning, a family reunion after church, and then at six o'clock, their plane left for the return to Dallas.

She shut her eyes tightly. It was only for two days. Monday morning everything would be right back to normal. Beau lived in a make-believe world of "everything is wonderful and everyone is going to love everyone else" but that kind of Cinderella syndrome didn't happen in real life. Even though he had an earring in his pocket it wasn't a glass slipper and it didn't mean all of his family was going to drop down on their knees and slobber on her toenails. She wasn't fair-haired Cinderella with a pumpkin coach and a dozen horses, and at midnight she was still the same old Milli.

"So why did you name our daughter Katy Scarlett?" Beau asked when they were in the sky.

Now, just exactly why did he think of that now? All these weeks and he'd never asked about her choice of names.

"Have you ever read *Gone With the Wind?* Or seen the movie? It's old. Vivien Leigh and Clark Gable star in it."

He shook his head. "Saw a lot of old westerns on late night television, but not that one."

"It's not a western. It's a story of the South after the Civil War, and the main character in it is Katy Scarlett O'Hara. She's full of spit and vinegar and steps right up in a man's world and makes a place for herself at a time when it wasn't the thing to do."

"So you named our daughter after a character?"

Milli set her jaw and challenged him with flashing brown eyes and drawn eyebrows. "Yes, don't you think she can fill the shoes?"

"I just think it's strange." He didn't back down from her gaze. The battle lines were drawn and even if he didn't win, he would have the fun of making up later.

"Strange! I don't think a fine old southern name like Katy Scarlett is strange," she huffed.

"Katy Scarlett sounds like a character in a book. It doesn't sound like a real name. Look at her, Milli. She looks like an Adelida or a Ruth, or something that has stability."

"Katy Scarlett sounds like a fine southern…"

The baby whipped her little head around and stared up at her mother with big blue eyes. Milli giggled, realizing that every time they said her name she turned to see what they wanted. "Besides, I couldn't very well name her Beau or Beauetta, now could I? Or even Antoinette, since I didn't know your first name was Anthony. We weren't exactly dragging family skeletons out of the closet that night she was conceived. I just picked out what I liked, and you can learn to live with it. Besides, my middle name is Kathryn and Katy is a nickname for that," she declared.

"I get to name the next one, then," he said.

"Over my dead body. The next one will be a joint effort from start to finish, and we'll agree on a name. And, dear hearts, it won't be Anthony!"

"Anthony was my great-uncle's name," Beau said sharply.

"I don't give a royal two-sided flip if it was the name of the governor of the great state of Texas or if it was the greatest, richest man in the whole state of Louisiana. I'm not having a little boy named Anthony."

"Then we'll name our next daughter Toni with an 'i' instead of a 'y.' They do that now, you know, name girls with boy's names." He fanned the fires of her anger just so he could watch her eyes dance. "Amelia Toni Luckadeau. Has a nice ring to it. Then she'll be named after what I thought your name was and me, too."

She rolled her eyes toward the ceiling of the plane. "It almost worked. You almost made me mad enough to forget that in a few minutes I have to meet all your relatives."

He smiled and his dimple deepened. "Who says I was joking? But we will be meeting them soon. I'll give you a few more minutes' reprieve, though. I told them that no one could come to the airport to get us. I've got a rental car reserved and we'll drive out to the place by ourselves."

They drove north and then back west into a sparsely populated area covered with gorgeous, tall pine trees. Beau stole glances at Milli often and noticed she kept straining her head to see the tops of the trees.

"Pretty impressive, aren't they? Sometimes when I look at the scrub oaks I miss the elegance and grandeur of these pines. Some of them are as old as the land, I'm sure." He reached across the console and took her hand in his, just about the time Katy leaned forward in her car seat and upchucked everything she'd eaten for two days.

"Good grief!" Milli turned quickly. "The medicine didn't work this time."

Beau pulled the van off on the side of the road. "What medicine? Is she all right? Do I need to turn around and go back to the hospital?"

Milli was as calm as a mid-summer breeze. "No. She gets sick every time we fly, but most of the time she does pretty good if I give her the medicine. Grab that box of tissues and the plastic trash sack, and I'll get this cleaned up in short time. It's all right, sugar, Mommy is here and we'll clean you all up in a minute."

"Katy's sick," she said. "Yuck."

"You must have flown a lot for it to affect her so little," he said.

"That's right," Milli said.

Beau turned around in the seat and watched as she unzipped a suitcase and dragged out a bright red sunsuit with a matching bonnet, a diaper, and a square box of baby wipes. In a few seconds she had Katy all clean, hugged several times, reassured a dozen more times, and back in a clean car seat. Then she cleaned up the mess on the floor with the skill only a mother possesses, and tied the top of the plastic bag holding all the nasty tissues and wipes into a double knot.

Beau was slightly green around the mouth. "Whew, you're pretty good at that."

"There's more to babies than sweet-smelling baby lotion and picking out a cute little name. Katy never has flown well, but she'll be fine now. Once it's out of her system, she's hungry as a bear."

Beau put his hand over his own mouth and tried to block thoughts of food entering his mouth. "I think I'll put the sweet-smelling baby lotion on the kids and you can do that cleanup stuff. I've always had a weak stomach when it comes to upchucking. And I hate to fly, too."

"Oh, no, big boy. You make 'em, you help with the whole ball of wax. You name one, boy or girl, Anthony or Toni, and I do hereby promise I'll hide the medicine when we fly. Reason I don't like that name is because Amanda called you that, like Beau was beneath her dignity. I didn't like the way she said it. Now fire this bus up and let's go eat all that food you promised me. You did say there would be potato salad, baked beans, and enough brisket to feed Sherman's march to the sea. And did I hear something about coconut cream pie?"

"If you say another word, you vixen, I'm going to do what Katy did." He checked the rearview mirror and pulled back onto the highway.

"So that's where she got her weak stomach. We Torres and Jiminez folks can talk about heartworms and castration while we're eating a plate of spaghetti and meatballs. We wondered why she upchucks so easily."

"I swear Milli, if you don't hush…" He covered his mouth again and a funny little gaggy sound crawled out of his sexy mouth.

"Oh, all right—and they say men folks are the stronger sex."

By the time they reached the ranch his color was almost normal. The faint green around his mouth was subsiding and his face didn't look as if he'd just awakened from a nightmare to see a ghost curled up on the pillow next to him. When he drove into the driveway, people came out from every corner. Milli had the sudden urge to lock the doors and refuse to get out of the van.

He opened the car door for her first and then took a smiling baby from the car seat. He put his arm around Milli and the three of them went to face the lion's den.

"Hi, y'all," Beau said.

"Well, get on up here boy, and let us see this new grandbaby you been braggin' up all summer." Joseph reached out a hand to touch the baby's arm.

"Daddy. This is Milli, and this is our daughter, Miss Katy Scarlett."

A tall, blonde woman wiped her hands on the bottom of a white apron covering a pale blue shirtwaist dress. She was barefoot and her long, blonde hair was tied back with a blue bandanna.

"Come on in the house, Milli. I'm Joann. We've been

dying to meet you. All we've heard every time we talk to Beau is your name. He said you were beautiful, but he didn't prepare us for just how pretty you are. Maybe the next baby will have your big, brown eyes. I'd just love to have a grandson with brown eyes. Come inside and meet the Luckadeau women and bring that baby with you. Beau can give her up for a little while." She ushered Milli into the living room of the long ranch house, through a porch full of men.

Women covered every square inch of the great room, not unlike the living room, den, kitchen, dining room combination at the ranch house where she grew up. Milli knew she'd never, ever remember all the names. But every single one of them smiled at her and the fear that they'd kill her disappeared.

"Do you think she'd let me hold her?" Joann asked.

"Maybe," Milli said. She was amazed that she wasn't more selfish with Katy. She'd sure been so when Beau wanted to hold her.

Joann reached out. Katy went right to her. Instantly, Milli knew what Katy was going to look like when she was edging up on sixty years old. Looking at the two of them together was seeing the past and the future standing beside her in the present. Katy would someday be the image of this graceful, barefoot woman. Still, a devilish little thought toyed in her mind. Wouldn't it be something if someday she and Beau did have a son who was the image of her Mexican father, with coal black hair and the banty rooster attitude that goes right along with short men?

Joann finally found her voice, but it still had a crack in it. She went to the front door. "Look, Grandpa. Granny got to hold the granddaughter first."

"Yep, but when she sees the pony I bought for her, she'll like me better," he teased.

"Pony? Ride, peas. Daddy, ride," Katy reached for Beau.

"What pony?" Beau asked.

"Oh, a little white Shetland. Them old boys can't have horses and Miss Katy not have one of her very own. Got her a sidesaddle made, too, but it won't be finished 'til next week 'cause I had the man tool her initials into the leather. KSL. You are meanin' to change that last name, ain't you, son?"

A hush fell over the entire room.

"As soon as possible," Milli answered.

Beau shot her a look that melted her heart.

An hour before the barn dance and party was to begin, Sami, one of the sisters-in-law, showed Milli to a bedroom at the end of a long hallway.

"This is the room Momma said to put you in. The door over there opens into a little nursery. Guess this is where they raised their boys. When a new one was born he would get the nursery, and the older one went to one of the other bedrooms. I bet Katy might appreciate a little nap before Beau, Grandpa, and Granny start showing her off like a prize calf. They're tickled with this new girl. You don't know how long this family has waited for a girl. I haven't got the heart to tell them that the doctor says this is probably a boy I've got." She patted her rounded tummy. "Already eleven rambunctious grandsons. You're a brave woman to bring that little girl in here amongst them all. All the relatives from here to Georgia and halfway across Texas are coming in to meet you, and oh, yeah, watch out for Jennifer. She's married to Beau's cousin, Dennis, and she's got the morals of an alley cat."

"Oh?" Milli raised a dark eyebrow.

"Yep, used to date Beau and threw him over for Dennis about two years ago. Dennis got the bad end of the deal. Woman ain't never been faithful to one man in her life. She grew up with my older sister, and she's got round heels. If a man breathes on her, she just rolls back on them heels and lands on her back!"

"Thanks for the warning, but she's married, you said," Milli laughed at the age-old joke with Sami. She undressed Katy, found her pacifier and laid her in the crib. Katy sighed loudly and shut her eyes, glad to be in something faintly familiar.

"Don't mean jack squat to her. And she's always had a soft spot for Beau, so watch out. See you in a little while. Bathroom is right there. Bet you're ready for a long soak and a few minutes of quiet."

The long bath and quietness did restore her nerves, but not as much as the acceptance of Beau's family. She dressed in a pair of black jeans and a black western-cut shirt with white snaps that had been tailored to fit her small waist. She laced a tooled leather belt through the loops and fastened the silver buckle, shaped like two entwining hearts, into the last hole in the belt. Then she pulled on black eel-skin boots. Finally she twirled her long dark hair up into a French roll and pinned the top with an ivory comb studded with diamond chips that her grandfather Jiminez had given her grandmother for a wedding gift.

She dressed Katy in a pale blue denim jumper with a pink and white checked shirt. Then she pulled up the golden curls with a matching pink lace bow. Just as she was sliding the silver bracelet on Katy's arm, Beau knocked once on the door.

He held his heart. "Whoooy! These are the finest-looking two women in the whole state. You look like something out of a magazine."

Milli eyed him from the shiny black boots, up past the skintight Wranglers with a sharp crease down the front of each leg, to the white shirt with pearl snaps, on past the bolo tie with a silver slide that matched his belt buckle, to his lop-sided, dimpled grin. "You look pretty fine, yourself."

"Ah, shucks, don't be sayin' things like that. You'll make me blush," he teased.

"You! You can't even playact that role, but you do look almighty handsome," she said.

"Thank you, madam. I intend to look just like this on our wedding day," he announced.

"And by then I'll be ready to help you shuck right out of those tight-fitting britches and do something other than look like the icing on a cake." She looped her arm though his and the three of them went out of the house and across the backyard to the Circle L sale barn.

"That kind of talk raises the temperature ten degrees." He pulled her close.

"Standing this close to you raises it twenty degrees," she said.

"Maybe we ought to elope rather than meet your parents and have a wedding."

"Don't tempt me. But honey, after all these blondes, I can hardly wait until next week when you meet all my folks. So eloping is out of the question until after that."

"Ah, shucks."

"Not even that poor old country boy 'ah shucks' attitude will change my mind," she said.

"Well, then, we might as well go on out to the party and let the rest of this part of the state meet my daughter and get a look at the prettiest girl ever to set foot in this area."

By midnight Milli had met so many family members and friends, her head was swirling. She missed Beau, but figured he'd disappeared outside for fresh air. The sisters-in-law were in the process of gathering up their own husbands and sons to take them home, and the band was putting away their instruments. Joann had taken Katy back to the house at ten and made sure she was sleeping soundly before she left the cook to watch her, and she and Joseph were outside bidding farewell to everyone who was leaving.

Milli wandered through the barn, not so very unlike the one on the Lazy T in west Texas, and only slightly bigger than the one at her grandfather's ranch in Oklahoma. Her thoughts were on how she'd handle the sale at the Bar M next year, and who she might get to cater the dinner, when she reached the back door of the barn and slung it open.

She stepped outside into the star-studded darkness of night and stood still for a minute for her eyes to adjust to the darkness. Then she heard the noise. When she turned to her left, there was Jennifer locked up in an embrace with none other than Beau, himself.

Her first reaction was to slip back into the barn and run away. Her second was a white-hot anger erupting from somewhere deeper than her toes, and spewing out over the top like an active volcano. So all men were just alike. Matthew wasn't a low-down cheating rattlesnake. He was just doing what they all did, and he got caught.

"Stop it," Beau pushed Jennifer away from him. "I'm not doing this and if I'd known this was what you wanted to talk about I would never have come out here with you. You're married to my cousin! And I'm engaged to Milli."

"And you still want me," Jennifer said snidely. "You never could keep your hands off me." She slid her left hand up his thigh.

Beau pushed her back at the same time he noticed a dark shadow on his right. "And I said no! Forget it. Go home."

"That Mexican bitch must be damn good if she's better than me," Jennifer said.

Beau realized the dark shadow was moving toward them. "Oh, no. Milli, let me explain."

She pushed him away and kept walking. "What did you call me?" She stopped two inches from Jennifer's nose.

Beau tried to step between them. "Wait a minute, Milli."

"Stand back, Beau. I'll deal with you later. Now, what did you call me?" She whipped around and faced the woman again. Jennifer was only slightly taller than Milli, but she had twenty pounds on her. Milli knew she might be sporting bruises next month on her wedding day, but she'd promised she'd stand up and fight for Beau, and she was damn well prepared to do just that.

"I said you were a Mexican bitch."

Another party came out of the shadows. "That's enough, Jennifer! Apologize to the lady for trespassing on her property, and we're going home."

"I will not," Jennifer glared at her husband.

"Yes, you will. We're going home and packing your bags. I've had all I'm taking. Beau don't need you interfering with him and the lady here has every right to slap the fire out of you. Now apologize, Jennifer."

"I won't." She sulked like a child.

"Then you can walk ten miles home and your stuff will be waiting on the porch. Your car keys will be in the ignition, and the divorce papers will be at your folks on Monday."

She took off in a run behind him. "Wait, Dennis."

"Now, what have you got to say for yourself?" Milli turned on Beau.

"Not a thing. I should have had more sense than to follow her out here when she said she needed to talk to me. But I got to admit I'm glad I did," he smiled brightly.

"You are what?" she yelled.

"Glad I did. I wondered when she kissed me if I'd see stars like I do with you, and I didn't."

"You really are out of your mind, just like Slim said. But honey, next time a woman calls me a bitch twice you'd better step back because I will knock the hell out of her." She put her arms around his neck and drew his mouth down for a kiss.

And the stars were there for both of them.

Chapter 20

"WE TAKIN' MY TRUCK OR YOURS? FLYIN' OR DRIVIN'?" Beau asked the next Friday night when he and Milli were taking turns pushing Katy in the swing.

"You arranged for last weekend's trip. I'm taking care of this weekend. You just be here at seven o'clock in the morning with your bags packed and ready," she said.

"And is there a Jennifer I'm goin' to have to take care of out there in west Texas?"

"No. I never did crawl between the sheets with anyone named Jennifer. And I don't think I'll be out behind the barn letting some female mess with my silver belt buckle."

"You know what I mean. Got any old boyfriends coming to the engagement party out there? Trying to entice you out in the yard to lure you away from me?"

"Never know."

"You are never going to give me a moment's peace. I'll be walking on eggshells the whole time we're married."

"Good. Then you won't get bored. It's your turn to push Katy."

His captivating grin made her whole body ache with desire. The past two weeks hadn't been easy for either of them. It was a busy time of the year, there hadn't been a drop of rain to draw them back to the barn, and neither Mary nor Hilda had jumped right in and said, "Why don't you two just go away for the weekend?"

Mary and Hilda talked about receptions, caterers, and flowers. They floated around with stars in their eyes just thinking about Milli living right next door. Where she used to hear Beau's name a hundred times a day, now it was wedding plans. But no one seemed to think about Milli and Beau wanting to have some time alone.

He sat in the lawn chair a few more seconds, watching Milli in tight, cut-off blue jean shorts and a cotton shirt tied up in the middle, showing off a couple of inches of midriff. He shut his eyes and imagined damp, tangled sheets in the back room of a trailer house, and the fire that had burned for more than two years even when he thought she was nothing more than a dream. Then the smell of rain and fresh hay sent his senses reeling as he remembered the morning they spent together in the barn. It was beginning to look like they wouldn't have time to be together now until after the wedding. Not even for a simple dinner and a couple of hours in a motel.

She leaned down and kissed the scar on the top of his head where the new hair was still shorter than the rest of his unruly mop of curls. "Whatever are you thinking about?"

"Loving you," he answered honestly.

The next morning Milli was ready to go and opened the door as Beau raised his hand to knock. "Come on in. Maybe we'll make a motel stop on the way."

"With Katy?"

"Just kidding, but I wish I wasn't. Granny, is Katy finished with breakfast?" she called over her shoulder. "Don't forget to give her a teaspoon of the medicine on the table."

"Oh, so we're flying?"

"Yep, we're flying."

Mary carried Katy into the living room and handed her to Beau. "Here she is, fed and doped up for the trip. Y'all be careful now. And give us a call when you get there, Milli. I know you're careful, but I always worry."

"Sure thing, Granny."

"Let me have the baby and you grab your bags."

"My truck or yours?" he asked.

"Mine."

"Got a kiss for me before you go?" Jim asked.

She hugged him tightly and planted a kiss on his forehead.

"See you late tomorrow or Monday morning, depending on the weather. Traveling ought to be a breeze. You could stay a couple of days extra. Just a few more acres of hay and the boys could take care of it," Jim said.

"Are you trying to get rid of me?"

"Just trying to give you some time away from all us old codgers," Mary said. "A couple of more days wouldn't hurt a thing. Few parties. Little courting. Lord, y'all ain't had time to even kiss each other good night since you got engaged."

Now's a fine time to notice. Milli almost groaned.

"We'll see." She waved good-bye one more time.

"Where's your stuff?" Beau asked when he put his suitcase, garment and boot bag in the back of her truck.

"Already loaded." She drove the truck around the house and down a dusty lane toward the open back pasture.

He held onto the door handle as they bumped along the rough path with only tire tracks for a road. "Hey, this ain't the way to west Texas."

"Yes, it is. See?"

"Where did that come from? I didn't know Jim had a plane."

"Jim don't. I do. There ain't no sense in us driving all the way there. Flew it in here at the beginning of summer. Poppy don't really like for Katy to fly, but it's faster and I thought I might need to do a little crop dusting for him while I was here. So we flew and one of the hired hands brought my truck and Wild Fire in for me. Haven't done any dusting yet, but Katy and I did fly home last month while you were up in Kansas. But surprise, surprise. You get your own crop duster in the marriage contract. And I won't even make you sign a paper saying that you won't try to get half of my plane if we split the blanket in a few years."

"You are the pilot?"

"You're lookin' at it. Like I said last week, it's your turn to chew your fingernails."

Beau really didn't like to fly, not even in the big commercial planes. The only time he'd been up in something this small was with a crop duster once, and he swore on a stack of Bibles he'd never set foot in anything that small and bumpy again.

She opened the truck door. "Oh, stop your worrying. I've got the manual in the cockpit that's got a whole section of troubleshooting if we have a problem. You can read it to me and we'll work everything out."

"How long you been doing this?"

"Oh, I've been up alone two or three times now."

"Milli…"

She opened the door to the passenger side of the truck. "Beau, if you're going to marry me forever amen, you've got to trust me. Get the baby and follow me. I promise I won't do any stunts and make you or Katy upchuck."

His eyes were as big as flattened cow patties. "Stunts?"

She unhooked the seat belt from Katy's car seat. "Come on, sweetie. Let's show Daddy the world between here and Hereford, Texas."

His feet were concrete inside his boots as he climbed into the plane. It had one small seat in addition to the pilot and co-pilot seats. Katy squealed with delight when Milli put her into her familiar place. She picked up a stuffed elephant and hugged it close and looked up out of the bubble-type window, waiting for the big, puffy white clouds she liked so much. Beau wished that same exuberance could replace the chunk of cold steel taking up the space where his stomach used to be.

"You are the co-pilot, Beau. Sit right here beside me. And you are given permission to pop your little thumb into your mouth anytime and begin to chew your nails or even suck your thumb if it makes you feel better. I didn't bring any security blankets, though."

"Milli…"

She put her hands on his cheeks and turned his face so that he had to look right into her eyes. "Beau, today, I'm the pilot and you're the co-pilot. We're a team, like we're going to be forever. I've been flying for ten years. I did my first solo when I was thirteen years old, and I've been stunt flying for three years. Trust me, darling."

He buckled up the seat and watched her adjust everything as she got ready for takeoff. "Okay. Is there anything you can't do?"

"I don't knit."

"Knit?"

"That's right. I do not knit. I tried it once. My English grandmother said all young women should knit and in thirty minutes I was so damned mad and she was so frustrated, we threw the whole thing in the corner. Rotten string wrapped itself around my fingers and tried to crawl up to my throat and choke me plumb to death. Acted like some kind of python snake, trying to smother me, so Grandy and I decided I'd just have to be imperfect. You're not going to break the engagement because I'm not perfect, are you?"

"Ain't damn likely." He managed a weak chuckle as they took off, making a smooth ascension up into the light blue summer sky complete with a few marshmallow clouds just for Katy.

The drop on the concrete runway at the Lazy T ranch was just as smooth, and Beau looked out to see two pickup trucks and a silver Cadillac parked and waiting.

"What's all this?"

She shut off a dozen buttons, and turned to look at Katy. "They've come to meet you and to take us to the house. Katy is awake. That's wonderful. Usually she sleeps part of the trip and at least an hour after we get home."

"My daddy. Want my daddy." Katy reached for Beau.

They stepped out of the plane like they went everywhere lately: Katy hugged up to Beau's left shoulder and his right arm possessively around Milli's shoulder. But the minute Katy saw her grandmother, she held out her arms and wiggled so hard Beau about dropped her.

The woman kissed her all over her fair face. "Nanny missed you so much."

"Momma, this is Beau," Milli said with a note of pride in her voice. "And Beau, is my dad, John Torres."

"Pleased to meet you both." Beau shook hands with John, but Angelina insisted on a hug.

Angelina Torres was the same height as Milli, but her eyes were a lighter shade of brown. John was only a couple of inches taller, but his handshake was firm and steady, and Beau could tell he'd put in a lot of hard days on the ranch by the way his shirtsleeves hugged his biceps.

Milli introduced the next two people in the line. "And this is my brother Andy and his wife, Jana. They've have been married ten years."

"Since you first flew."

Andy's handshake was firm. "That's right. She was a hellion even back then. She should have been a firstborn son instead of a baby girl."

Milli pushed him but he didn't waver. "You're just jealous because you can't fly."

"And these are our daughters," Jana said. "Tammy is eight and Casey is six."

Tammy's brown eyes glittered in adoration when she looked at her aunt. "And I'm going to fly just as soon as Aunt Milli can teach me. And someday I'm going to do the stunts at the fair."

"I bet you will," Beau said. "You, too, Casey? You going to fly?"

"Hell, no," the prissy little girl said. "Ain't no damn way I'm going up in a plane like that. I'm going to marry a millionaire and drip diamonds and have a jet airplane to take me everywhere."

Her mother swatted her on the bottom. "Casey, I'm

going to make you stay in your room at the party tonight if you cuss any more."

Casey winked the same way Milli did. "Oh, all right," she said.

The other brother stepped forward with his hand extended. "And I'm James. I can sure tell you're Katy's daddy. It's amazing how much she looks like you."

"Thanks," Beau beamed.

"And this is my wife, Laura, and our kids—Jimmy, who is six, just like Miss Potty Mouth. And Jeremy, who's five."

"And that's the whole bunch of us right now," Milli said. "Not so formidable now, are we? There's only eight new faces. There were ten million at the Circle L last week, Daddy. And I'm only exaggerating a little bit. There were so many blondes there it scared me. Felt like I was the only chicken at a coyote party. And, Momma, he's got five brothers and they've all got kids and you can't kick a bush over in that part of the country without a dozen Luckadeaus running out and they're all blond except for one who has a white streak in his hair. And I'm never going to remember all their names."

She put her arm around her mother's shoulders and they started off toward the Cadillac. She grabbed Beau's hand and dragged him along.

"Come on Beau. Don't just stand there. They'll all find their way out of here. And you know what else, Momma? There ain't one baby granddaughter except Katy and she's going to be so rotten the garbageman won't even haul her to the dump by the time she's grown."

Milli and Angelina crawled into the big back seat and chattered all the way to the house about the wedding. John shook his head and grinned at Beau. The ranch house wasn't so very different from the one on the Bar M—long and low, but a wide porch wrapped around it on three sides. Beau liked the porch so well he began making plans to add a verandah to his house.

John showed him to a room at the end of the hall. "This is your room. Bathroom is through there and if you need anything, holler right loud. And Beau, we're glad things are working out for you and Milli. Been a long time since she's talked that much. Just got quiet and serious and we didn't see many smiles this past two years. We're glad you've put the glow back in her face and the shine back in her brown eyes. If she would've told us who you were, I promise you would have known about Katy a lot sooner, but she's as stubborn as a mule when she sets her head," John told him.

"She sure is. If I'd known about Katy I'd have been here, too, sir. I've been hopelessly in love with your daughter for two years. I looked all over the southern half of the state for her. But I thought her name was Amelia Jiminez."

"Life sure has a funny way of dealing the cards, don't it, son? When you quit looking, there she was on the farm right next door. We got a community party tonight. Women been working all week on the barn, trying to make it look like a fancy hotel. Band cranks up at six and it'll be daylight before some of these folks go home. Us Mexicans make a party out of everything we can, and make it last as long as possible."

John shut the door gently and Beau could hear Milli's clear laughter floating down the hall as she and her mother disappeared into a room right across the hall from him.

He exhaled forcefully and plopped backwards onto the bed. She was a good pilot, and he hadn't minded the ride any more than if he'd really been in big plane. Who knew how many more surprises she would pounce upon him in the next few years? Life with her was sure going to be a roller coaster. He heard a faint tap on his door but before he could sit up and say a word, she'd slipped into the room.

She stretched out beside him on the bed. "Wasn't so bad, now was it? Nobody brought a new rope to string you up from the nearest mesquite tree, and Daddy didn't even load the shotgun."

She snuggled closer to his side, unbuttoned a couple of buttons in the middle of his shirt so she could slip her hand inside to feel the hair on his chest.

"You got two hours to stop that."

She kissed the end of his nose and fluttered a butterfly kiss across his cheek. "In two hours, darlin', we'd be doin' more than this. Get on your work boots and jeans and a T-shirt. We're going out to look at my herd and discuss what we want to do with it."

He wrapped his arms around her. "I'd rather stay here and start a new herd."

She was on her feet before he could kiss her again. "Me, too, but it won't happen in this house, trust me."

She gave him the royal tour of the ranch, introducing him to all the hired help along the way, and showed him her herd of registered white-faced cattle.

"What do you think?"

"Good cattle. Jim wouldn't cull a one of them."

"We can transport them to the Bar M without too much trouble. Take a couple of trips, but the ranch owns two cattle semis."

"We'll section off a chunk of land for them and keep them separate from the Angus. You've got some prize stock here, lady," he said.

"I'm lookin' at prize stock. Those are just cows," she teased.

"Much more talk like that and honey, I'm going to do a Indian rain dance right here," he said.

"What?"

"Rain, honey. I see a barn right over there, and if it was raining too hard for us to get back to the ranch…?"

"Can you show me how to do that dance?" she asked.

Her father drove up on a four-wheeler before he could answer and talk went to cattle and ranching. Before long they were ushered back to the house to get ready for the party. The band had arrived and the first few strands of music were drifting across the yard from the barn, when he heard another rap on his door, and opened it to find Milli standing before him in the same lace dress she had worn to the wedding. Her hair was up and he gasped, knowing if he blinked even for a minute, she would be gone like a puff of smoke on a clear, sunny day.

He had part of the buttons fastened on his shirt. Her fingers strayed to the soft fur on his chest. Surely nothing could go wrong at a Torres party, but she'd thought the same thing the previous week. Everything was perfect and nothing could ever make her have a single doubt again. Then there was Jennifer in the shadows with her hands all over Beau, and for a moment, the old fears had returned with a vengeance.

"Let me help you with those buttons. Now, you look just like one of those good-lookin' men on the Marlboro commercials in the magazines. All you need is your horse and a felt hat. I better go polish my six-gun. All these female cousins of mine are going to see a tall, blond feller and make a play for you. I'll need something to keep them at bay."

"You mean there's more just like you? Is there one who's not so blasted stubborn? Maybe I'd be willin' to work out a deal."

"Over my dead body, cowboy. You look cross-eyed at one of those girls and I'll scratch her eyes out and shoot you graveyard dead. Either you belong to me or you belong to no one."

"Sounds like you better chase your pretty little butt on out to the barn and get the branding iron and heat it up. Womenfolks see a brand on me, they might not be in the mood for rustling."

"If they think they can rustle what belongs to me, they'll end up just like your sweet little Amanda. On her scraggly old rump in the dust. Now let's go. If we stay in here too long Andy and James will come bustin' in the door with a shot gun and a preacher."

"Sounds like a winner to me. We wouldn't have to wait another day," he said.

And I wouldn't have to worry that someone might still come along and steal you right out from under my nose. There's always the old "lucky in everything but not lucky in love" thing sitting on my shoulder, and I'm scared out of my boots that I'm going to lose you, my darling.

He took her arm and they went out to the barn.

"And now here comes our honored couple," the lead singer said into the microphone and everyone clapped loudly when they walked through the doors.

Beau was surprised to see so many people. The barn was filled to capacity and those on the dance floor parted to let Milli lead him into the center.

"Milli has requested a special song to dance with her fiancé on this night. So here it is, an old song by Trisha Yearwood. She says it's the song that made her realize she was about to make the biggest mistake of her entire life. Beau, you are a lucky man," the female lead singer said.

Milli looked up into his eyes as they danced to "How Do I Live" and there wasn't anyone else in the barn. They were alone in their own world where only two hearts beat in unison. At the end of the song, she kissed him gently. Beau really was branded. Milli Torres had her mark on him forever.

The applause brought them back down from the clouds to reality and they bowed gracefully as the band started to play the song one more time just like she'd told them. She wrapped her arms tightly around his neck and snuggled her face into his chest where she sang softly to him as they swayed gently to the music one more time.

When the song ended the band broke into a lively number by Shania Twain, "Any Man of Mine."

Milli stepped back and shook her finger at him as she sang loudly with the singer and he crossed his arms across his chest. She danced around him, teasing him with her movements until all he could think about was taking the gypsy-looking hussy to bed.

The singer finished the song and said, "Folks, John says the food is ready at the back side of the barn now. So dance if you want to, or line up at the buffet. We'll keep playing. If you're really good, you can dance and eat at the same time."

Milli took his hand. "Come on, you've got a lot of folks to meet. You're a good sport, Beau. Thanks for the dances."

"Thank you for the first two. I'm not so sure about the last one. We'll see how good I can walk a line. I'll probably set my heels. I've got a determined streak and don't like the idea of being henpecked."

"If I could henpeck you, I wouldn't want you."

Just after midnight, Beau was dancing with his future mother-in-law, but his eyes kept going back to Milli. He'd never get tired of looking at her. The grace with which she moved. The way she intermingled with family and friends. She was truly a rancher's wife.

First she talked to her older brother. Her feisty niece, Casey, said something that made her toss her head back and laugh. Then she visited with Laura, her sister-in-law, and from the hand movements he figured they must be discussing the wedding dress. Milli shook her head no when Laura made signs like a big white dress, and Laura looked toward Angelina. Then a man slipped inside the barn. Beau couldn't tell if he was an uncle or a cousin, but Milli bristled when she saw him.

Evidently he'd made her angry about something, because if looks could have killed, a bullet would have shot out of her eyes and entered his heart in a split second. He nodded toward the door and she nodded. He started across the barn to her and she followed. When she reached his side, he said something and reached for her arm. She shook it off like so much dirt and followed him out the door.

"Who's that?" Beau asked Angelina.

She just caught the back side of a well-cut western

suit and the familiar boots with silver heels and tips. She
swore and stomped her foot. Her face was as pale as a
half-Mexican lady could get. "Good Lord. What is he
doing here? Damn it all to hell and back anyway. Pardon
me, Beau. I've got to talk to my sons."

"I think maybe I better go see what is going on."

"Maybe so. But I think I'll still talk to James and
Andy." She was off like a flash of lightning.

Beau went out the open doors at the front of the
barn and stopped, letting his eyes adjust to the darkness after being inside all evening. He heard Milli and
it didn't take an expert to know she was so mad she
could commit homicide. She was standing beside a
black Porsche and the man was only a foot away from
her. Beau eased over closer so he could hear the words
as well as the tone.

"I made a mistake two years ago, Milli," the man said.
"I wasn't thinking straight. My father said it was time for
me to marry and I should look for someone with dignity to
bring to our family. He said I could play around as long as
I wanted with whomever I pleased, but when it came time
to choose a wife, she had to be a virgin. And I had to be
married by the time I was thirty. I chose you and it made
him happy. But I wasn't ready for marriage. I still had a
lot of wild oats to sow. I'm ready now and I'll do whatever you say. Trust me, darling. We'll make a wonderful
couple, and I'll adopt the little girl you have. I won't ever
mention that you weren't ready to settle down either, and
that you had a few wild oats, too."

"You can go to hell, Matthew," she told him emphatically.

How could she have ever loved him? He looked like a
slimy slug standing there promising her the moon.

He edged close enough to her to run his hand across her cheek. "Oh, come on, darling. I can give you more than that poor old Okie."

A low rumble of disgust rose in her throat. "Don't you touch me."

"You like for me to kiss you. Evidently by that child you have, you like a lot more, too. All you had to do was tell me you wanted sex before we were married. I would have gladly taken care of it. If you'd just told me you were already sexually active, you could have been in the motel with me every night. Father must have been wrong when he had the investigators check out your background. Got to say one thing. You are sly and very sneaky, because everything he found said you were pure as the driven snow."

She opened her fist just before it made contact with his jaw or it would have broken the bone. "I said don't touch me. Now get off my land and don't come back. It was over the day I gave you back the ring at the motel room. Remember, Matthew? You had another woman in the room and were engaged to me. And don't talk about Beau like that. He's my daughter's father, and, honey, he can make my body sing when all you could possibly hope to do is make it puke."

"You are a fool and you'll be sorry."

Beau stepped out of the shadows. "The lady said for you to leave, and I think maybe that's the best thing you can do before you really get into trouble."

Andy and James appeared from the darkness.

"Got a problem here?" James asked.

James didn't stop walking until he was inches from Matthew's nose. "What in the hell are you doing here tonight? You're not welcome on this ranch. I heard you were getting married next week. What's happened? Another girl find out how much she can trust you?"

"I'm leaving. But when the going gets rough, remember what you could have had," he said flippantly to Milli.

"Sure, I will. And I'll drop down on my knees every morning and give thanks I didn't get any part of you."

Beau turned on her just like she did him the week before. "Now what have you got to say for yourself? Why did you come out here in the dark with that bucket of worthless manure?"

She looked up into his eyes in the moonlight remembering saying the same thing to him when she discovered him with Jennifer.

"I don't have a damned thing to say for myself, but I'm glad I came out here. There will never be a time when I look back and wonder what it would have been like to have married him. I happen to be in love with you, Beau, and that's a fact."

He kissed the tip of her nose. "Then let's go back to our party."

Her mother met them inside the barn. "What's happened? Your brothers said you took care of it?"

"I did, Momma, and he won't be back. Now I'm taking this man out on the dance floor and dance with him until the last song is sung. I think I might be in love with him, Momma. When do you know for sure?"

"Oh, get out of here, and quit teasing your momma. No, wait a minute, Milli. Beau, go find a taco or an enchilada and get some strength to dance. I need to talk to Milli a minute."

"What is it, Momma?"

"I think it is time you two had some time together," she said. "You got everything all turned around in your lives. A baby before you know each other, and then a courtship with a baby underfoot. How many times have you been off away from everyone all by yourselves since you found each other again?"

"Only a couple of times."

"I see," her mother nodded. "And what kind of honeymoon are you planning?"

"Well, this is a bad time of year for a real honeymoon. Maybe later we'll get away for a day or two, but Katy…"

"An affair before you know each other. A baby before he even knows your name. Everything is backwards, but then who am I to judge? Maybe this is what it took to bring you together finally. I think it is time for you to have a few days with just you two. Do you like him?"

"I love him," Milli said.

"I didn't ask you if you loved him. I asked you if you liked him. Love is important but like is more important. If you don't like him, all the love in the world can't make you have a good relationship. We are keeping Katy for a few days, and tomorrow morning you can get in that little plane of yours and fly down to the cabin on the shore in Mexico. Stay with him, with no one else around from Sunday until Wednesday, and then come home. If you've got stars in your eyes, I'll know you like him as well as love him. If you fly home and time and familiarity has killed the love, then it wasn't meant to be."

"Momma, you're telling me to go on a honeymoon before the wedding."

"Exactly. You had a baby before the wedding. Why not have the honeymoon now and make sure?"

Milli kissed her on the cheek. "Thank you, Momma. I love you."

"And we'll have a big wedding?"

Milli threw back her head and laughed. "So I'm to pay for the honeymoon? Yes, Momma, you plan whatever you want... except the dress. I'm wearing something very simple. I already have a daughter and besides, Beau is wearing jeans, and I don't want to overdo it. Flowers, catering, band, whatever else, I leave in your hands... if I bring him back alive."

Chapter 21

MILLI SET THE PLANE DOWN ON A CRUDE RUNWAY OF hard, baked earth right next to a small cabin on the water's edge. At first Beau couldn't believe they were actually going away for a few days, and he couldn't believe her mother was the one who insisted they have some time alone. But there they were with a rough wooden cabin and a lot of water in front of them. No baby between them. Even though he adored his daughter, he had to pinch himself to realize he had three days alone with Milli.

"You flew better this time. You didn't even make your knuckles white squeezing the hell out of the arm of the seat. A few more times and you'll want to take over the controls for me."

"Not on your life, darlin'. Pinch me. I know this is a dream for sure."

He held his arm toward her. She grabbed a chunk of skin and pinched hard.

He jerked it back. "Ouch!"

"Just doing what you said. Are going to sit here forever, or are we going inside the cabin and make love?"

She was out of the plane and walking before he could get his seat belt undone.

"Wait a minute," he called out.

He dropped the suitcases at the front door

She fished in her purse for a key and opened the door.

He picked her up and carried her over the threshold.

"I think this is what they do in the movies and, even though the paperwork isn't finished yet, this is our honeymoon." He kicked the door shut with the back of his boot. The kiss began when the door slammed and didn't end until he laid her on the bed.

"Paperwork?" she asked.

"Yes, paperwork. In my heart I'm already married to you and have been for a while, Miss Camilla Torres. We just have to have a marriage ceremony and do the paperwork to make you Mrs. Beau Luckadeau." He kicked off his boots.

"Well, kind sir, you don't intend to waste any time, now do you?"

"No, ma'am. You going to unbutton this shirt or you want me to do it?"

His blue eyes were hungry and his body already hard in anticipation. She looked him in the eye and started unsnapping his shirt—slowly, a snap at a time, kissing bare skin with every snap. He moaned and began to undress her just as slowly, tugging her jean shorts down to her ankles, tossing them on the floor and kissing his way back up to her belly button.

She shuddered.

Somehow he shed his shirt and socks and finished undressing her without breaking the kiss. His tongue slipped between her full, sexy lips and found its soul mate waiting. She tugged at his hips, her body begging him to make the aching need go away.

Two starving souls searching for fulfillment found it again. Just like in the back bedroom of a trailer. Just like in the hay. They fell asleep in each other's arms, sleeping that deep, contented rest that comes only after weeks of pure sexual starvation are satisfied.

Her stomach woke her up, growling and threatening real starvation if she didn't find something to feast upon other than Beau's muscular, sensual body. She snuggled closer to him and kicked at the thin sheet tangled up at their feet. She tried to go back to sleep and ignore her stomach's demands. She was too tired to crawl out of a love nest and cook lunch.

"Hungry?" he said.

"Starving. Momma said she'd have someone stock the cabinets and the fridge but I'd rather do this all day." She nibbled on his earlobe and hoped her growling stomach would be quiet.

He sat up on the edge of the bed just about the time a spider floated down from a web on the ceiling to land beside Milli's hand. "This kind of activity makes me ravenous. Let's make lunch and then lie on the beach like honeymooners."

She opened her eyes and saw the big, black furry bug at the same time.

"Kill it!" she gasped.

"What? My superwoman who can do anything but knit is afraid of a plain old house spider?"

"Kill it now!" she demanded.

He smashed it and then gathered her shaking body close to his. "Hey, it's just a bug. It's more scared of you than you are of it."

"Wanna bet? I hate them sumbitches. I'd rather square off with a coiled rattler than a spider. They're only slightly smaller than King Kong and meaner than a grizzly with an ingrown toenail."

"Okay, honey, I'll kill the spiders and you fly the airplane and we'll get along fine. Now, let's see what's hiding in the refrigerator and make lunch."

She slung her legs off the side of the bed and opened one of the suitcases. She pulled on a pair of bikini panties and a kimono-style, black silk robe, sashed the middle, and padded barefoot to the refrigerator.

The whole cabin was one room, with a bed and dresser on the west end and the kitchen area on the east end, and a small sitting space between the two. It was furnished with leftovers from her Jiminez grandparents' home. A floral love seat, two mismatched recliners, a four-poster bed and a dresser that didn't match. Milli loved every piece and had childhood memories of each one.

Beau slipped into a pair of underwear and cut-off jean shorts and followed her.

"Eggs, bacon, cheese, onions, peppers, picante, tortillas… even if they are packaged and not fresh. We'll have breakfast burritos and then stretch out in the sun for the afternoon and see if I like you."

He pulled out a cane-bottomed chair and sat down at the small kitchen table. "Like me? I love you and you want to see if you like me after what we just did?"

"Yep, Momma says these three days are to find out if I like you. She says it's evident I love you, but a marriage can't be built on love alone. We have to like each other. You earned a bunch of brownie points when you killed the spider, so I think I may like you. We'll go to the beach for a while and see if we continue to like each other. Who knows what might happen? We usually end up fighting every time we get together with no one else around." She cracked the eggs and waited for the butter to melt in an iron skillet she put on the stove.

"I see. Well, bring on a horde of spiders and let me redeem myself in the like business. What can I do to help? I'm a pretty damn good cook myself. I can make omelets to die for."

She leaned forward and the belt of the robe came undone, showing her naked body from the top of her bikini underpants to her neck. She stopped what she was doing, straddled his lap, and kissed him soundly.

"Someday, darlin', I'll let you cook, but right now you just sit here and regain your strength. I may need to have another session in bed before we go out to the beach. So, do you want to argue about this cooking?"

"No, ma'am," he grinned.

She kissed him and very, very slowly went back to the stove.

"How far are we from civilization?" His voice was only a little hoarse. That was good. He was afraid he'd be unable to do anything but growl and drag her back to bed.

"About two city blocks, but don't worry, unless we want to see people, we won't see anyone. Momma's parents own this place and they live a little ways over the dunes back there." She nodded toward the north. "We might be gracious enough before we leave on Wednesday morning to go thank them for the supplies. That is, if we like each other by then. If we don't and we decide to call off the whole marriage, then it's best you don't meet them. Momma might be understanding about a honeymoon before the wedding, but Grandpoppy Jiminez would probably shoot you or stick a knife in your liver if he thought you'd just slept with me all these days and didn't intend to marry me. Now, how hot do you like your eggs?"

"You can't make them too hot for me."

"Oh, yeah? Well, big boy, we'll see if I can't make you eat your words. Habaneros have brought many a good Anglo to his knees."

"What the hell is a habanero?"

"It's the hottest pepper in the whole world," she said.

"Ain't nothing hotter than jalapeño."

"We'll see."

Beau braced himself, but he was ready for a mouthful of spicy, wonderful eggs wrapped up in a tortilla shell. What he bit into was a mouthful of pure hell. His eyes watered, his nose ran, and his stomach came close to sending the first mouthful right back up.

Milli sat across from him and watched his expressions intently. "Hot enough for you?"

He yanked up the napkin and wiped his eyes, then blew his nose loudly on a paper towel he found on the cabinet. When he found his voice again, hiding somewhere down deep, next to his rebellious stomach, he coughed and sputtered.

He exhaled and sucked in a mouthful of air to cool his burning tongue, then grabbed up the glass of tea she'd set on the place mat before him.

"Guess maybe it is hot enough." She kept eating.

He nodded because he couldn't force enough wind from his fiery esophagus to utter a single word. Even the tea didn't seem to soothe the blistery feeling.

She buttered one side of a tortilla and rolled it up like

a crepe before she handed it to him. "Try a bite of this. It'll help, I promise."

He knew she was lying. Nothing would help. Nothing short of major surgery to replace the first degree burns from his tongue to his colon.

Oh, my god! When this stuff hits bottom it's going to set me on fire again.

It took all the trust he had to believe her. He bit off a chunk of the tortilla and was amazed at the soothing effect it had on its way down to his stomach.

"It's the butter. It takes the fire out. Here, give me your burrito and I'll eat it. I made one with jalapeños for you."

He finally found his voice. "That was the hottest sumbitch in the world. I'm not so sure I do like you right now. You damn near killed me, woman."

She pointed her fork at him. "Don't be calling me woman. I'm Milli or sugar or honey or sweetheart, but I'm not 'woman.' That's what white trash call their wives. Pretty hot little sucker, ain't it?" She bit off a second bite of the burrito and then followed it with a piece of buttered tortilla.

"I ain't about to fight with anyone who can eat something that hot. Where do those things grow? On the back forty in hell?"

"Somewhere close to that, I'm sure. And I ain't about to fight with anyone who can whup a big mean spider, so I guess we aren't in trouble, yet. Chow down. I promise I didn't even cut up the jalapeños with the same knife I used on the habanero, so it's mild."

"There is a heaven!" He took a bite of the burrito she put in front of him. "I'd begun to think there was only hell."

She grinned.

She remembered when she was a little girl at her grandparents house on this same property and they introduced her to the habanero pepper. She thought she would suffocate to death before she chased it with a buttered tortilla. She thought about the hacienda where they were probably taking an afternoon siesta right now: her very brown grandfather, who was full-blooded Mexican, and her grandmother, who at the age of seventy-two was as blonde as Beau and had eyes just as blue.

He refilled their tea glasses. "Penny for your thoughts."

"Remember, pennies don't buy my thoughts. They cost you a helluva lot more than that."

"I see where Casey gets her sweet little feminine way of saying things," he laughed.

"Got a problem with the way I talk?"

"No, ma'am. You ready to swim off some of these calories?"

"Peppers ain't got no calories. That's the one good thing about them. Eat them all day and never worry about weight. Do you think I'm fat?"

"What in the world brought that on? Of course you're not fat."

"I told you the story already. I was in the sixth grade and a couple of blonde-haired snooty little girls called me a fat Mexican bitch. I got expelled from school for three days."

"Why did you get expelled because they were rude?" He led her to the door, picking up a couple of beach towels from a hook beside the door on the way.

"Because I knocked Myrna's front tooth out and broke Lisa's nose." She said it as if she was telling him the sky was blue and the clouds were white. "And I decided right then nobody was ever going to call me that name again. You really don't think I'm fat? Wait a minute. I've got to put my bikini on."

"Why, you can't tan in the nude?"

She dropped the robe in the middle of the floor and stretched a bright yellow bikini top on. "Not on your life. If Grandpoppy decided to sneak a peek at us with his binoculars I'd better have something on my body, even if it's a bikini. Besides, stretch marks from the baby aren't all gone."

He trailed a row of kisses down to her naval. "Hey, you're beautiful, stretch marks and all. Sure you want to swim?"

"No, but we'd better at least put in an appearance on the beach."

They laid on their stomachs, holding hands across the warm sand separating them, for an hour. He was glad, as he laid there in the warm sand with the hot sun beating down upon his back, that things had worked out the way they did.

"Hey, tell me about your grandparents who live just two blocks back there."

Her grandmother had told Milli the love story so many times, Milli knew it by heart. She wondered if her grandfather ever tricked her English grandmother with a habanero pepper, and chuckled at the memory of Beau's blue eyes swimming in tears.

"What's so funny?"

"Nothing, darlin'. I was just thinkin' that if you get

hateful with me and start calling me 'woman,' I can always just dump a few habaneros in your supper."

He picked her up and waded out into the water. "You're a vixen. Say you'll never, ever be mean to me or I'll dunk you."

She wrapped her arms tightly around his neck. "And when you do, you'll go down with me. Where I go, you shall go. My dunking shall be your dunking." She intoned like a preacher at a revival.

"Then we shall go together." He fell backwards with her and water covered them both.

She came up spluttering. "And now we are no more Methodists, but full-fledged Baptists. And my hair will be a fright for the rest of the day. We'll see if you like a wicked sea witch by the end. Which reminds me—I forgot to tell you, there is no phone, no television, no radio, no CD player, or anything else from the outside world in the cabin. I do believe there are a few cattle books left there by Grandpoppy, who must have a little reprieve from boring sex when he brings my grandmother here."

He kissed her neck and saw a glimmer of light behind the cabin. "Well, maybe I won't get so bored I have to read old cattle magazines. Don't look now, but I think he's checking to see if you have on your bikini."

She wiggled closer to him and saw the light reflecting. So one or both of them couldn't wait to see what the new grandson-in-law looked like. She bet her grandmother was dancing a ring around herself as she looked at this good-looking blond giant. She'd wanted a blond, blue-eyed son so badly, and all she got was a house full of dark-haired beautiful daughters.

"You were going to tell me about them," Beau reminded her.

"It's a love story with a bittersweet ending. Grandmother came from Rio County, Texas. That's one of the border counties over in Texas. Anyway she came to the University of Mexico to study Spanish. She made friends with my grandfather's sister and went home with her for a weekend and there was her older brother. She says they were both thunderstruck. She says he looked like a darker version of Clark Gable and he says she looked just like a goddess with her blonde hair and blue eyes."

"Blue eyes?" Beau was stunned.

"Yes, blue eyes. They were in love, but do you know what it was like in the '40s for a rich, white Texas girl to fall in love with a full-blooded Mexican boy? Even if his parents were every bit as rich as hers? I can tell you, it wasn't easy. I guess her father came close to a heart attack when she told them she was marrying a Mexican. He disowned her and refused to have her name mentioned in his house ever again. So they lived in Mexico, right back there for about eight years; then her parents both died in a plane crash and, since she was the only child, the property was hers. So she and my Grandpoppy took all five girls to Rio County to raise them in the United States. They kept their place here and came for vacations and holidays. Now that they're retired they spend a lot of time here and less in Rio County. Momma is the oldest. You met some of the sisters at the party Saturday night. When Momma went to college in the panhandle, she met Daddy and they settled down right there. Aunt Gloria met a man in college a couple of years after that. His parents were of the hippy generation and never married. Anyway, I guess Grandpoppy like to have died when he found out Uncle Jim was illegitimate. I figured he'd go up in smoke over Katy, but he didn't. I guess after Grandmother set him straight about Uncle Jim's heritage, it didn't matter about Katy so much."

"I sure wouldn't want Katy dating some lowlife, either."

"Hey, Uncle Jim is a medical doctor now. He's not a lowlife, even if his mother is a little eccentric and never got married," she snipped back.

"Well—" he snapped.

"And Katy is illegitimate, too. Or had you forgotten?"

"She won't be for long. Besides that's not what I asked. What changed his mind?"

"Grandmother reminded him about what happened to them and he straightened up pretty quick. I guess Grandpoppy didn't want to lose a daughter."

"Smart man. I can't imagine doing anything to lose Katy."

Milli resisted the urge to wave at them. "Now stand up gently and carry me back to the cabin, kissing me all the way. Let's at least give them something to make a long distance call back to west Texas about. It would be a shame if they missed their siesta and didn't see anything. Make it look just like a scene from the movies. Betcha we can hear them sighing if you do."

He rose to his full height then swooped her up with one arm to hug her close to his chest. Then as if she were no more than a feather pillow, he picked her up dramatically and kissed her long and sensuously as he carried her to the porch. If they turned their heads just right both of them imagined they really could hear sighs.

"That's enough. That should fry the telephone wires between here and Texas. Bet they're racing to the house to see who gets to talk first. And Grandmother will be in hog heaven when she tells them how beautiful you are."

His eyes never left her face as he reached around and unhooked the top of her bikini. "It'll be enough when I say it's enough. Besides, they might be waiting out there to see if we come back out and they'll know it was all a farce."

"Was it a farce, Beau? It felt pretty damned real to me."

"Darlin', everything between the two of us is real, and right. Even a little exaggeration for your grandparents is real, and don't you ever doubt it."

Chapter 22

BEAU FOLLOWED THE PREACHER FROM THE BACK DOOR of the sale barn to the platform. All five of his brothers walked slowly behind him. James, who was in charge of the music, put a tape into the stereo system and Conway Twitty's gravelly voice came through singing "The Rose." Three of his sisters-in-law, and both of Milli's brothers' wives, appeared at the front door of the barn. All of them had been bridesmaids several times and they floated down the aisle with grace and dignity even in their flannel shirts, jeans, and sneakers. Then Casey, who was standing in for Milli, appeared at the door on the arm of John Torres.

An hour later the wedding rehearsal was over. They practiced the whole thing twice with Milli watching from the front row of folding chairs. The entire building had been transformed from a cattle sale barn to a wedding chapel. The walls were literally draped with thousands of yards of ivory illusion. Hurricane lamps burned brightly on all the tables already laid with ivory lace tablecloths, and tomorrow the florist would bring fresh roses, freesia, and trailing English ivy to encircle the lamps. Huge pew bows with silk roses held drapes of tulle from the balcony where buyers usually looked down upon the cattle being offered for sale.

"Well, son, this is sure enough a transformation." Milli's maternal grandmother took Beau's arm and smiled at him, still in awe that she finally had a relative who looked like her. And even more so that in the past half century, society had changed enough that two cultures could meet in the middle of this barn tomorrow night, and all that would be offered would be blessings and love.

"Yes, ma'am." He searched for Milli in a sea of dark hair and every shade of blond in the world.

"So did you decide you like each other?" The grandmother's blue eyes glittered.

"Yes, ma'am," Beau smiled. "But there was a moment there when I wasn't too sure when I was trying to figure out if she'd plumb killed me graveyard dead with that damn hot pepper."

Grandmother Jiminez laughed loudly. "I remember the first time Carlos talked me into eating one of those demons. Lord, I thought the devil had grabbed me by the ankle and pulled me straight down to hell. It told him I would never trust him again."

"I know the feeling," Beau nodded.

Milli appeared from nowhere to hug him close. "You monopolizing my groom?"

"If I could, I would. Pretty as he is, you'd better not let him out of your sight. But that old Mexican over there wouldn't let me stand close to him for very long without making an excuse to see what we were talking about. He's still jealous, you know, even after more than fifty years. Now, where have you two put my fair-haired great-granddaughter? All this time I thought my genes had finally come through to mark one of the Jiminez children. Then I find out Katy's father is a fair-haired, blue-eyed cowboy."

"Oh, Grandmother, you know she got those pretty eyes from you. Beau gave her the dimples."

"Don't you believe it. She's the spitting image of this man. Now go on and get some food. Just before midnight you two have to go your separate ways, you know. You better enjoy these moments, and besides, tradition has it that the bride and groom must be served first. You are holding up the line."

"Yes, ma'am," Beau said.

Milli whispered as they made their way to the tables, "Aren't you glad we've already had the honeymoon? It would be a helluva thing to endure all this and be thinking of nothing but a bed in a motel room."

He tilted her chin up for a kiss. "Hey, I'm always thinking of ways to get you to the bedroom, but tomorrow night it will be legal, the paperwork will be finished and formally filed, and honey, it don't matter where we are, it will be a wonderful honeymoon."

"Oh?"

"That's right. Our bedroom will be a honeymoon for the next fifty or sixty years. And then maybe we'll go back down to the beach to refresh our memories of when we decided to like each other." He bent forward just enough to kiss her again, oblivious to all the relatives.

"Oh, I've got a present for you." She pulled an envelope from her purse and handed it to him.

"To open now?"

"Yep, right now. They'll wait another minute for us. I was going to give it to you in private later, but we probably won't have a more private time than right now. They're going to eat and visit and then it will be midnight. They all say I can't see you from midnight tonight until the wedding tomorrow night. Momma says it'll bring bad luck to the marriage. And she's not about to have something happen right here at the end to sabotage the marriage. So open it."

He tore into the envelope to find a check made out to the Bar M Ranch for a hundred thousand dollars and it was signed by Milli Torres.

"What is this?"

"That is what my herd brought. You are going to reinvest it in Angus cattle. I know you said that you'd fence off a section for my cattle, but a house divided cannot stand. So we won't have a ranch divided, either. Katy is legally a Luckadeau as of today when the papers were signed, and I'll be legally a Luckadeau tomorrow night. The Luckadeaus raise Angus cattle. So buy more Angus cattle for our ranch, darling."

"But."

She laid a finger over his lips. "No buts. And don't be thinking I'm going to let you go buy cows all by yourself. Remember, whither thou goest, I shall go, if it's under the water or to the cattle sale. Besides, I know a good Angus as well as you do. And you're not using my money for a bunch of low down, useless culls."

"You sayin' I don't know how to buy cattle?" he challenged.

"I'm sayin' you might be a Luckadeau, but I'm a Torres and we cut our teeth in a sale barn, so I'm goin' with you. Besides, by damn, you never know when Amanda or Jennifer or some barroom rosy just like them might take a fancy to what's hiding under your belt buckle. And darlin', I don't share what's mine with nobody. And that's a fact."

John Torres heard the last of the argument as he came to inform them supper was ready to be served. "Just say 'Yes, dear.' She gets that temper from the Jiminez side of the family. And I'm tellin' you right now, it don't mellow with age. The only redeeming quality is that they're passionate in everything they do."

He winked and looped an arm through his daughter's arm and his son-in-law's, and walking between them, he led them to the table laden down with a combination of Mexican and Anglo foods.

Beau lay on his back in the bunkhouse, surrounded by the snores of both his and Milli's male relatives. Soft rain peppered the metal roof and then a low rumble of thunder sounded in the distance. Thank goodness, the wedding was going to be inside the barn. It wouldn't matter if the grass was wet or if it stormed—like it had that morning when he found Milli in the pasture putting Jim's tractor in the barn.

One memory led to another. There she was in the off-white lace dress, sitting in a chair on the edge of the reception room at the wedding; in his arms at the trailer; cussing at him and threatening to shoot him; when his heart remembered her and he couldn't; hot habanero peppers; three wonderful days of honeymooning; and coming home. Suddenly he wanted to ride out to the barn where they met that morning when they made love for the second time. She wouldn't be there, but he could stand in the doorway and smell the soft rain and hay and besides, he couldn't sleep anyway. Call it nervous jitters or just plain fear that something would go wrong at the last minute, since it always did. Like they all said, "He's lucky in everything but he sure ain't lucky in love."

Milli turned the covers back on the four-poster oak cannonball bed, and heard the low rumble of thunder just as her head hit the pillow where she would spend every night for the rest of her life. Only starting tomorrow night, Beau would be right beside her, and the bed wouldn't seem nearly so big and empty.

Before she turned out the light, she looked at the dress hanging in the closet. She'd argued with her mother, declaring the whole time she was going to be married in the off-white lace dress Beau saw her wearing first, but in the end she lost the argument. Although she steadfastly refused to wear a big, white dress and veil, she did let her mother talk her into a simple ivory satin sheath with a wide portrait collar of lace. She would wear satin lace-up boots and Jana was styling her hair in a French roll with rosebuds worked into the curls at the top of the twist.

She went to the dresser and picked up the satin box holding her wedding present from Beau: a replica of the Bar M brand in 18 carat gold and diamonds, hanging from a gold chain. He told everyone at rehearsal she legally belonged to the ranch now, but in private, when he kissed her good night one last time before they were married, he told her it was to remind her where her heart was for all eternity.

She forgot about the dress, and laid the diamond brand down. She heard another low rumble of thunder and remembered the day it stormed and she met Beau in the barn. She hummed "How Do I Live." The singer asked how she would live without him. Milli wondered how she'd live without Beau. It wasn't something she wanted to answer, because life without him wasn't life at all.

She threw back the covers and opened the drapes to watch the raindrops fall in the light between the window and the glow of the porch light in the bunkhouse. He was just fifty yards across the lawn and through that door, and in twenty-four hours, all the relatives would be gone. She shut the curtains and sat on the edge of the bed. She had the strangest notion to saddle up Wild Fire and race out to the barn.

She slipped her jeans back on and found her work boots in the closet. She didn't bother putting on a bra, since no one was going to see her anyway. She saddled Wild Fire in the dark and in minutes she was racing across the pasture. They cleared the first fence with the expertise of an English lady riding to the hounds in hot pursuit of the foxes. She thought she'd better fit the mold of a gypsy out chasing coyotes in the moonlight and rain. All she needed was a big flowing skirt of many colors and a toe ring. She already had the dark hair and eyes and a wild streak a mile wide.

The barn door was open when she arrived. The wind must have blown it open. Anyone in their right mind wouldn't be out on a rainy night like this. All the relatives were sleeping soundly in the house. The bunkhouse on both the Bar M and Lazy Z and several motels in Ardmore were full. If a bunch of kids, who'd been out chasing coyotes, holed up in this barn, they'd better be on their knees with their little hands together in a prayerful pose when she got there. Because if they'd cut the fences again, she intended to read them a piece of her mind they wouldn't want to hear.

She rode inside with intentions of tearing up a bunch of half-grown boys, and was surprised to find the barn empty except for Beau's horse nibbling from a feed bucket and tethered to a support post.

"Hey, you better get on back home before you see me or I see you in better light and we have bad luck the rest of our lives." His voice floated down from the loft.

"What are you doing here?" She was climbing the ladder to the loft before he could say another word.

"Same thing you are. My heart said 'go to the barn' and smell the hay and listen to the rain, and remember the day that turned your life around. So I listened to it and here I am."

She put her arms around his waist and hugged him as if he was a lifeboat in a wild and windy ocean. "I heard the same thing. I love you so much it hurts."

"But do you like me?" He pushed her back, yet held both her hands so she wouldn't disappear in a foggy vapor.

"I'd like you even better if you'd allow me to unbutton that shirt. I promise I'll button it right back when I'm finished with your body." She shook her hands free from his and started unfastening the top button.

"With my blessings, but you know we have to be at home before daylight, safe in our beds. I sure don't intend to face your mother if she finds out we cheated on the midnight rule. That'd be one helluva way to get started off in the Torres family. Your brothers might even take me to the nearest oak tree and hang me with an old worn-out rope."

"So we'll get married right now and there can't be any bad luck. I promise to love you, treat you with respect, and make you a wife you can be proud of. I promise to give you enough hell every day so that we can make up and have heaven every night." She looked into his eyes as she recited her vows.

"And I promise to love you with my whole heart, never leave you, and give you tit for tat, for the rest of our lives," he said.

The next evening the preacher put the finishing touch on the marriage in front of their families and friends. "By the authority vested in me by the state of Oklahoma I now pronounce Camillia Kathryn Torres and Anthony Beau Luckadeau man and wife. Beau, you may now kiss your bride."

"Yes, sir." Beau took Milli in his arms. "The spell is broken, my lady. I'm now lucky in love and will be throughout all eternity."

He kissed her.

She gave him her heart and soul forever.

The End

About the Author

Carolyn Brown, an award-winning author of more than forty books, credits her eclectic family for her humor and writing ideas. She was born in Texas but grew up in southern Oklahoma where she and her husband, Charles, a retired English teacher, make their home. They have three grown children and enough grandchildren to keep them young.

For more from Carolyn Brown, read on
for a preview of

ONE *Lucky* COWBOY

GETTING *Lucky*

ONE *Lucky* COWBOY

SLADE TRIED TO INTIMIDATE THE PETITE, DISHWATER blonde with a glare meant to drop her stone cold dead on the spot. Even if it didn't work, she'd know exactly how he felt about the situation and that he wasn't buying into her act. The fair-haired con artist with pecan-colored brown eyes would be gone in twenty-four hours and that wasn't a threat; it was a solid promise. He might have just lost the first battle with his grandmother, but he'd be damned if he would lose the whole war.

Jane didn't blink when she and the tall, blond cowboy locked eyes. She needed a place to hide for six weeks and this was perfect. If he thought he could run her off, he had cow chips for brains. The opportunity had dropped in her lap at the bus station like an answered prayer from heaven. She could endure his cold accusations and he could damn sure live with the situation for a few weeks. She'd stay out of his way as much as possible. She'd just seen how the evil male brain worked and it was scary.

Nellie Luckadeau, Slade's grandmother, could have danced a jig in a pig trough half full of fermented slop. Never had she seen Slade so angry. He was the cold, calm, collected, and slow-moving cowboy who never had a temper fit. She'd begun to think he'd never feel anything again and suddenly he was ready to chew up railroad spikes all because she'd brought home a stray, homeless girl. Well, praise the Lord and pass the biscuits, her prayers had been answered.

Slade shifted his big blue eyes to his grandmother. "I can't believe you drove to Wichita Falls. I told you I'd be here as soon as I could."

"Ellen wanted to get home this afternoon and she'd have missed her bus. Damned near did anyway, what with the wreck and all. Don't get your underbritches in a wad. I drove. I backed out into a car. I've got damned good insurance that'll pay for the damages and if I didn't, I expect I could handle the amount. I was lucky to be sittin' there when Jane got off the bus. Now I've got a driver and you can get on back to your ranchin' and quit your bellyachin' about me hiring her. She told me on the way from Wichita Falls that this was her lucky break. Well, I reckon it's mine, too. And if you'll admit it, it's your lucky break because damn it all, Slade Luckadeau, you don't have to worry about drivin' me anywhere long as she's here."

"She's not a driver, she's a con artist. I bet Jane Day isn't even her name. It's so close to Jane Doe that she probably picked it from the air when you asked her. It doesn't even show any imagination. She's here to swindle you, Granny. Wait and see. She'll end up with everything you own before she leaves." He stormed out of the house. His boots sounded like bolts of thunder and his spurs jingled like a wind chime as he stomped across the wooden porch.

"Don't worry about him, Jane. He's just got a burr in his britches. He'll get over it. Let me show you to your room. But before I do, look me in the eye and tell me you aren't a con artist," Nellie said.

Jane took a step forward, looked up, and met the tall older woman's eyes. "I am not a con artist. I'm not here to rob you of anything. I just need a place to stay for a few weeks. I'm grateful for the job and I'll work like a mule."

"That's all I need to know," Nellie said. "Follow me."

Jane picked up a stuffed duffel bag and carried it through a living room that looked seldom used, a dining room with a long table that could easily seat a dozen people, a den where most of the living went on by the look of the well-used, overstuffed sofa and recliners, and down a hallway. She would never have guessed she'd end up on a ranch south of Ringgold, Texas when she left Greenville, Mississippi two days before. But she wasn't about to look a gift horse in the mouth. Like she'd said, she'd work like a mule for six weeks and then go back home to settle matters.

"Old house started out as a two-bedroom frame back in the beginning," Nellie said. "My husband's father built it for his new wife. Then the kids came along and they added this wing with an extra three bedrooms. When my husband bought out his sibling's interest in the ranch and we got married, he added another wing for us. It's got a sitting room and a bedroom. Sitting room turned into his office and my sewing and quilting room pretty quick. My boys lived on this wing the whole time they was growing up. We saved the original two bedrooms for guests. Slade lives in this room."

She motioned toward a shut door. "Here's where you can toss your belongings and sleep at night. Reckon the rest of the time I'll keep you busy. Make yourself at home and get settled in. We serve up three meals a day.

We'll start dinner in an hour. That's for the whole work crew. Part of the deal we've always made on the Double L: a good salary and dinner at twelve sharp. Supper is flexible depending on what's going on. If Slade is cutting hay, we might not eat until eight or nine. If he's able to get in early, it's around six. It's not as big as dinner because the help all goes home to their families. Just the three of us at that time. You. Me. Slade. Sometimes my sister, Ellen. She spends a lot of time over here. Ignore Slade if he gets testy."

"Yes, ma'am. I'll be out there in an hour to help you," Jane said.

"Might want to stretch out. Don't reckon you got much sleep on that bus, did you?"

"No, ma'am, I didn't. And thank you," Jane said.

"And no thanks due. You'll work for the money I promised you and you'll have a room and board as long as you want to stay here." Nellie shut the door.

Jane threw herself on the full-sized bed, laced her hands behind her head, and stared at her surroundings. It had definitely been a boy's room at one time. Cranberry and ecru plaid curtains hung at the window. A piecework quilt using the same colors covered the bed. The iron headboard and footboard had been painted a soft buttery yellow. A mirror hung above a six-drawer dresser with family pictures arranged from the larger eight by ten sizes at the back down to small ones in the front. The light tan carpet had been replaced recently and still looked new. The walls were painted a soft antique white but were bare.

She glanced at the door. No lock. She shared a wing with the abominable grandson, Slade, with no way to keep him from sneaking into her room and smothering her to death at night. At least she would know there was a possibility she'd be dead by morning and it wouldn't come as a total surprise from the hands of the man she'd promised to love forever amen.

Tired beyond words, she couldn't be still. She popped up and opened the duffle bag. Three pair of jeans, three T-shirts, a dozen pair of underpants, three bras, two pair of Nikes, and a few pair of socks. She had the whole thing unpacked and put away in one empty dresser drawer and the closet in less than ten minutes. She could easily make do with that much for the next few weeks. If she needed anything for a special occasion, she could always purchase it with the money she'd be paid each Friday night.

That almost brought a smile to her face. Who would have thought a week ago that she'd be working for a hundred dollars a week plus room and board? It would have been the biggest joke in the whole state of Mississippi. Ellacyn Jane Hayes working on a ranch for a tiny fraction of her normal salary, without her fancy clothes, cars, and credit cards.

She dug around in her purse for her cell phone to call her best friend Celia and whined out loud. She had vowed she wouldn't miss her bank account or the credit cards she'd been wise enough to leave behind, or even her business, if she could just be safe. But she really, really did miss that cell phone.

"Damn you, John," she mumbled. She missed her friend, Celia, even more than all the clothing in her closets, more than the laptop computer that she relied on so heavily, even more than chocolate.

She'd thrown the phone out the window somewhere between Dallas and Wichita Falls when she found the tracking device hidden under the battery flap. Finding it had been a fluke. She'd dropped the phone on the floor and the back fell off. When she picked it up, she recognized the little shiny metal thing immediately. She'd slung the phone out the window into the tall grass along the roadside and berated herself for all the expensive subterfuge she'd already sacrificed. The plane ticket from Jackson to New York hadn't been cheap and had eaten up most of her cash. She'd left her Cadillac in the airport parking lot and taken a taxi to the bus station, where she'd bought a ticket to Dallas. No one would look for her on a bus.

She'd written a note that she had gotten cold feet and was on her way to New York for a few weeks to think things through. John would have gone there immediately if it hadn't been for that damned cell phone tracker. Oh, well, it had happened and it couldn't be helped. Now she was as safe as possible, hidden away on a ranch near Ringgold, Texas, population one hundred according to the history lesson Nellie had provided on the drive from Wichita Falls to the Double L Ranch.

She pulled the curtains back and got a view of Black Angus cattle just outside the fenced yard. Farther out she could see Slade on a horse rounding cattle into a huge semi truck. It was definitely a working ranch and Slade was a bona fide cowboy. He cocked his head toward the house and she dropped the curtain faster than if it had been on fire. Surely he couldn't have seen her, but that glare he'd settled upon her when he found out his grandmother had picked her up in the bus station like a stray puppy was enough to give her cold chills. On second thought, those blue eyes could most likely see well enough through trees, cattle hind ends, and glass windows to fry her where she stood.

To say that Slade was angry was the understatement of the century. He'd never been so mad in his whole life. Not even the day his mother shoved him crying out of the car and disappeared with her new husband in a cloud of Texas dust. Granny had no business driving more than thirty miles to Wichita Falls to the bus station in the first place. All she had to do was exercise a little patience and he'd have taken Aunt Ellen to catch the bus back to Amarillo. Damn it all, he'd have taken time to drive the feisty old lady all the way to Amarillo, if Granny would have given him a chance.

But oh, no, she had to take matters in her own hands and get behind the wheel even though she couldn't see jack shit. It had been a year since the doctor had told her about the macular degeneration and said she wasn't to drive anymore. Slade should have taken her license away from her then, but he'd thought she had more sense than to endanger her own life as well as others. Well, he'd been wrong but he'd see to it he had that license in his possession before nightfall. And that little blonde was going right back to the train station come morning. He'd never liked brown-eyed women and he could see through a con from a mile away on a foggy day.

Heat rose up from the ground in waves but he didn't notice it or the sweat pouring down his back, soaking the chambray shirt in big wet circles. It was June in north Texas and sweat was part of life.

"What you so mad about? Never seen you act like this," Vince Johnson asked. His father was the foreman of the Double L Ranch and the tall, gangly young man had worked for Slade in the summers since he was barely big enough to sit a horse.

"Granny drove to town, backed into a car, drug home a stray woman, and is acting like nothing happened," Slade said.

"It's the woman that's making you the maddest. Granny has driven to town before. She's had accidents before and you've never gotten in a snit like this."

Slade turned his horse to gather in another bull without answering. Damn kids these days. What made them so wise, anyway? He didn't remember being that smart when he was sixteen. So what if it was the woman that brought on the fury? Granny had no right to hire live-in help without consulting him. They had always talked things over, hashing through the pros and cons until an agreement was reached.

He pulled a bottle of water from his saddle bag and drank long and deep, frowning at the house the whole time. He'd never liked being reminded of his vulnerability where his mother was concerned and he'd hated the idea of being blindsided. Not that Jane Doe or Day or whatever fictitious name she pulled out of her ass was anything like his mother, who was a tall, gorgeous blonde and could put Marilyn Monroe to shame. Pretty enough to be a model. Trashy enough to entice men. Smart enough to know the difference between rich and poor men. These days she had her nails and hair done in Los Angeles and the line of ex-husbands was longer than his arm.

Jane Day was pretty in an impish sort of way. She had dirty-blonde hair cut in layers from her chin to her shoulders, big brown eyes with perfectly arched brows, and a wide full mouth that would appeal to some men but reminded Slade too much of the pouting Marilyn look. It was that mouth that reminded him of his mother and brought on the memories.

The resemblance ended there, though. He would give credit where it was due and admit she had some redeemable qualities in that short little body with a waist so small he could span it with his big hands. After all he wasn't blind. Neither was he dumb. The woman was after something, and she wasn't finding it on his ranch.

Available November 2009

From

GETTING *Lucky*

JULIE DONAVAN, THE NEW KINDERGARTEN TEACHER, was on her knees consoling a little boy named Chuck on the first day of school when she noticed movement coming in the door. She gasped when she looked up. Her eyes widened and high color filled her cheeks. The most striking cowboy she'd ever laid eyes on just walked through the door. Well, she had laid eyes upon him one time before, but that time they'd been two point five sheets to the wind. One less drink that night and they'd have stopped before they got to the motel. Two more and neither would have remembered a damn thing. But the combination had been just right and he was there in her kindergarten classroom in Saint Jo, Texas.

Her first thought was "Damn, he even looks better with hair."

Her second was "What in the hell is he doing in Saint Jo, Texas?"

Her third was, "Oh, shit, what do I do now?"

The man stopped in front of her and looked down. "Hello, we are the Luckadeaus. This is my daughter, Lizzy; she's in your class this year."

And I'm the woman you met in Dallas six years ago, she wanted to shout at him. *Remember me? I'm Red.*

Griffin waited for her to finish with the little boy, his pulse racing and his heart thumping. God Almighty, he'd never been attracted to a redhead before. That was his brother's choice of women. No one told him the new kindergarten teacher was knock-down-gorgeous or that she had eyes that could see straight into his soul. Desire shot through his body, or was it plain old lust? Either one was something he hadn't allowed in a very long time, and he determined he would get control of it before he spoke again.

Julie's daughter, Annie, came running from across the room, her jet black pigtails bouncing on her shoulders, the white poliosis streak in her hair parted so that the majority of it was on the left side. She stopped dead in her tracks in front of the other little girl.

They eyed each other for several moments, mirror images of each other, doubles in almost every sense of the word. Jet black hair with a white streak from the forehead back several inches, crystal clear blue eyes, a slight dent in their chins.

Finally Annie grabbed Lizzy's hand and said, "Come sit by me. My momma is the teacher, she won't care."

Lizzy let go of her father's hand and ran off with Annie, her jet black pony tail waving from one side to the other, the white streak in her hair slicked straight back.

Both parents couldn't peel their eyes away from the two little girls giggling together. Julie felt the world tilt backwards on its axis and the concrete floor of the St. Jo, Texas, elementary school tremor as if Texas was having a rare earthquake.

"Who are you?" Griffin whispered. Desire took a back seat to shock. That little girl had to be a Luckadeau. His blue eyes narrowed into slits. Who was the redhead and where had that child come from?

"I'm going to be your child's teacher but we knew each other a long time ago. You don't remember?"

He shook his head. "I've never met you before in my life, but that little girl could be my Lizzy's sister with that white forelock."

"It's time for school to start. We'll have to discuss this later. Guess they each just met their double," Julie said. If he wanted to play dumb as a box of rocks, then she could do the same thing.

He spun around and marched out the door without a backward glance.

Julie would have liked nothing better than to follow him screaming like a fish wife, but she had a classroom of kindergartners waiting. However if G. Luckadeau thought he'd gotten off easy, then he'd best think again and this time with the head on his shoulders instead of the one behind his zipper. That visual sent her staggering backwards to hold on to her desk and look out over more than a dozen little children all looking to her with a bit of fear in their eyes. She had to get her raw nerves under control and teach a class. She had to put aside the multitude of sinful thoughts ... the foremost of which was homicide at that point. Not far behind it was anger and running a close race was the urge to pick up Annie and run as fast and far as she could.

"Okay, class, it's time for us all to meet each other," Julie said. Her words come out like she'd been running a mile but she took two deep breaths and composed herself. "This is Chuck Chester and he's five years old. Can the rest of you stand up beside your desk and tell me what your name is?" She led Chuck to the desk directly in front of hers and settled him in. She always had one child in her classroom like Chuck. Backward, dressed poorly, almost malnourished but not enough to call the authorities, unsure of himself. It broke her heart but it happened every year.

Both Annie and Lizzy turned to look at the little boy. Lizzy on his left. Annie on his right. Annie popped up from her seat and said, "I'm Annie Donavan and that is my mommy." She pointed at Julie.

"But in the classroom I'll be Miss Julie, won't I?" Julie's naturally lovely smile was strained amid the turmoil in her chest. She tried to control the inner chaos tearing up her nerves like a class five tornado ripping across Texas but she was so pissed off it was impossible. She wanted to strangle Mr. Luckadeau until his pretty blue eyes popped out and rolled around on the floor like ping-pong balls. How in the hell had he come to life right there in Saint Jo and more importantly why? He had to live close by for his daughter to be enrolled in her classroom. How many more little white forelocked kids were running around the county and how many more women had he sweet-talked into sleeping with him?

Lizzy hopped to her feet and said, "I'm Lizzy Luckadeau. My daddy is Griffin Luckadeau, and I almost didn't get to come to school but I cried and cried and Marita said I would be safe."

The principal, Mrs. Amos, stuck her head in the open door. "Could I have a word with you?"

Julie motioned her inside. One hour into the first day and Julie was sure she was already fired. G. Luckadeau had most likely gone straight to the big dog in the office when he saw Annie and insisted that hussy mother of hers be fired on the spot.

Mrs. Amos stopped in front of Julie's desk and lowered her voice considerably. "I want to make you aware of special arrangements with Lizzy Luckadeau. Her father, Griffin, was going to home school her but finally agreed with lots of talking from me and his housekeeper that Lizzy needed to come to school. That's why you didn't see her name on the student sheet. He just made up his mind last night. She is not to leave this school with anyone other than Griffin or Marita. I'll point her out to you if she comes to pick up Lizzy. And Lizzy is never to ride the bus home."

"May I ask why?" Julie asked softly.

"Protection against abduction. That's as much as I can say. Amazing how much Lizzy and your Annie look alike. You sure you've never been in these parts or ever known Griff?"

Her boss knew the secret. Her twinkling eyes said it all. The very thing Julie was running from had circled back around and taken a huge bite out of her ass when she least expected it.

"No, ma'am. Didn't even know Saint Jo existed until I heard about the job," she said.

"Well, they say everyone has a twin. Guess those little girls found theirs early on in life," Mrs. Amos said as she left the room.

By the end of the day Lizzy, Annie, and Chuck were inseparable.

When the last bell sounded a thin woman with dyed blonde hair and four inches of dark brown roots appeared in the doorway and yelled at Chuck to hurry. He cringed at the sight of her and dropped his glasses in his rush.

"You break those again boy and you're gettin' in big

trouble. They said if you had to have another pair, we'd have to pay for them. So if you break 'em, you won't be able to see. Now get a move on. We've got places we need to go."

Chuck rushed out and they were gone.

Julie wanted to mop up the floor with that woman. Her hair did resemble a mop that had been left out on the clothes line to dry, and Julie was tired of seeing children mentally as well as physically abused, and she'd taught long enough to recognize the signs of both. She'd barely cooled down from that episode when the light was completely obliterated in the doorway with one Griffin Luckadeau. Would the day never end? From lust to shock to anger and now back to lust. Damn! He was every bit as fine a cowboy as he had been a soldier. And still he had a puzzled look in his eyes like he'd never seen her. Well, he'd best think hard and long because he'd seen every square inch of her and they'd done a hell of a lot more than exchange phone numbers. Annie was proof positive of that.

Lizzy ran to his side, grabbed his hand, and started to chatter about Chuck and Annie being her new friends. Griffin picked her up and hugged her close then shot one more look over his shoulder at Julie. He'd remember someone that pretty even if had been a long time ago. He'd racked his brain all day and not one memory surfaced. Why would she think she'd known him?

Julie hoped he choked to death when Lizzy went running in their house telling *her* mother about the little girl in the classroom that looked just like her. Mr. Griffin Luckadeau was fixing to find out just what it meant to face off with a mad woman. His wife would never believe that he hadn't been unfaithful when she clapped eyes on Annie.

And that made Julie the other woman, a part that she never, ever intended to play after the pain of confronting the other woman in her husband's life. In her defense, she hadn't known Griffin was married when she wound up in bed with him six years before. He wasn't wearing a wedding band. She might have had a few drinks too many but she did remember checking for that particular item and there wasn't even a white ring where it should have been.

After all the students were gone, Julie and Annie shut and locked the door and headed home. Julie's hands shook as she put the key in the ignition of her truck. For a long minute she sat in stunned silence, her head on the steering wheel while she tried to tame a million memories and racing thoughts. It was a useless endeavor; taming her thoughts was like attempting to take the wild out of a Texas Long Horn. Some things simply weren't possible.

"Momma, why does Lizzy look just like me? And Chuck didn't like that stuff they put on his plate in the lunch room today so I gave him half my sandwich," Annie said.

Julie started up the engine and headed north toward her new home. "Let's go home, baby. We've got lots of things to do. You aren't the only little girl in the world with a white streak in their hair. We just haven't seen any of the others. And why didn't Chuck eat his lunch?"

Annie exhaled in impatience. "Because he don't like fish sticks. He said they make him puke. I gave him half of my sandwich."

"What did Lizzy bring?"

"She had ham and cheese with mustard just like me. And potato chips and a cookie and chocolate milk," Annie said.

Julie started the truck and backed out of the school parking lot. Surprisingly enough, the sun still hung in the sky and the world had not come to an abrupt end. It had been a day of miracles. She had kept her cool when Griffin Luckadeau waltzed in her classroom. Mrs. Amos didn't fire her. And she didn't try to mop up Main Street of Saint Jo with Chuck Chester's mother. All in all, not as bad as it could have been.

"Lizzy gave Chuck half her cookie," Annie said.

"Well, I suppose Chuck ate well today," Julie said.

"Yes, he did. I like him and Lizzy. They are my bestest friends," Annie said.

Children were wonderful. They had no preconceived notions of who to like or not like. Money or the lack thereof didn't affect them at all. From the looks of Lizzy, she came from a comfortable family. Chuck, according to Mrs. Amos, when they discussed her students the day before, lived in a trailer south of Saint Jo, and his father had been arrested multiple times on drug charges.

A person had to pass a test to get a driver's license. They had to prove they were credit worthy to buy a house. But any drug dealing son-of-a-bitch could be a father.

Or any handsome soldier on his way to Iraq. Julie's jaw clamped shut. A woman couldn't even berate an SOB without her guardian angel putting in her two bits.

By the time Julie stopped at the local grocery store

and picked up supplies, then got to her new property a mile north of St. Jo, she had convinced herself that Griffin Luckadeau had really been three sheets to the wind that night, and he didn't remember the night he'd spent with her in the hotel room.

That was her blessing for holding her temper all day. He flat out didn't remember. Thank God! She sure wouldn't ever bring it up to him. That was a solid fact.

Available January 2010

SEALed
with a Kiss

BY MARY MARGRET DAUGHTRIDGE

THERE'S ONLY ONE THING HE CAN'T HANDLE, AND
ONE WOMAN WHO CAN HELP HIM...

Jax Graham is a rough, tough Navy SEAL, but when
it comes to taking care of his four-year-old son after
his ex-wife dies, he's completely clueless. Family
therapist Pickett Sessoms can help, but only if he'll
let her.

When Jax and his little boy get trapped by a hurricane,
Picket takes them in against her better judgment.
When the situation turns deadly, Pickett discovers
what it means to be a SEAL, and Jax discovers that
even a hero needs help sometimes.

"*A heart-touching story that will keep you smiling and
cheering for the characters clear through to the happy
ending.*" —Romantic Times

"*A well-written romance...simultaneously tender and sensuous.*" —Booklist

978-1-4022-1118-8 • $6.99 U.S. / $8.99 CAN

SEALed
with a
Promise

BY MARY MARGRET DAUGHTRIDGE

NAVY SEAL CALEB DELAUDE IS AS DEADLY AS HE IS CHARMING.

Professor Emmie Caddington's quiet intelligence and quirky personality intrigue him. When he discovers that her personal connections can get him close to the man he's vowed to kill, will their budding relationship be nothing more than a means to revenge…or is she the key to his salvation?

Praise for *SEALed with a Kiss*:

"This story delivers in a huge way." —Romantic Times

"A wonderful story that will have readers experiencing a whirlwind of emotions and culminating with an awesome scene that will have your pulse pounding." —Romance Junkies

"What an incredibly powerful book! I laughed and sniffled, was turned on and turned inside out." —Queue My Review

978-1-4022-1763-0 • $6.99 U.S. / $7.99 CAN

Romeo, Romeo

BY ROBIN KAYE

Rosalie Ronaldi doesn't have a domestic bone in her body...

All she cares about is her career, so she survives on take-out and dirty martinis, keeps her shoes under the dining room table, her bras on the shower curtain rod, and her clothes on the couch.

Nick Romeo is every woman's fantasy— tall, dark, handsome, rich, really good in bed, AND he loves to cook and clean...

He says he wants an independent woman, but when he meets Rosalie, all he wants to do is take care of her. Before long, he's cleaned up her apartment, stocked her refrigerator, and adopted her dog.

So what's the problem? Just a little matter of mistaken identity, corporate theft, a hidden past in juvenile detention, and one big nosy Italian family too close for comfort...

"Kaye's debut is a delightfully fun, witty romance, making her a writer to watch." —*Booklist*

978-1-4022-1339-7 • $6.99 U.S. / $8.99 CAN

Line of
SCRIMMAGE

BY MARIE FORCE

SHE'S GIVEN UP ON HIM AND MOVED ON...

Susannah finally has peace, calm, a sedate life, and a no-surprises man. Marriage to football superstar Ryan Sanderson was a whirlwind, but Susanna got sick of playing second fiddle to his team. With their divorce just a few weeks away, she's already planning her wedding with her new fiancé.

HE'S FINALLY FIGURED OUT WHAT'S REALLY IMPORTANT TO HIM. IF ONLY IT'S NOT TOO

Ryan has just ten days to convince his soon-to-be-ex-wife to give him a second chance. His career is at its pinnacle, but in the year of their separation, Ryan's come to realize it doesn't mean anything without Susannah...

978-1-4022-1424-0 • $6.99 U.S. / $8.99 CAN

Love at
FIRST FLIGHT

BY MARIE FORCE

What if the guy
in the airplane seat next to you turned out
to be the love of your life?

JULIANA, HAPPY IN HER CAREER AS A HAIR STYLIST, IS ON HER
WAY TO Florida to visit her boyfriend. When he tells her
he's wondering what it might be like to make love to other
women she is devastated. Even though he tries to take it
back, she doesn't want him to be wondering all his life. So
they agree to take a break, and heartbroken, she goes back
to Baltimore.

Michael is going to his fiancee's parents' home for an
engagement party he doesn't want. A state's prosecutor,
he's about to try the biggest case of his career, and he's
having doubts about the relationship. When Paige pulls a
manipulative stunt at the party, he becomes so enraged that
he breaks off the engagement.

Juliana and Michael sat together on the plane ride from
Baltimore to Florida, and discover they're on the same
flight coming back. With the weekend a disaster for each of
them, they bond in a "two-person pity party" on the plane
ride home. Their friendship begins to blossom and love,
too, but life is full of complications, and when Michael's
trial turns dangerous, the two must confront what they
value most in life...

978-1-4022-2006-7 • $6.99 U.S. / $7.99 CAN

IN OVER HER HEAD

by Judi Fennell

"Holy mackerel! *In Over Her Head* is a
fantastically fun romantic catch!"

—Michelle Rowen, author of *Bitten & Smitten*

∘ ∘ ∘ ∘ ∘ ∘   **HE LIVES UNDER THE SEA**   ∘ ∘ ∘ ∘ ∘ ∘

Reel Tritone is the rebellious royal second son of the ruler
of a vast undersea kingdom. A Merman, born with legs
instead of a tail, he's always been fascinated by humans,
especially one young woman he once saw swimming near
his family's reef…

∘ ∘ ∘ ∘ ∘   **SHE'S TERRIFIED OF THE OCEAN**   ∘ ∘ ∘ ∘ ∘

Ever since the day she swam out too far and heard voices
in the water, marina owner Erica Peck won't go swimming
for anything—until she's forced into the water by a shady
ex-boyfriend searching for stolen diamonds, and is nearly
eaten by a shark…luckily Reel is nearby to save her, and
discovers she's the woman he's been searching for…

978-1-4022-2001-2 • $6.99 U.S. / $7.99 CAN

The WILD SIGHT

BY LOUCINDA McGARY

"A magical tale of romance and intrigue. I couldn't put it down!" —Pamela Palmer, author of *Dark Deceiver* and *The Dark Gate*

HE WAS CURSED WITH A "GIFT"

Born with the clairvoyance known to the Irish as "The Sight," Donovan O'Shea fled to America to escape his visions. On a return trip to Ireland to see his ailing father, staggering family secrets threaten to turn his world upside down. And then beautiful, sensual Rylie Powell shows up, claiming to be his half-sister...

SHE'S LOOKING FOR THE FAMILY SHE NEVER KNEW...

After her mother's death, Rylie journeys to Ireland to find her mysterious father. She needs the truth—but how can she and Donovan be brother and sister when the chemistry between them is nearly irresistible?

UNCOVERING THE PAST LEADS THEM DANGEROUSLY CLOSE TO MADNESS...

"A richly drawn love story and riveting romantic suspense!" —Karin Tabke, author of *What You Can't See*

978-1-4022-1394-6 • $6.99 U.S. / $8.99 CAN

50 Ways to Hex Your Lover

BY LINDA WISDOM

"A magical page-turner...had me bewitched from the start!"

—Yasmine Galenorn,
USA Today bestselling author of *Witchling*

JAZZ CAN'T DECIDE WHETHER TO SCORCH HIM WITH A FIREBALL OR JUMP INTO BED WITH HIM

Jasmine Tremaine is a witch who can't stay out of trouble. Nikolai Gregorivich is a vampire cop on the trail of a serial killer. Their sizzling love affair has been on-again, off-again for about 300 years—mostly off, lately.

But now Nick needs Jazz's help to steer clear of a maniacal killer with supernatural powers, while they try to finally figure out their own hearts.

978-1-4022-1085-3 • $6.99 U.S. / $8.99 CAN

BY LINDA WISDOM

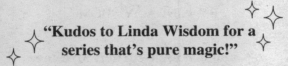

> "Kudos to Linda Wisdom for a
> series that's pure magic!"

—Vicki Lewis Thompson,
New York Times bestselling author of *Wild & Hexy*

**JAZZ AND NICK'S DREAM ROMANCE HAS
TURNED INTO A NIGHTMARE…**

FEISTY WITCH JASMINE TREMAINE AND DROP-DEAD
GORGEOUS vampire cop Nikolai Gregorovich have a
hot thing going, but it's tough to keep it together when
nightmare visions turn their passion into bickering.

With a little help from their friends, Nick and Jazz are in a
race against time to uncover whoever it is that's poisoning
their dreams, and their relationship…

978-1-4022-1400-4 • $6.99 U.S. / $7.99 CAN

Wicked by Any Other Name

BY LINDA WISDOM

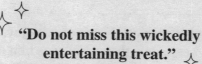

"Do not miss this wickedly entertaining treat."

—Annette Blair,
Sex and the Psychic Witch

STASI ROMANOV USES A LITTLE WITCH MAGIC IN HER LINGERIE shop, running a brisk side business in love charms. A disgruntled customer threatening to sue over a failed spell brings wizard attorney Trevor Barnes to town—and witches and wizards make a volatile combination. The sparks fly, almost everyone's getting singed, and the whole town seems on the verge of a witch hunt.

Can the feisty witch and the gorgeous wizard overcome their objections and settle out of court—and in the bedroom?

978-1-4022-1773-9 • $6.99 U.S. / $7.99 CAN

call of the
highland
moon

BY KENDRA LEIGH CASTLE

A Highlands werewolf fleeing his destiny, and the
warm-hearted woman who takes him in…

Not ready for the responsibilities of an alpha wolf, Gideon
MacInnes leaves Scotland and seeks the quiet hills of
upstate New York. When he is attacked by rogue wolves
and collapses on Carly Silver's doorstep, she thinks she's
rescuing a wounded animal. But she awakens to find
that the beast has turned into a devastatingly handsome,
naked man.

With a supernatural enemy stalking them, their only hope
is to get back to Scotland, where Carly has to risk becom-
ing a werewolf herself, or give up the one man she's ever
truly loved.

**"*Call of the Highland Moon* thrills with seductive
romance and breathtaking suspense." —Alyssa Day,
USA Today bestselling author of *Atlantis Awakening***

978-1-4022-1158-4 • $6.99 U.S. / $8.99 CAN

DARK
HIGHLAND
FIRE

BY KENDRA LEIGH CASTLE

A werewolf from the Scottish Highlands and a fiery
demi-goddess fleeing for her life…

Desired by women, kissed by luck, Gabriel MacInnes has
always been able to put pleasure ahead of duty. But with
the MacInnes wolves now squarely in the sights of an
ancient enemy, everything is about to change…

Rowan *an* Morgaine, on the run from a dragon prince who
will stop at nothing to have her as his own, must accept
the protection of Gabriel and his clan. By force or by
guile, Rowan and Gabriel must uncover the secrets of their
intertwining fate and stop their common enemy.

**"This fresh and exciting take on the werewolf
legend held me captive."**

—NINA BANGS, AUTHOR OF *ONE BITE STAND*

978-1-4022-1159-1 • $6.99 U.S. / $8.99 CAN

WILD
HIGHLAND
MAGIC

BY KENDRA LEIGH CASTLE

She's a Scottish Highlands werewolf

Growing up in America, Catrionna MacInnes always tried desperately to control her powers and pretend to be normal…

He's a wizard prince with a devastating secret

The minute Cat lays eyes on Bastian, she knows she's met her destiny. In their first encounter, she unwittingly binds him to her for life, and now they're both targets for the evil enemies out to destroy their very souls.

Praise for Kendra Leigh Castle:

"Fans of straight up romance looking for a little extra something will be bitten." —*Publishers Weekly*

978-1-4022-1856-9 • $7.99 U.S. / $8.99 CAN

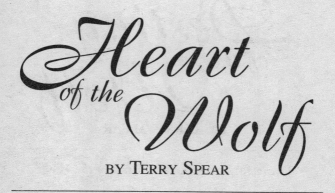

Heart
of the
Wolf

BY TERRY SPEAR

A *Publisher's Weekly* Best Book of the Year

"A fast-paced, sexy read with lots of twists and turns!" —Nicole North, author of *Devil in a Kilt*

THEIR FORBIDDEN LOVE MAY GET THEM BOTH KILLED

"Red werewolf Bella flees her adoptive pack of gray werewolves when the alpha male Volan tries forcibly to claim her as his mate. Her real love, beta male Devlyn, is willing to fight Volan to the death to claim her. That problem pales, however, as a pack of red werewolves takes to killing human females in a crazed quest to claim Bella for their own. Bella and Devlyn must defeat the rogue wolves before Devlyn's final confrontation with Volan. The vulpine couple's chemistry crackles off the page, but the real strength of the book lies in Spear's depiction of pack power dynamics…her wolf world feels at once palpable and even plausible."

—*Publisher's Weekly*

978-1-4022-1157-7 • $6.99 U.S. / $8.99 CAN

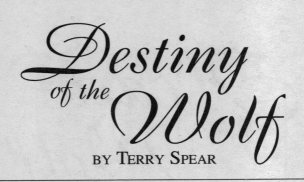

Destiny
of the
Wolf

BY TERRY SPEAR

Praise for Terry Spear's *Heart of the Wolf*:

"The chemistry crackles off the page."
—*Publisher's Weekly*

"The characters are well drawn and believable, which makes the contemporary plotline of love and life among the lupus garou seem, well, realistic." —*Romantic Times*

"Full of action, adventure, suspense, and romance... one of the best werewolf stories I've read!" —*Fallen Angel Reviews*

ALL SHE WANTS IS THE TRUTH

Lelandi is determined to discover the truth about her beloved sister's mysterious death. But everyone thinks she's making a bid for her sister's widowed mate...

HE'S A PACK LEADER TORMENTED BY MEMORIES

Darien finds himself bewitched by Lelandi, and when someone attempts to silence her, he realizes that protecting the beautiful stranger may be the only way to protect his pack...and himself...

978-1-4022-1668-8 • $6.99 U.S. / $7.99 CAN

SLAVE

BY CHERYL BROOKS

"I found him in the slave market on Orpheseus Prime, and even on such a god-forsaken planet as that one, their treatment of him seemed extreme."

Cat may be the last of a species whose sexual talents were the envy of the galaxy. Even filthy, chained, and beaten, his feline gene gives him a special aura.

Jacinth is on a rescue mission… and she needs a man she can trust with her life.

PRAISE FOR CHERYL BROOKS' *SLAVE*:

"A sexy adventure with a hero you can't resist!"

—Candace Havens, author of *Charmed & Deadly*

"Fascinating world customs, a bit of mystery, and the relationship between the hero and heroine make this a very sensual romance."

—*Romantic Times*

978-1-4022-1192-8 • $6.99 U.S. / $8.99 CAN

WARRIOR

BY CHERYL BROOKS

*"He came to me in the dead of winter,
his body burning with fever."*

EVEN NEAR DEATH, HIS SENSUALITY IS AMAZING...

Leo arrives on Tisana's doorstep a beaten slave from a near extinct race with feline genes. As soon as Leo recovers his strength, he'll use his extraordinary sexual talents to bewitch Tisana and make a bolt for freedom...

PRAISE FOR THE CAT STAR CHRONICLES:

"A compelling tale of danger, intrigue, and sizzling romance!"

—Candace Havens, author of *Charmed & Deadly*

"Hot enough to start a fire. Add in a thrilling new world and my reading experience was complete."

—*Romance Junkies*

978-1-4022-1440-0 • $6.99 U.S. / $7.99 CAN

ROGUE

BY CHERYL BROOKS

Tychar crawled toward me on his hands and knees like a tiger stalking his prey. "I, for one, am glad you came," he purred. "And I promise you, Kyra, you will never want to leave Darconia."

"Cheryl Brooks knows how to keep the heat on and the reader turning pages!"
—Sydney Croft, author of *Seduced by the Storm*

PRAISE FOR THE CAT STAR CHRONICLES:

"Wow. Just…wow. The romantic chemistry is as close to perfect as you'll find." —*BookFetish.org*

"Will make you purr with delight. Cheryl Brooks has a great talent as a storyteller." —*Cheryl's Book Nook*

978-1-4022-1762-3 • $6.99 U.S. / $7.99 CAN

OUTCAST

BY CHERYL BROOKS

Sold into slavery in a harem, Lynx is a favorite because his feline gene gives him remarkable sexual powers. But after ten years, Lynx is exhausted and is thrown out of the harem without a penny. Then he meets Bonnie, who's determined not to let such a beautiful and sensual young man go to waste...

PRAISE FOR THE CAT STAR CHRONICLES:

"Leaves the reader eager for the next story featuring these captivating aliens." —*Romantic Times*

"One of the sweetest love stories...one of the hottest heroes ever conceived and...one of the most exciting and adventurous quests that I have ever had the pleasure of reading." —*Single Titles*

"One of the most sensually imaginative books that I've ever read... A magical story of hope, love and devotion" —*Yankee Romance Reviews*

978-1-4022-1896-5 • $6.99 U.S. / $7.99 CAN

THE
PRINCE
OF
MIDNIGHT

BY LAURA KINSALE
New York Times bestselling author

INTENT ON REVENGE, ALL SHE WANTS FROM HIM IS TO LEARN HOW TO KILL

Lady Leigh Strachan has crossed all of France in search of S.T. Maitland, nobleman, highwayman, and legendary swordsman, once known as the Prince of Midnight. Now he's hiding out in a crumbling castle with a tame wolf as his only companion, trying to conceal his deafness and desperation. Leigh is terribly disappointed to find the man behind the legend doesn't meet her expectations. But when they're forced on a quest together, she discovers the dangerous and vital man behind the mask, and he finds a way to touch her ice cold heart.

978-1-4022-1397-7 • $7.99 U.S./$8.99 CAN

MIDSUMMER MOON

MOON

BY LAURA KINSALE

New York Times bestselling author

"The acknowledged master."
—*Albany Times-Union*

IF HE REALLY LOVED HER,
WOULDN'T HE HELP HER REALIZE HER DREAM?

When inventor Merlin Lambourne is endangered by Napoleon's advancing forces, Lord Ransom Falconer, in service of his government, comes to her rescue and falls under the spell of her beauty and absent-minded brilliance. But he is horrified by her dream of building a flying machine—and not only because he is determined to keep her safe.

"Laura Kinsale writes the kind of works that live in your heart." —Elizabeth Grayson

"A true storyteller, Laura Kinsale has managed to break all the rules of standard romance writing and come away shining."
—*San Diego Union-Tribune*

978-1-4022-1398-4 • $7.99 U.S./$8.99 CAN

SEIZE THE FIRE

BY LAURA KINSALE

New York Times bestselling author

"Magic and beauty flow from
Laura Kinsale's pen." —*Romantic Times*

AN UNLIKELY PRINCESS SHIPWRECKED
WITH A WAR HERO WHO'S GOT HELL TO PAY

Her Serene Highness Olympia of Oriens—plump, demure,
and idealistic—longs to return to her tiny, embattled land
and lead her people to justice and freedom. Famous hero
Captain Sheridan Drake, destitute and tormented by nightmares of the carnage he's seen, means only to rob and abandon her. What is Olympia to do with the tortured man
behind the hero's façade? And how will they cope when
their very survival depends on each other?

"One of the best writers in the history of the
romance genre." —*All About Romance*

978-1-4022-1396-0 • $7.99 U.S./$8.99 CAN

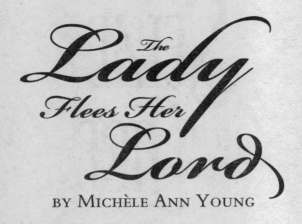

The Lady Flees Her Lord

by Michèle Ann Young

DESPERATE FOR PEACE AND SAFETY...

Lucinda, Lady Denbigh, is running from a husband who physically and emotionally abused her. Posing as a widow, she seeks refuge in the quiet countryside, where she meets Lord Hugo Wanstead. Returning from the wars with a wound that won't heal, he finds his estate impoverished, his sleep torn by nightmares, and brandy the only solace. When he meets Lucinda, he thinks she just might give him something to live for...

Praise for Michèle Ann Young's *No Regrets*

"Dark heroes, courageous heroines, intrigue, heartbreak, and heaps of sexual tension. Do not miss this fabulous new author." —Molly O'Keefe, *Harlequin Superromance*

"Readers will never want to put her book down!" —Bronwyn Scott, author of *Pickpocket Countess*

978-1-4022-1399-1 • $6.99 U.S. / $7.99 CAN

No Regrets

BY MICHÈLE ANN YOUNG

"A remarkable talent that taps your emotions with each and every page." —Gerry Russel, award winning author of *The Warrior Trainer*

A MOST UNUSUAL HEROINE

Voluptuous and bespectacled, Caroline Torrington feels dowdy and unattractive beside the slim beauties of her day. Little does she know that Lord Lucas Foxhaven thinks her curves are breathtaking, and can barely keep his hands off her.

"The suspense and sexual tension accelerate throughout." —*Romance Reviews Today*

978-1-4022-1016-7 • $6.99 U.S./$8.99 CAN

A *Duke* TO *Die For*

BY AMELIA GREY

THE RAKISH FIFTH DUKE OF BLAKEWELL'S UNEXPECTED AND shockingly lovely new ward has just arrived, claiming to carry a curse that has brought each of her previous guardians to an untimely end…

Praise for Amelia Grey's Regency romances:

"This beguiling romance steals your heart, lifts your spirits and lights up the pages with humor and passion." —Romantic Times

"Each new Amelia Grey tale is a diamond. Ms. Grey…is a master storyteller." —Affaire de Coeur

"Readers will be quickly drawn in by the lively pace, the appealing protagonists, and the sexual chemistry that almost visibly shimmers between." —Library Journal

978-1-4022-1767-8 • $6.99 U.S./$7.99 CAN

Lady Anne
AND THE
HOWL
IN THE
DARK

by Donna Lea Simpson

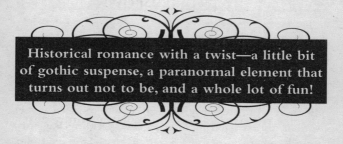

Historical romance with a twist—a little bit of gothic suspense, a paranormal element that turns out not to be, and a whole lot of fun!

LADY ANNE ADDISON IS A RATIONAL AND COURAGEOUS woman. So when she's summoned by a frightened friend to Yorkshire to prove or disprove the presence in their woods of a menacing wolf—or werewolf—she takes up the challenge.

Lady Anne finds the Marquess of Darkefell to be an infuriatingly unyielding man. Rumors swirl and suspects abound. The Marquess is indeed at the middle of it all, but not in the way that Lady Anne had suspected…and now he's firmly determined to win her in spite of everything.

978-1-4022-1791-3 • $6.99 U.S. / $7.99 CAN

Hundreds of Years to Reform a Rake

by Laurie Brown

His touch pulled her irresistibly across the mists of time

Deverell Thornton, the ninth Earl of Waite, needs Josie Drummond to come back to his time and foil the plot that would destroy him. Josie is a modern career woman, thrust back in time to the sparkling Regency period, where she must contend with the complex manners and mores of the day, unmask a dangerous charlatan, and in the end, choose between the ghost who captivated her or the man himself—but can she give her heart to a notorious rake?

"A smart, amusing, and fun time travel/Regency tale."
—*All About Romance*

"Extremely well written…A great read from start to finish." —*Revisiting the Moon's Library*

"Blends Regency, contemporary and paranormal romance to a charming and very entertaining effect." —*Book Loons*

978-1-4022-1013-6 • $6.99 U.S./$8.99 CAN

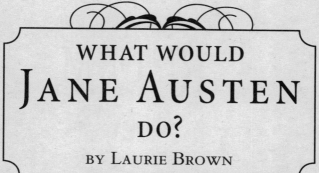

WHAT WOULD JANE AUSTEN DO?

BY LAURIE BROWN

Eleanor goes back in time to save a man's life, but could it be she's got the wrong villain?

Lord Shermont, renowned rake, feels an inexplicable bond to the mysterious woman with radical ideas who seems to know so much…but could she be a Napoleonic spy?

Thankfully, Jane Austen's sage advice prevents a fatal mistake…

At a country house party, Eleanor makes the acquaintance of Jane Austen, whose sharp wit can untangle the most complicated problem. With an international intrigue going on before her eyes, Eleanor must figure out which of two dueling gentlemen is the spy, and which is the man of her dreams.

978-1-4022-1831-6 • $6.99 U.S. / $7.99 CAN